Fireweed Glow

Fireweed Glow

Jeanette F. Chaplin

Copyright © 2001 by Jeanette F. Chaplin.

Library of Congress Number:	00-193171
ISBN #: Softcover	0-7388-5354-2

All rights reserved. No part of this book may be reproduced or transmitted in any form or by any means, electronic or mechanical, including photocopying, recording, or by any information storage and retrieval system, without permission in writing from the copyright owner.

This is a work of fiction. Names, characters, places and incidents either are the product of the author's imagination or are used fictitiously, and any resemblance to any actual persons, living or dead, events, or locales is entirely coincidental.

This book was printed in the United States of America.

To order additional copies of this book, contact:
Xlibris Corporation
1-888-7-XLIBRIS
www.Xlibris.com
Orders@Xlibris.com

Contents

PART ONE

Prologue 13
Chapter 1 19
Chapter 2 29
Chapter 3 39
Chapter 4 50
Chapter 5 61
Chapter 6 68
Chapter 7 78
Chapter 8 85

PART TWO

Chapter 9 97
Chapter 10 105
Chapter 11 115
Chapter 12 126
Chapter 13 135
Chapter 14 145
Chapter 15 158
Chapter 16 170

PART THREE

Chapter 17 183
Chapter 18 190

Chapter 19	200
Chapter 20	212
Chapter 21	220
Chapter 22	229
Chapter 23	237
Chapter 24	246
Epilogue	254

DEDICATION

To my daughters, Rachelle and Andrea, who encourage me.

To Jo, who encouraged me to write.

To Bo, who encouraged me to write mysteries.

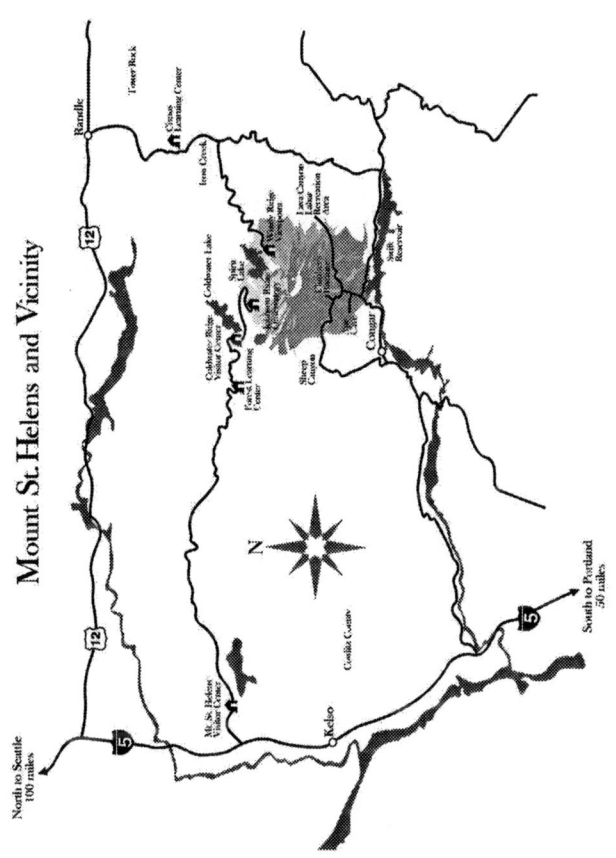

MAP OF MOUNT ST. HELEN'S AREA

PART ONE

MUTANTS

Prologue

MOUNT ST. HELENS: 1986

The moon hung listlessly in the mid-morning sky—a translucent gauze echo of the full brilliance it had displayed the previous night. A lone hiker scrambled to gain footing on the loose pumice of the barren landscape surrounding the dozing volcano. A check of the watch indicated three hours into the hike. Straight ahead lay the shattered remnant of the summit of the volcano. Just a few more yards before resting and taking a drink of precious water.

To the north, the colorless landscape traced the path of destruction. A plain of pumice and hummocks of lava occupied the former paradise. Once-verdant forests alive with scurrying wildlife and birdsong had been replaced in seconds with devastation and destruction. Still, the mountain loomed majestically over the landscape and the urge to conquer its heights was, if anything, more compelling since the eruption. The second most-climbed mountain after Mount Fuji, the mountain invited novice and expert alike to conquer its summit.

This adventurer sought a more challenging pursuit—one of the forbidden canyons that had been set aside for scientific research. Of course it was not wise to climb alone, but this would be the last chance for a long time and not many campers were still around this late in the season. Besides, no one could be trusted to take part in this clandestine adventure. Occasional tremors were also a concern—mild earthquakes had continued to assault the site since the 1980 eruption. Although most scientists thought they had subsided by now, an occasional one still threatened the area. The climber decided that experience and prudence would compensate for any inherent dangers. Leaving the well-traveled Loowit trail that encircled the mountain would protect the hiker from discovery by any late season tourists or hard-working scientists while exploring one of the obscure canyons.

Refreshed after a brief lunch break, the climber looked furtively around for observers, left the trail, and headed toward the canyon. Keeping up a brisk pace, the hiker soon neared the goal. Breathing in deeply the fresh mountain air and the exhilaration of conquest—observing sights few had ever seen: striated canyon walls, trickling streams, and still-bubbling mud flats.

Seeing a natural pass in an outcropping of rock, the hiker decided to ascend for a better view of the hummocky plains below. At that instant a tremor violently shook the unsuspecting climber and loosened many of the huge rocks above. There was nothing to do but hunker down and wait until the tremor passed. A lava boulder offered temporary protection until the clamor of an avalanche reached the tentative refuge and dislodged boulder and hiker in one screaming instant, hurtling both to the floor of the canyon.

A faint glimmer of consciousness allowed the hiker to glimpse the waning moon in the jet sky before slipping again into the swimming void of pain and nothingness.

The second return to reality proved more fruitful. Now it was daytime and no remnant of moon hung in the sky to provide a clue as to the passage of days. The hiker tried to assume a half-sitting position. Why was it so hard to breathe? Nothing seemed to be broken. The sensation of sinking into a warm and comforting bath was overwhelming—evidently a hallucination.

Then as the hiker began to regain full consciousness, it became evident that the sensation was not imagined—the hiker was sinking slowly, into the terrible tentacles of an area of quicksand, or more accurately, quick mud. Several of these patches had remained since the volcano, gradually cooling and hardening, but many still soft and warm—posing a danger for the unsuspecting.

The urge for survival jump-started a tentative plan in the barely functioning brain: remain as motionless as possible, flatten the body, spread the arms, look for something to grab onto. With eyes wide, the victim scanned the perimeter of the death pit. Success: a fallen log just out of reach, but apparently stable. With a rush, the hiker lunged in the direction of the log, but missed. The second thrashing attempt attained the desired object and provided a tenuous hold and time to gain strength for the second phase of the escape. With a final desperate effort, the hiker reached the relative safety of the arid, ashy ground surrounding the bubbling pit, then sank into a numbing sleep.

With the sleep came a restoration of mental facilities and the hiker assessed the situation: backpack still intact with one strap torn loose; jeans ripped at the calf revealing a gaping tear in the skin; muscle intertwined with shards of lava. The bleeding had stopped, leaving a burning pain in its place. An examination of the wound revealed that no bones were broken. A tentative search of the backpack produced a half tube of ointment—enough for a casual scrape, but certainly not adequate to stem the infection that broiled under the exposed surface of damaged flesh.

Gingerly, the hiker extricated the foreign material from the wound with a camping knife, starting the bleeding again. After splashing the angry sore from the limited supply of water and applying the ointment and a gauze patch, the hiker was ready to attempt the painful walk back to the campsite. Stomach cramps were a reminder that the rations for the intended day hike were long gone. The hiker took a slow swig from the water bottle and eyed the nearby stream. Too saturated with pulverized stone to be drinkable. The little that remained in the flask would have to do. The hiker started tentatively but resolutely toward safety.

The next morning, after a cold night wrapped in a silver emergency blanket, the climber awoke to a dry mouth, fever, and a relentless throbbing in the wounded leg. The water was gone and the only hope of survival was to make camp by evening. Staggering steps slowed to a shuffle as the hiker began to weaken and finally stumbled and fell. After regaining the main trail, the hiker resumed the slow painful march and survival once again seemed possible. Lulled into a mindless rhythm of painful steps in the afternoon sun, the hiker misstepped and plunged downward in a second, more devastating fall, scraping the dressing from the tender sore. A gasp of pain escaped between parched lips. The hiker vomited dryly and drifted off into oblivion, to be roused by a faint droning. Struggling to perceive the source of the potential rescue, a helicopter maybe, the hiker raised an aching head and opened red, swollen eyes.

The droning was bees, hundreds of bees. Moaning, the hiker instinctively covered face and bare hands in anticipation of a painful ending to what had turned into a nightmare. But the bees ignored the intruder, evidently not perceived as a threat. Clear-headedness began to return slowly as the hiker analyzed this new threat—or maybe it wasn't a threat. Honey. Large swarms of bees meant hives—and honey.

* * *

The bees are returning from a lush field of Fireweed in a secluded corner of the vast Mount St. Helens Monument. Similar in appearance to the plant ordinarily found in areas that have been burned, this strain is bigger and more fragrant, hardier. This variety sprang from the force of the volcano itself. The immense blast that leveled 150 square miles of forest with devastating force caused the germination of prehistoric seeds that had lain dormant for thousands of years.

The same force that destroys also provides the means to reinstate the ravaged forest, for the seeds engendered a superior plant with a potent form of pollen. From the pollen, an errant swarm of bees produced a magnificent super honey—capable of nourishing the struggling survivors and hardy immigrants to the barren ash-covered hills. From the plants and the honey and on up the life chain, the super-charged nourishment promises health and renewed life for the delicate emerging ecological system.

As long as man doesn't interfere.

* * *

With the last ounce of will, the hiker raised to a crouch. The bees were hovering around one of the fallen logs that carpeted the blowdown area. The hiker pulled up sweatshirt hood and tightened it, leaving only eyes exposed, removed some essential from the backpack, and crept toward the log slowly so as not to alarm the bees. When the swarm had become accustomed to the foreign presence, the hiker tentatively reached a gloved hand into an opening in the log. When the hand emerged, it was covered with bees and was clutching a precious section of dripping honeycomb.

Grimacing from random stings, the hiker stifled the urge

to panic. Slowly, even more slowly, the hiker retired to a spot a few yards from the log, brushing bees tenderly from the treasure with a trembling hand. Finally the feast was secured and the life-preserving sustenance was devoured. One hand still smeared with honey, the hiker looked down at the newly exposed wound, the pain once again demanding attention, and cautiously applied the remains of the sticky liquid to the flaming flesh.

The traveler sunk into a deep, refreshing sleep and awoke with the moon overhead. The pains in the stomach were gone and the hiker rose thankfully and removed a flashlight from the backpack. Time to make the last leg back to camp. The honey was nutritious but wouldn't stave off dehydration for long. Cautiously the hiker rose to a standing position and tested the damaged leg. It seemed to be numb from the cramped sleeping position. The hiker started down the trail, cautiously lighting the way for each step. Favoring the leg, the hiker was astounded to realize that the pain had subsided. Sitting on a log by the trail to examine the wound, the hiker discovered that the pain and swelling had subsided and the angry redness had been replaced by a protective scab. Overnight the wound had changed from potential gangrene and amputation to a pain-free, rapidly healing, functional limb.

This was no ordinary honey.

With unexpected stamina and energy, the hiker returned to the campsite as the morning sun topped the nearby mountain ridge. This time the hiker was going home with far more than memories. This discovery would give the explorer's life an unexpected turn—and was destined to change the course of all that were involved in the drama of the recovering forest—man and animal alike.

Chapter 1

OLD GROWTH FOREST

MOUNT ST. HELENS: 1990S

Torrie Madison glanced at her watch for the third time in the last half hour: two-thirty and her double shot, amaretto latte with two percent was getting cold. This one didn't quite pack the punch as the two she'd had in the morning. Plus, the local residents were giving her strange looks for drinking coffee in the afternoon.

She looked around at the others sharing her oasis in the canyon of skyscrapers. Interstate Five hummed in the background, muffled by a necklace of foliage draped over the walls surrounding the open air patio in downtown Seattle. A tall glass building loomed green behind her. It was there that her cousin Morgan had gone for her first interview that morning and where they had agreed to meet about twoish after she finished her third one.

It had seemed like a good idea at the time. Since it was Torrie's first visit to the Northwest, she could shop around downtown while her cousin went to some job interviews. Morgan had just graduated from the University of Washington and had invited Torrie to fly out from Texas and help her celebrate. Neither had anticipated the flurry of interviews.

They had ridden the bus that morning amongst the commuters with noses buried in their books and newspapers. Morgan had pointed out the street leading to Pike Place Market and other places of interest for Torrie to explore while she waited. At first Torrie had been in awe of the bustle of a strange city—they had actually passed the Space Needle and gotten a glimpse of Puget Sound on the way. Morgan had given her a tourist map and told her where to catch the monorail back to the Needle. Torrie decided to save the ride to the top for a time when someone made her go—maybe at night when it was too dark to see just how high up she was. High buildings were not places Torrie went by choice.

Pike Place Market, however, was a dream world. She had arrived in time to observe the throwing of the fresh fish—hallmark of the fish mongers in the stalls of the famous market lining the rim of Elliot Bay. She had tried on vintage dresses and browsed bookshelves filled with Northwestern lore. She had purchased some handmade native silver jewelry and tasted some sleepless-in-Seattle tiramisu, near the actual spot she thought she recognized from the movie. She admired the neat rows of fresh fruits and vegetables and bought some dried cranberries to snack on. The displays of cut flowers drew her with their fragrance, myriad hues, and variety. Some were familiar to her: irises, tulips, daffodils, and glads, but she most enjoyed the ones she had only read about: brightly colored snap dragons and the exquisitely-colored aromatic lavender.

In an impulsive moment she had bought a spray of flowers to take to her Aunt Lorna—never considering she would have to carry it around all day while she waited on Morgan. After a few minutes of close contact with the unidentified species, she began a spasm of sneezing and dropped her coin purse down a storm drain. When she bent to try to retrieve it, she brushed the plants into the face of a nearby child, whose hysterical mother insisted had nearly poked out her child's eyes. In her eagerness to leave the scene of her embarrassment, she knocked over someone's coffee at a sidewalk café. Finally, in desperation, she donated the bouquet to a beggar on a street corner. She never realized innocent flowers could cause so much trouble.

Rid of the attractive nuisance, she set out to buy some practical souvenirs. When she ducked into a building to escape the first rain shower of the day, she found herself in an outfitters and bought a crushable rainproof cap to match her eyes and a hooded Seattle sweatshirt, along with some thick socks and the sandals the Northwest is famous for.

Loaded with purchases she began to wish she had worn her daypack after all. Morgan had tried to convince her she wouldn't be out of place; now that she observed the well-dressed workers on their way to the office in suit and tie or stylish dresses and equipped with a backpack and athletic shoes, she realized her cousin had been right.

The highlight of the day had been a noon-hour string concert. She watched in amazement, and longed for a camera, as a bearded man in a mini-skirt performed an impromptu scarf dance. She seemed the only one in the audience who noted his presence in the otherwise artful performance. Now after a morning of hiking up and down steep sidewalks dodging skateboarders and helmeted bikers, Torrie was ready to go back to the Parker's house and take a well-deserved nap. But it was hard telling when her none-too-considerate cousin would show up.

She tried not to be too annoyed with her cousin's interviews. After all, getting a job was the whole point of finishing a degree. But she had taken two weeks off from her own job, and other than the graduation ceremony, they still hadn't done anything she had come out here for.

Their original plan had been to camp out on the beautiful Oregon coast at Coos Bay, then go to a concert at the Columbia River Gorge. Torrie, at age twenty-five, had eagerly been awaiting her first sight of the Pacific Ocean. After the interview delays, plans had changed again when Morgan had received an urgent phone call from a university classmate, a graduate student in botany, pleading with her to bring some additional notes and books that she needed for her environmental research at Mount St. Helens.

Morgan had been excited about the change in plans. "It'll be fun," she had assured Torrie. "We can camp out there just as well as at Coos Bay, and you'll get to see an active volcano." Torrie's alarmed reaction brought the admission that it wasn't exactly active—just smoking and rebuilding its shattered dome with frequent belchings of steam and ash.

Torrie was not pleased. Camping in a forest with acres of blown-down trees resembling a moonscape was not her idea of a vacation. She'd seen the gray pictures of the former jewel of the Northwest.

But she couldn't remember any time during their childhood that Morgan hadn't gotten her way, so Torrie sighed and resigned herself to a dreary camping trip. Maybe after they had delivered the precious pile of notes to the budding botanist, her cousin would tire of the desolation and monotony and decide to go on to the coast after all. As long as she could make Morgan think it was her own idea. As the older cousin, Torrie had always been good at that.

Two days and four interviews later, Torrie found herself squirming around in the seat of the not-quite-new Porsche to get a better look out the window. Morgan was driving the way Torrie expected her to drive the sporty graduation present: never under the speed limit and rarely on her own side of the road. They were traveling through dense forest and it was impossible to see if anything was approaching from the opposite direction until they skimmed around the curves.

Torrie had tired of reminding her of the speed limits and of pointing out yellow signs with arrows resembling earthworms. But she did have to admit her cousin knew how to drive in the mountains.

In the meantime, she was attempting to enjoy every inch of the surviving forest before they reached the blast zone. She was still in awe of the endless miles of tree-lined mountain ranges, interspersed with glimpses of solitary peaks: Mount Baker, Mount Hood, Mount Adams, and of course, the most famous of all, Mount Rainier reigning, or raining, supreme over the Washington landscape.

Morgan Parker had taken a few electives in environmental studies—that was how she had met Astrid, her graduate student friend. The older girl had been a lab assistant at the time and had tutored Morgan extensively when she was in danger of failing a course in ecology. Morgan had sailed through the rest of the class and now considered herself quite an authority on the entire ecological movement.

Torrie turned back from the window to catch the rest of Morgan's lecture on the plight of the forests in the Pacific Northwest; she was secretly reaping the benefits of her cousin's expertise, but of course would never admit it to Morgan. It was like having her own private tour guide—until Morgan slipped back into the role of spoiled younger cousin.

The forests had been the scene of controversy, Morgan was saying, long before anyone had heard of the spotted owl: timber interests were interested in the bottom line; tourists wanted their pristine vacation spots preserved; hunters and fishermen wanted their game protected; and the native Americans wanted to maintain their culture and gain respect for their ancestors' way of life. Far away in the other

Washington the lawmakers were trying to make decisions about an area of the country most of them had never seen and didn't understand—attempting to keep voters happy until the next election rolled around. It seemed that every perspective had been considered except what was good for the forest.

* * *

The forest stands solid after hundreds, thousands of years; it is a survivor in every sense of the word. The eruption at Mount St. Helens, tragic and devastating by human standards, was a mere annoyance to an ecosystem acquainted with glaciers, flood, fires, and the ultimate predator—man. Just five years after the massive blast, large animals like elk and deer had returned to the area in numbers sufficient to replace those of their species lost to the blast. Step by step the magnificent forest began to regain the 150 square miles that had been literally leveled with the force of 20,000 atomic bombs. Regrowth was the key: by colonizers, fast-growing weeds, immigrant species, hardy insects, scavengers, and so on up the line.

On the surface, everything is developing according to plan; the forest once again settles into a comfortable routine of seasonal change. Everything should be at peace. But it isn't. Somewhere, deep within the recesses of the sylvan grandeur something is amiss. Some small species is uneasy. Some minute element of the delicate balance is disturbed—a member so small as to almost be insignificant. Almost. But the forest can sense it. That small nagging irritation like a case of sniffles portending a greater outbreak. It is there, persistent, growing, and the forest will not feel at ease until the problem goes away.

* * *

Morgan drove with the window down, gesturing and pointing with one arm out the window. Her straight dark hair caught the wind, creating an ever-changing frame for even features set in a flawless complexion that always managed to look tan, even in this sunless climate. Torrie thought it quite ironic that she herself lived in the sunbelt and could never get a tan. And the same wind that was creating interesting patterns in her cousin's practical, blunt-cut style was tangling Torrie's fine hair into a mass of unruly curls. She got out her new cap and jammed it on her head in self-defense.

Morgan continued expounding on the intricacies of the politics surrounding the allocation of the riches of the Cascade Mountain Range. The girls had been following a narrow winding roadway that sliced through an impressive stand of fir, red cedar, and hemlock. The sky was overcast—no surprise for Washington State—but occasional breaks between the trees allowed glimpses of the misty sky, painting a silvery cast on the moss-hung trees. Torrie was reading the guide book they had purchased at the ranger station, hoping to find a place where Morgan would be willing to stop and enjoy the scenery—and give Torrie's stomach a chance to stop flip-flopping.

They hadn't stopped at all during the long drive from Seattle, not even after they had turned off Interstate Five for the long drive east past endless farmland, and finally into the foothills and the edge of the forest. After a late start—Morgan never had been a morning person—they had been under pressure to find the campground before dark so they could stay with Astrid in her small travel trailer.

Torrie had at least convinced her cousin to stop at the ranger station in Randle to get information on the forest. As long as they had to be here, they might as well know what sights were worth seeing, if any.

They hadn't received a particularly warm welcome. They had pulled up in front of the plain wooden building just before closing time and the staff was eager to get off work and do whatever it is that people do in Randle after dark. A surly attendant appeared from the back room. She looked like she was having a bad hair life: the straight dark hair was too black for her pale face and had the look of a self-inflicted style. Morgan asked where they could get the best view of the volcano and began chatting about Astrid's research before asking for directions to the Tower Rock campground.

Bad Hair gave them a map of the area and pointed without comment to the road that led into the Gifford Pinchot National Forest. When they asked about day passes they were told they could wait and purchase them at Cascade Peaks the next day—if they were sure they wanted to drive up to Windy Ridge. While Morgan idly surveyed an aerial view of the forest, Torrie had started toward the back of the building looking for a restroom, and was icily told to use the facilities outside. Just before they left, Torrie hurriedly purchased a slim guide book, to the obvious annoyance of Bad Hair, who made a great show of laboriously taking out her cash box for the inconvenient purchase.

"I hope that's not your typical ranger," commented Torrie as they left.

"I can't believe she was so rude," agreed Morgan. "She didn't act like she was too thrilled to have us visiting her forest."

"Was it my imagination, or did she clam up after you mentioned Astrid's research?"

"No, I think she was just in a hurry to close up and go home."

"Probably has a hot date tonight," Torrie deadpanned.

"And think how long it'll take her to look good," added Morgan.

The girls started laughing hysterically and Torrie barely made it to the outdoor privy in time.

Back in the Porsche, the girls turned off the main highway onto the secondary route leading toward the forest and the monument. At a fork in the road, Morgan read the sign: "'*Mount St. Helens Monument—Straight Ahead,*'" and triumphantly sailed onto the park road. After several miles of driving, Morgan began searching in her purse with one hand while executing the curves with the other.

Alarmed, Torrie asked her what she was looking for.

"The directions to Astrid's campground. I know I brought them."

"Let me look for them," offered Torrie, preferring a two-handed driver maneuvering the winding road.

"They're in my planner. That red book in the side pocket of my purse."

"Is this it?" Torrie asked, pulling out the bulging planner.

"Yeah. Find today's date. They should be on a sticky note."

"Here it is. Do you want me to read . . ."

Morgan snatched the paper from her and stuck it to the visor. She started reading between curves. *"Take Hwy 25 out of Randle.'* Is that what we're on?"

Torrie searched the road for an indication of the highway number. Nothing but tree-lined curves in sight. "I can't tell."

"Look in the glove box," Morgan instructed. "There should be a Washington map in there. And a flashlight."

As she produced the map and refolded it to display the southwestern quarter of the state, Torrie realized uneasily that darkness was fast approaching. "Here's Gifford Pinchot," she said. "And Mount St. Helens. So Randle must be to the north. What are we looking for?"

"Twenty-something. Unless you'd rather look for 'twenty-somethings.'"

"Not now, Morgan," replied Torrie, annoyed. "Oh, here it is. Twenty-five. It's the one that goes up to Windy Ridge."

"Uh, oh," responded Morgan.

"Uh, oh, what?" asked Torrie, turning to study her cousin

in the fading daylight.

Morgan squealed to a stop in the middle of the road and pulled down the sticky note. "We shouldn't be on twenty-five; we're supposed to take twenty-three to get to Tower Rock."

"Well, I don't even see Tower Rock campground on here," said Torrie. "This map doesn't show the park roads."

"Here," said Morgan. "Try this little map the rude Randle ranger gave us.

Torrie studied it for a moment. "*Voila!* Here's a connecting road that leads to the campground. Do you think we've come to it yet?"

"I don't think so," answered Morgan, shifting into low for a power jolt start which sent them fishtailing for a few feet, much too close to the narrow shoulder for Torrie's comfort. "Love a car with spunk," Morgan said.

Another mile and they both spotted an approaching intersection. Morgan actually took her foot off the accelerator. Both women studied the signs.

"Highway seventy-six," Morgan announced. "And there's a sign pointing to Tower Rock Camp Grounds. Yes!"

They high-fived and Morgan turned up the radio. They started singing along to an oldies station: "*Drove my Chevy to the levee, but the levee was dry.*" which soon became, "Drove my Porsche to the forest, but the forest was fried."

Without warning, Morgan stopped singing and braked to a halt in front of a blockade.

"What on earth . . ." began Torrie.

"'*Bridge Out,*'" read Morgan. "Just what we need."

Chapter 2

IRON CREEK

"Now what?" asked Torrie.

"I guess this must be what that aerial photograph in the ranger station was about," said Morgan. "It said something about winter storms damaging some of the bridges."

"You mean you knew about this?" said Torrie, anger edging her tone.

"Well, not exactly," replied her cousin. "I couldn't tell which areas were washed out—it's not like I know this area. And an aerial view isn't like a map."

Torrie sighed. Never could pin anything on Morgan. And she did have to admit that it was the ranger's responsibility to tell them that the bridge was out. She was still certain that Bad Hair's attitude changed when they mentioned Astrid's name.

Morgan turned on the overhead light and looked at her watch. "It's after eight," she said. "Astrid will probably be in bed by the time we get there."

Morgan backed up, and to Torrie's relief turned the little sports car around without leaving the roadway.

They returned to the intersection they had greeted with such joy minutes earlier, and Morgan started to make a right turn back towards Randle.

"Wait a minute," said Torrie. "There's a sign for a campground pointing left. What does it say?"

Morgan slowed. "'*Iron Creek*,'" she read.

"Looks like it's just around the corner," said Torrie, studying the local map again.

Morgan put the car into neutral and drummed long slender fingers on the steering wheel. She turned to Torrie. "Do you think we should make camp here tonight? It's hard telling how long it'll take us to find Astrid's camp ground in the dark. And she may already be in bed. She's an early riser." Morgan grimaced.

"Will she worry about you?" asked Torrie.

"I doubt it," replied Morgan. "She's probably so involved in her research she hasn't even noticed we haven't showed up yet."

"She'd better notice," Torrie retorted. "We came all the way up here just to bring her that precious box of . . ."

"Box of what?" asked Morgan defensively.

"Never mind," replied Torrie. "It's up to you. She's your friend."

She turned away from Morgan and stared out the window without seeing.

Morgan drummed a few seconds more, then threw the car into gear. "Let's stay at this campground," she said, making a decided left turn. "If we're lucky we can get the tent up before dark."

They weren't quite that lucky, but they did find the mobile home near the entrance, marked "*Manager*," and there were plenty of spaces available since it was midweek.

After the manager had told them that the campgrounds

had been filled to capacity on the weekends, Torrie felt a little guilty about the fuss she had made about the change in plans. Funny how the things that upset you most have a way of turning around. They would have had trouble finding a place to camp if they had come on the weekend as they had originally planned. So Morgan's delays had worked to their advantage after all. At least this time.

Morgan borrowed the phone and called home to leave a message for Astrid, in case her friend called to ask where she was; then they drove on to their campsite.

Their tent site was close to their parking space, so they were able to set up their blue and gray dome tent aided by the headlights of the Porsche. With the help of their flashlights, they located the primitive toilets and cold water showers. They showered in record time. Neither one washed her hair, and they raced each other back to the campsite.

"I love car camping," said Morgan as she unscrewed the valve on the self-inflating mattress. "It's a lot easier than packing everything for miles on your back."

Torrie nodded agreement although she hadn't done either. The Northwest branch of the Morgan family was really into the outdoors mode. Every summer they had pictures and slides to show from their latest adventure: hiking Mount Baker, mountain biking, ferrying to the San Juan Islands, whale watching. Torrie had been overjoyed when Morgan had invited her to come out for her graduation. "Just bring your hiking boots and come on out," her aunt had said. "We'll take care of all the rest." It would be the first time that Torrie had visited her Uncle Stuart and Aunt Lorna on the west coast, and they were all eager to show off their rainy paradise.

While the girls were young the family used to get together every summer at the farm in Iowa. Their grandmothers were sisters—Minerva and Katherine, or Minnie and Kate to anyone who knew them for more than five minutes. The women had gone through the depression and were determined to pass along their survival skills to all their offspring and the extended family. Grandma Kate had moved West with her young husband just before the second world war, while Torrie's grandmother and her husband, Grandpa Madison, remained on the Morgan farm in the Midwest. The two sisters remained close for over half a century, with Kate's side of the family making a yearly trek back to Iowa; no one dared miss a Morgan family reunion. When Kate passed away, the reunions came to an end and the two cousins had lost contact, except for a constant stream of letters. Torrie could hardly believe they hadn't seen each other for ten years. She was delighted when she received the invitation to Morgan's graduation and had looked forward to the trip and the reunion. But now she was beginning to remember their childhood spats that had resulted in tears and threats—and usually isolation from each other for several hours.

Now with the tent and its contents readied for occupancy, the girls took an armload of firewood from a bin in the trunk of the Porsche and placed it in the fire ring. Morgan built the fire while Torrie got the food from the cooler and began to prepare their supper. Their camping spot was in a pine-needle-carpeted clearing in a circle of trees that stretched into infinite darkness above their heads. The sparks catapulted up into the night, aspiring to be stars, but fading as they reached the dark vastness at the fringes of the circle of light.

After the girls finished their cleanup they sat holding Styrofoam cups of hot chocolate with tiny marshmallows and enjoying the warmth of the fire on their faces. Each sat quietly with her own thoughts, mesmerized by the soothing crackle of the fire.

When the fire died down, they prepared to go to bed. Torrie gathered up her snack bars and a bottle of water from the cooler and headed toward the tent.

"Where do you think you're going with those?" asked

Morgan and lectured Torrie on the procedure for keeping bears away from the campsite. She didn't even allow her to bring her fruit-scented lip balm into the tent. "Nothing that smells like food. Everything has to be locked in the car."

"Why? Do the bears open the car doors?" asked Torrie wryly.

"You wouldn't think it was so funny if you heard one outside your tent at night," Morgan retorted. "Believe me, I know. I guess you don't have any *big* animals to worry about in Texas—just possums and armadillos."

Torrie opened her mouth to reply, thought better of it, then returned her snacks to the car, making sure she had a flashlight.

With an argument narrowly averted, the cousins settled down in a cathedral of fragrant cedar, lulled to sleep by the gurgling of a nearby stream and the chorus of night noises from the forest inhabitants.

Torrie awoke the next day to the early-morning chatter of birds, and left the tent quietly so as not to disturb her sleeping cousin. She plugged a coffee pot into the cigarette lighter of the Porsche and spooned in the fragrant freshly-ground beans. Nothing like Seattle coffee for inspiration, she thought.

She began writing in her journal—a habit initiated with the Christmas gift of a diary from Grandma Minnie when Torrie was twelve, and modified by an eighth grade English teacher into journaling. Morgan had received the same gift, but her only entries were from December 26th to January 8th: *"I'M HAVING SO MUCH FUN I DON'T HAVE TIME TO WRITE IN MY DIARY!!!"*—one word on each page. Torrie, on the other hand, had been writing faithfully ever since, recording feelings, descriptions, and impressions of every phase of her life.

This morning she sat at the picnic table in the quiet dawn and captured the jumble of sights and sounds that had been assaulting her senses since they had entered the forest. The peacefulness of the unscathed natural surroundings soothed her unease of the previous week. The lush forest was an unexpected joy after anticipating the barrenness she had imagined Mount St. Helens would be. She decided she might be able to relax and enjoy what little was left of her vacation after all. But a distant rumble of thunder cast doubts even on that slim hope.

After finishing her second cup and her journaling, she poured another cup, entered the tent and sat on her rumpled sleeping bag. She waved the coffee cup near Morgan's face. "Wake up cuz. It's time to see the forest."

Morgan raised her eyebrows without opening her eyes and made waking-up noises. Her short dark hair fanned out becomingly on the little camping pillow.

Great, thought Torrie. Her hair looks better than mine and I've been up an hour. Morgan had always had the ability to look good even when she was painting the garage in her dad's old paint-smeared shirt and ragged jeans, or trudging back from a sweaty afternoon of picking strawberries in Grandpa Madison's garden. Of course it helped that she had been amply endowed with the proportions the Morgan sisters had been noted for. At an age too young to appreciate it, Morgan had always been surrounded by boys. Torrie hadn't minded all that much—she preferred to be "one of the guys" anyway. She could blend in with her unremarkable build, mousy brown hair, and plain face; her only outstanding feature was her startlingly amber eyes, which seemed to glitter when they caught the light.

What had irked Torrie was that Morgan got to carry the family name. Their grandmothers had no brothers, so with no boys to carry it on, Aunt Lorna had salvaged at least that remnant of a once numerous family when she named her older daughter.

Torrie continued her prodding, gently shaking Morgan's shoulder, who frowned and pulled away, murmuring in her sleep.

"Fine," said Torrie. "I'll go see the moonscape by myself." She raised to a crouch at the tent door and asked, "Do you want anything out of the car before I leave?"

Morgan sat up immediately and shook the blur of sleep from her head. "Don't even think about driving my car," she warned, with eyebrows raised, eyes still closed.

"Well, I guess I know how to get you up," Torrie said smugly.

An hour later they had vacated the campsite and were ready to be on their way. Morgan guessed that Astrid would be out doing field research by now, so there was no point in looking for her until tonight. They decided to do the Windy Ridge loop while they were on this side of the mountain, and then let Astrid be their guide to the immense volcano monument area for the rest of the week. After skimming through the guide book, and eyeing the gray sky, they dressed for hiking, and just in case, placed their rain gear in the little back seat where it would be handy.

When they stopped by the caretakers' mobile home to check out he had told them there was a "big storm brewin' on the mountain today." With concern he had asked if they were sure they wanted to head up that way.

Morgan had responded without hesitation, jangling the keys to her prized possession. "I can drive in anything the weather gods send my way," she said, and they were back on the winding forest road.

"I really want to see that old growth forest," said Morgan.

"I'd think you'd have seen plenty of them," answered Torrie.

"No, not really. There's not many left in the Northwest anymore. Except in the Olympic Peninsula, and the only place I've been out there is Hurricane Ridge and La Push on the coast."

"Well, I'm up for that. I've never seen a tree too big to put my arms around—at least since I've been grown."

Morgan raised an eyebrow. "Better be careful about tree-hugging remarks around here. Some people get pretty testy about it."

"Okay, I'll try to refrain from showing affection to any of the sylvan inhabitants. Do you have any you can drive a car through?"

Morgan gave an exasperated sigh. "Do you see why we don't like tourists around here?"

Torrie grinned and returned to her admiration of the dense forest surrounding them. Streaks of light would shoot unexpectedly through a clearing, illuminating clumps of the pale green feathery moss that hung in so many of the trees, then darkness would prevail for a few more miles. They were steadily climbing and Torrie's ears began to pop. She took out a piece of gum for herself and offered Morgan one.

Morgan shook her head. "Watch for signs to Iron Creek Falls," she said. "It's supposed to be just a short hike." She settled into a rhythm, taking the curves smoothly while Torrie peered this way and that to enjoy the view. They reached the parking area for Iron Creek and pulled off. "Ready for our first official hike?" she asked, and pulled out her new Canon, another graduation present.

They entered the silent womb of the forest and Torrie hardly dared breathe. It seemed almost a sacred place. Wordlessly, they penetrated the dark recesses of the ancient woods, the darkness of the secluded path broken only by the flash of Morgan's camera.

Torrie was halted by Morgan's uplifted hand. She looked in the direction Morgan pointed and saw a moss covered dead log with numerous small trees growing from it. "Nurse log," she whispered, as though the slumbering log might awaken and shake its young charges to the ground.

Around the next bend they were delighted to find the falls, twinkling and sparkling in the gloom. They sat on a cold rock and breathed in the moist mountain air. Torrie read from the guide book: "'*This is one of the few areas in the Mount St. Helens region where you can observe an old growth forest.*'" She stopped reading. "If this is an old growth forest, where are all the big trees?"

"I don't know," admitted Morgan. "Doesn't your book explain it?"

"No, it just goes on more about the eruption and how some of the young trees were protected in the snowbanks and started regrowing soon after." Torrie looked around. "What did you call that log back there? A nursery log?" she asked.

"Nurse log. That's how the new trees get their start. When an old tree decays and falls the new seedlings get their start by growing on it. Eventually the whole log rots away and all that's left is a row of young trees, all in a neat row."

"Sad." The former majestic sentinel of the forest had been reduced to an inert source of nutrients, Torrie thought. Life springing out of death. One of the principles of the forest. Yet she had to admit it was a reassuring thought.

* * *

Life out of death. Yes, that is the cycle, but that cycle moves inexorably toward the next phase: death out of life. The super Fireweed that had supplied the nutrients for the repropagation of the wounded forest is now acting as its agent of destruction. For some inexplicable reason, its cellular structure has undergone an irrevocable chemical change. Now unwitting insects are feeding on its succulent leaves—leaves that now harbor a sinister chemical induced by spiraling mutations and unpredicted changes.

The food chain is about to succumb to the vagaries of its weakest link.

* * *

The coldness of the rock they were sitting on soon seeped through their clothes and into their stiff muscles, so the girls reluctantly left their vantage point and headed toward the waterfall. Morgan resumed her pictorial documentation closer to the stream. She had only moved several feet along the path when she abruptly stopped. "What's this?" she asked, looking down at the ground.

Torrie looked down, expecting to see some flower she might be able to identify in the guide book.

Morgan had stooped down and was picking up what looked like fish eggs. "This stuff is cold."

"Cold?" said Torrie, puzzled. Maybe somebody had dumped out their ice chest here.

Then Morgan stood up and shoved a handful of the mysterious substance under Torrie's nose.

"I knew we were in for something strange today," said Torrie. "It's hail!"

Chapter 3

HEROES

"If it's hailing, maybe we shouldn't go up to Windy Ridge," suggested Morgan.

"You're worried about a little hail?" said Torrie. "That's nothing compared to the thunder that was rumbling early this morning."

"What thunder?" replied her cousin as she started back up the path toward the road.

"Don't tell me you actually slept through all that."

"That's impossible. We don't have thunderstorms in Washington."

"It may be impossible, but that's what it was doing. Unless it was your snoring I heard."

"Well you must have brought it with you from Texas," concluded Morgan as she picked up her pace. "Come on, let's get back to my car. If it's going to hail I want to get it under shelter."

Torrie rolled her eyes. "I thought it was your favorite cousin you were concerned about."

Morgan had already started back down the trail in the direction of the precious Porsche, when a sudden spate of showers sent them both dashing for the safety of the vehicle.

Breathless, Morgan reached for the map. "How far is the closest shelter?" she asked.

Torrie leaned over the open map and pointed out their present location. "We're right here," she said, indicating the spot, and here's where we started this morning."

Morgan studied the map and wrinkled her brow. "Don't tell me. According to the map, that road we just came on was straight. I'd hate to think what the curvy part is going to be like."

After further study of the map they decided to go on up to Bear Meadow and look for shelter there. They continued up the steeper, more winding road, meeting sheets of rain and dozens of vehicles heading down, and passing in and out of patches of mist. The road likewise was mottled with dry spots and dark stretches that Torrie worried could be turning to ice.

"Do you get the idea we're the only ones going up the mountain?" said Torrie.

"Maybe they know something we don't." Morgan switched on the radio and punched buttons, but received only static and snatches of melodies. She finally switched it off. "Guess we'll have to wait until we find a ranger for a weather report."

"If they're from Randle, they'll probably tell us it's going to be clear and sunny."

"Right," agreed her cousin. "Oh, look. Here's Bear Meadow," she said as she whipped the steering wheel to the left and came to a rapid stop at the interpretive center.

"I don't see any shelter," said Torrie, looking around the parking area. "But it looks like the rain has stopped for now."

The girls got out of the car and walked over to the large sign overlooking a meadow teeming with an array of purplish flowers and ending abruptly in a wall of mist.

Morgan started reading the sign. "This is where a couple of photographers were watching during the blast," she explained.

"Oh, no," said Torrie soberly. "Were they killed?"

"No," Morgan answered, continuing to read. The blast separated and went in two directions. It missed this spot."

"Wow," said Torrie. "That gives me goose flesh."

"Goose flesh," said Morgan indignantly. "You're starting to talk like a Texan."

"That shouldn't come as a surprise, I've lived there for ten years." Torrie made a good-natured swipe at her which Morgan agilely ducked. "This is incredible," Torrie concluded as she finished reading the sign to herself. "What a narrow escape. So on a clear day this would be our first view of Mount St. Helens."

"Right. On a clear day. If you hang around Washington until August you might actually see a clear day."

Back in the car they continued their climb up the winding roadway with Torrie narrating from the guide book. The hillsides were carpeted with a stand of young fir trees and a profusion of the same deep mauve flowers they had seen in the meadow, along with a scattering of yellow and white flowers and splashes of Indian paintbrush.

"I hadn't expected it to be this green," commented Torrie.

"Actually, this is an unusual look for a forest," explained her cousin. "There should be more variety. And of course, the trees should be bigger."

Torrie continued her visual scan of the reemerging wildlife. "There's an animal up there," she said excitedly.

"A big one?"

"No. About the size of a cat."

"A fox?"

"No. It looks more like a beaver."

"Beaver, huh. Well, there's certainly plenty of wood for them."

"And they wouldn't even have to cut it," suggested Torrie.

"But what would a beaver be doing way up on the side of the mountain? It should be down by a river. Oh, look. Here's a lake," said Morgan, pointing to the sign. "Shall we stop?"

The sign said it was the site of the Miner's Car, whatever that meant. Relieved when the Porsche came to a stop, Torrie jumped out before Morgan could change her mind and resume the crazy zigzag careening up the mountainside. They looked with dismay at the charred remains of a car that had been blown sixty feet in the volcano's 1980 blast. Everything that wasn't made of metal had been instantly disintegrated, and the tires had been vulcanized. The family that had parked it there to walk to a nearby miner's cabin had all perished instantly. "All the statistics don't mean much until you actually see the results," said Torrie with a shudder.

She hurried to catch up with Morgan who had already started toward the lake. They walked on a wooden walkway constructed along the beach of what had previously been a living, well-stocked lake. The desolation overwhelmed them at every step, even though a newly constructed path made the walking easy. The rain was spitting again as they returned to the parking lot, and they were startled to see a lone figure examining the car.

"Who's that by your car?" whispered Torrie, nudging Morgan.

"I don't know, but I'm going to find out," replied Morgan, striding purposefully over toward the stranger.

As they neared the car they could see that it was a forest ranger, clad head to toe in a hunter green Gore-tex jacket. He was hunkered down against the rain beneath a fur-lined hood, probably imitation, which obscured his face from view.

"Excuse me," said Morgan boldly as they approached him.

He turned and fixed them with ice-blue eyes. He had finely chiselled features with a firm jaw and a hint of a daily-emerging beard. His expression was stone serious. "This is a fee area," he said with a deep resonant voice.

"Fee area?" asked Torrie blankly, turning to Morgan.

Morgan stood up straighter. "Yes, we Washingtonians are not too happy about paying fees to enjoy our own state," she explained to Torrie with a sidelong glance at the ranger. To him she said, "We tried to buy a pass yesterday at the ranger station, but they told us to wait until today—if we decided to come at all."

The ranger nodded knowingly. "Because of the weather." It was a statement.

Torrie and Morgan exchanged concerned glances. "The weather?" prompted Torrie.

"Thunder and lightning, hail, with reported gale force winds," he said. "Just like they predicted."

"You mean they knew this was going to happen?" said Torrie in disbelief.

"And they didn't tell us?" responded Morgan.

The ranger raised an eyebrow at their rapid-fire exchange and there was a flicker of a smile in his ice blue eyes. "It sounds like you've been to Randle," he surmised. "But you still need a pass."

"Can you sell us one?" asked Morgan, giving him a look that could only be described as flirtatious.

He directed them to Cascade Peaks, farther up the road they had been following, and the closest place to purchase a pass and find shelter if need be. He tried to dissuade them from their planned outing since there had even been snow flurries at the higher elevations. Torrie turned to face the mist-shrouded volcano. She had come too far to turn back now and miss out on her chance to see the ragged summit of the once perfectly conical peak.

Meanwhile, Morgan had edged around Torrie until she was standing next to the ranger. She turned to face the lake. "What are those?" she asked, indicating a patch of the red-violet flowers they had been admiring all the way up the mountain.

"Those are the heroes of the forest," he replied.

"Heroes?" said Torrie.

"Yes, it's an awesome story." He raised his arm and made a slow circle indicating the emerging growth that surrounded them on all sides in the drizzle. "All of this was made possible by this lowly little weed, along with some of its helpful friends."

"It's just a weed?" asked Torrie in amazement.

"How did they do that?" asked Morgan, just short of fluttering her eyelashes at him.

"Let's go over here," he said, pointing to the path they had just come from near the lake and gently nudging Torrie's elbow to propel her in that direction.

The two girls gladly moved away from the guilty car with its pass-less windshield and started down the path. Morgan gave Torrie a thumbs-up sign behind his back.

They had discovered his passion. For half an hour he talked non-stop, describing the reforestation process and the part played by the beautiful plant—yes, classified by some as a weed—but he preferred to call them the colonizers. Soon after the eruption, the wind had carried the hardy seeds into the barren landscape on delicate tufts and the reforestation process was begun. The early plants started adding their nutrients to the soil to make the area more habitable for less durable species.

Its partner in the process was the pocket gopher. Safe in their burrows deep below the surface, these creatures were among the handful of survivors of the devastation. Soon they were feasting on the tender roots of the plant newcomers, and bringing rich soil to the surface from beneath the thick carpet of ash in the process of their construction process. In a surprising twist of nature's inter-relationships, the miles of tunnels became home to some unusual guests. The gopher played unwitting host to the salamanders, frogs, and newts that had initially survived the devastation under water. When the amphibians emerged to find hostile ash fields, they became subterranean dwellers rather than stay in the inhospitable terrain.

The rest of the food chain followed the encroaching colonizers, and within five years most of the species originally populating the area had returned to forage and re-establish a semblance of their former existence.

* * *

Beneath the floral enchantment surrounding the lake, a busy gopher is remodeling her den. The tunnels are quiet now, not like the post-eruption years when strange visitors roamed the unaccustomed haunts. Now the problems she faces are of a more serious kind. The plants she has long relied on for nourishment for her brood are suspect. The Fireweed that once served as her co-laborer in rebuilding has taken on the role of villain, supplying toxins destined to destroy. Now the desperate gopher spends long hours searching for wholesome nourishment. If things don't improve, she will have to resort to desperate measures . . .

* * *

The path the ranger led them on for the informal lecture wound around the gentle curve of the lake, and soon they drew near the parking area again. As they neared the Porsche a green Department of Natural Resources truck pulled up with the large DNR logo on its door, and a perky blond female ranger jumped out. Their ranger walked over to confer with her while Torrie and Morgan discussed their stroke of luck—he had forgotten all about their day pass. As they got back into the car, he walked over in their direction again, and Morgan rolled down the window.

"We just got an all-clear on the weather," he informed them. "I've been summoned back to the trails to lead interpretive hikes again." He gestured almost apologetically in the direction of the tall blond. "So it's probably safe to go on up to Windy Ridge."

Morgan thanked him and started to pull away.

"You probably won't get a look at the mountain, though," he shouted to Torrie.

She responded with an expansive two-handed shrug.

"I think he likes you," said Morgan, simulating a pout.

"He was just doing his job."

"No, he was definitely eyeing you."

"You have an overactive imagination. Besides, you were the one who was flirting with him."

"I wasn't flirting. I was just trying to keep his mind off the visitor's pass."

"So, you were using him," accused Torrie.

"Oh, don't be naïve," said Morgan. "Guys like to feel useful."

Their mock quarrel was interrupted when they arrived at Cascade Peaks. They got out and purchased some souvenirs, and, of course, the requisite pass. They picnicked out of their cooler at the next scenic area and spent the rest of the afternoon stopping at the various overlooks. The last leg up to Windy Ridge consisted of a series of switchbacks with a chasm on one side and a steep bank on the other studded with trees poking out at all angles and looking as if they could fall at any moment. Finally they reached Windy Ridge, and Torrie got out on shaky legs.

To their disappointment, the volcano was still enveloped by the persistent bank of clouds.

"I guess your Ranger Rick was right," commented Morgan.

"*Ranger Rick*," said Torrie, with a touch of nostalgia in her voice. "I had forgotten about that magazine. I suppose Grandma Kate gave you a subscription every year, too."

"Of course. That and the matching housecoat and pajamas she always made us. Yeah, Meagan and I always fought . . ." Her voice trailed off and she looked away. "It still isn't easy to remember her, after all these years."

"I know," agreed Torrie, and walked over to the sign that described the view they should have had from that spot.

Torrie left Morgan alone with her memories for a few moments. Morgan's younger sister had tragically drowned when she was ten and Morgan still carried the ache. Torrie herself hadn't come to grips with the death, and she suggested they climb the ridge. "For a better view of the clouds," she quipped, but really to get their minds off Meagan.

Narrow wooden steps ascended into the clouds with a Jack-in-the-beanstalk promise. They climbed steadily for several minutes and rested at the first landing that had a bench. Two small boys clambered up past them with eyes fixed on the steps. "Two hundred thirty-one, two hundred thirty-two, two hundred thirty-three . . . ," they heard them counting as they hurried past.

"I don't *even* want to know how many steps there are," said Morgan.

"I want to know where they get all that energy," commented Torrie.

As they started up the next flight, they had to move aside for a swarthy young man coming down from the overlook at the top. He was dressed in gear resembling a wet suit, red and black from head to toe, with a dark parcel tucked under his arm.

His bearing was regal and his expression imperious. Torrie casually greeted him in passing, but his gaze never faltered in its cool, controlled firmness. He didn't even give Morgan a passing glance. His eyebrows and short spiky hair were coal black and his eyes a deep unsearchable brown. His gait was smooth and effortless as he descended the steps and walked across the parking lot.

"I wonder what he was dressed for," said Morgan. "Was that scuba diving gear?"

"Maybe somebody warned him about the weather," suggested Torrie.

"He's built like a swimmer," observed Morgan.

"Leave it to you to notice."

"Why don't we go ask him if he wants to double date," Morgan said. "Which would you rather have, the swimmer or the ranger? Or we could even triple date. Astrid has mentioned a 'colleague' that I'm willing to bet is a man. I intend to find out as soon as we get to her place."

No surprises there, Torrie thought as she scowled at her cousin—Morgan was always prying into other people's relationships, even when there was nothing there to pry at. Then they heard a distant roar and turned to look down the steep incline they had just conquered. Far below they saw a motorcycle leave the lot, piloted by a red-and-black-clad driver.

Morgan laughed. "A motorcyclist. That explains his strange clothes."

"Of course," agreed Torrie. "That was his helmet under his arm."

They resumed their climb and eventually reached the observation point where several other tourists lingered hopefully in the vicinity of the temporarily-useless binoculars installed on the deck. The billowing white mass refused to release its prey to view, so the two began the long trek back down. They were passed again by the scampering children and Torrie called out to ask how many steps there were.

"Four hundred and thirty-two," was the reply.

"You had to ask," groaned Morgan.

Back in the car they began the return trip down the mountain. When they returned to the fields of colorful flowers, they realized that the ranger had never told them the name of his "heroes." "I know there are some pictures of flowers in this road guide," said Torrie, taking it out. She thumbed through and found the page she was looking for. "Goatsbeard, lupine, false dandelion—definitely not dandelion—pearly everlasting..." She stopped suddenly. "Of course. Why didn't I think of that?"

"What? What kind is it?" asked Morgan impatiently.

"Think about it. It's the same kind of plant that starts growing after a fire."

"And...," Morgan prompted.

"And the conditions after a volcano would be like it is after a fire. Only a hundred times worse. I thought you liked guessing games."

"So, the name of this flower is..."

"You're not trying hard enough. The ranger said some people call it a weed," she said, emphasizing the last word. "And it starts growing after a F-I-R-E."

"Give me that book," said Morgan in exasperation. She snatched at it as she engineered a steep curve, throwing up gravel at the edge of the pavement.

"Okay, you win," said Torrie. "Just keep your eyes on the road and I'll tell you: it's called *Fireweed*."

Chapter 4

APE CAVE

"Fireweed," said Morgan. "I should have guessed." She pretended to be concentrating on her driving. "I know why you're picking on me. It's because I'm driving and you know I can't do anything to you."

"No, that's not true," replied Torrie. "I'm picking on you because I'm your older cousin. That's part of the job description."

"Now that I think about it," Torrie continued. "I remember reading about plants that can only germinate after an immense amount of heat has softened the hull of the seed. So it makes sense that the devastation of a volcano would be followed by the same pattern: plants—and animals—finding a way to survive against impossible odds."

Morgan shrugged her disinterest, so Torrie dropped the subject.

They were retracing the switchbacks Morgan had driven up earlier. Patches of welcome sunshine were beginning to break through the fog, with the unsettling result of revealing deep chasms off to Torrie's right. Just as Morgan rounded yet another curve, the cloud cover opened up and an enormous double rainbow loomed just ahead of them, tickling the emptiness from end to end.

The conversation abruptly halted and Morgan said, "Get a picture."

"You know I'm not a photographer," protested Torrie.

"This camera's foolproof. And besides, you can't convince me that the daughter of a world-renowned photojournalist didn't inherit a little bit of that talent."

"That subject's *verboten*," said Torrie brusquely and reluctantly fumbled for the camera. She quickly snapped several shots of the unexpected beauty. The silence was only interrupted by their sounds of admiration as they made their way back down the mountain.

Morgan stopped again at Bear Meadow, trying for one last chance at a view of the majestic remains of the mountain. They sat in the car for awhile. No luck. The brief appearance of the sun had been fleeting and the peak was still shrouded.

"What a disappointment," said Morgan. "You came all this way and didn't get to see it."

"Well, we got to see something even better," Torrie reminded her. "The rainbow. The universal symbol of promise. That's pretty ironic."

"What?" asked her cousin.

"The earth is never supposed to be destroyed by flood again, but for all these people—and animals—it was destroyed by volcano. So for them the rainbow is more like a promise that life will go on after the destruction, like the ranger explained to us."

Morgan started the car. "You always have had a strange way of looking at things, Torrie Madison."

Torrie didn't pursue the conversation, but she knew she would have a lot of thoughts to add to her journal tonight.

Since the weather had discouraged the rest of their sightseeing and hiking plans, they decided to go see Ape Cave—it wouldn't matter whether it rained or stormed while they were down there. They were back in the untouched part of the forest and the highway wended its narrow path through the evergreen splendor. When they emerged, they followed the shore of a reservoir for several miles, catching an occasional glimpse of the sparkling water when patches of sunshine coincided with openings in the forest.

They arrived at Ape Cave just in time to take the last tour. The cousins joined a group of about a dozen adults and children already assembled. The guide had half a dozen Coleman lanterns at her feet and was orienting her assembled group on cave etiquette. She stressed the importance of adequate preparation: wear a jacket or sweater, hat, and sturdy shoes, and take three sources of light. In order to protect the cave environment, no artificial lighting had been installed, so explorers were required to import their own. Torrie volunteered to carry a lantern, but Morgan wanted to keep her hands free for taking pictures.

The guide reassured the children that there were no apes in the cave; it had been named after a group of young outdoorsmen known as the St. Helens Apes who had explored the cave. The cave itself was actually a lava tube formed from an eruption of the volcano about 1900 years ago. A stream of molten lava had carved it out of the earth, and cooling on the outer edges, it left a solid surface which became the cave walls after the still hot liquid continued its descent and eventually emptied the newly-formed tube. At over 12,000 feet, the guide pointed out, Ape Cave is the longest lava tube in the continental United States, but the tour itself would cover only the 4000 feet of the lower cave—a less-challenging climb than the rock-strewn upper cave tackled by experienced cavers.

People carrying lanterns were interspersed the length of the tour group and everyone was admonished not to touch the walls unless absolutely necessary—in order to protect the living things growing on the walls. Torrie scrupulously obeyed, especially since the guide had not yet told them exactly what it was that was living in the cave; the guide would tell them at an opportune moment when they neared the end of their trek.

Torrie and Morgan huddled into their warm jackets against the forty degree temperature and the continual light breeze. The ancient lava flow had followed the easiest path downhill—the course of the stream—so it twisted and tumbled over the extinct stream bed, making walking treacherous. At one particularly steep place, Torrie lost her footing on the slippery boulders and had to be steadied by another tourist, an attractive older man.

"Want me to get a picture of him?" whispered Morgan, as soon as they stopped for the next interpretive session.

"Don't you think of anything else?" whispered Torrie back. "He's old enough to be my grandpa."

"Just trying to look out for my cousin," she replied, taking the promised picture and being rewarded by a wink from the amused man.

The inside of the cave had a very unique appearance since it was formed from lava, not limestone as most caves. The walls had been coated with a dark shiny glaze after hot gasses had melted the surface. In places the rippled pattern revealed where sections of the forming wall had slumped. The few remaining stalactites and stalagmites are very fragile, the guide explained. Most had long since fallen prey to souvenir hunters. The cave had a steam-cooked roof, in places showing a red ceiling where portions of the lava shell had fallen away and the baked reddish soil remained. "But nothing has fallen in recent years," the guide informed those who were looking apprehensively at the ceiling. She promised the clamoring children they would learn about the inhabitants of the cave at the next stop.

"It better not be bats," said Torrie. Several people turned and looked at her; and the elderly man shook his head reassuringly.

He was right. Bats no longer lived in the cave; they also were victims of the encroachment of human life into their habitat. Early explorers had to contend with bats, or vice versa. But contrary to popular myth, humans have very little to fear from bats, mostly because the animal's reaction time is very slow. If humans invade the bats' domain, it takes the nocturnal creatures half an hour to mobilize. By the time they are swooping about, the wise interloper will have left the scene.

* * *

Bats in a distant cave are suffering from another, more insidious human encroachment. At dusk, when they leave the protection of their new-found cave, they feed upon the insects that have been nibbling on a tasty, but deadly, new strain of Fireweed.

The unsuspecting bats return to their habitat, little knowing that they have become the next link in a rapidly deconstructing chain. The much-maligned little creatures may soon turn into vicious attackers as they are so often portrayed.

* * *

On the final stop of the tour, the guide invited the spectators to smell the walls, without touching them of course, to try to guess what was living on them. The few brave participants reported that it smelled like a storm cellar, or mushrooms, or mildew.

"Good," said the guide. "What causes those kinds of smells?"

"Fungus?" asked an alert eight-year-old.

"Exactly," she replied, and the crowd applauded.

"The creatures living on the walls are a form of fungus known as cave slime."

A choruses of disgusted "ooh's" and "yuk's" passed through the crowd. They had reached the end of the passable portion and at the guide's instructions, the little entourage turned and retraced its steps to the opening. They soon reached the entrance and Torrie was glad to extinguish her lantern and climb the steep steps leading back into the open air.

After leaving the cave, Morgan and Torrie started back toward Tower Rock and Astrid's trailer. They stopped and got gas and supplies at Cougar, their last chance before re-entering Gifford Pinchot Forest.

The return drive took nearly two hours and it was dark when they finally located the Tower Rock Campground. In contrast to the surrounding forest, the campground was located in a large clearing with a fish pond in the center. A silvery moon peeked over the top of a looming rock formation clearly visible in the fringe of trees surrounding the clearing. The owner directed them to Astrid's small travel trailer.

"Her pickup is here," observed Morgan. "She must be home. And the lights are on, so she's not in bed yet." She gathered up the box of books and papers she had brought and they knocked on the door of the trailer. They heard a staccato stream of frenetic barking inside. "Oh, good, she brought Tasha."

"Tasha? Just exactly how big is Tasha?"

"She's harmless," replied Morgan as the door burst open and Astrid's pleasantly freckled face and an overly enthusiastic sheltie greeted them.

"Come on in," she said, moving aside to let them enter the small space. "Tasha, sit."

Surprisingly, the miniature canine sat, wagging and waiting for her master's next command.

"Where do you want your stuff?" asked Morgan, looking around an area that was already cluttered with books, loose papers, and scattered piles of different colored notebooks, all of a uniform size and shape.

"Right here in my 'office,'" she said, indicating the top of a small built-in cabinet. She moved a bulging briefcase to the floor below.

Morgan deposited the overflowing box. "I hope I found everything you needed," she said. Then she looked at the pile of dishes in the sink." Looks like we missed supper."

Tasha leaped to her feet and wagged even more eagerly until Astrid repeated her order to sit and the dog slumped to the carpet again. "We spell out food words around here," she reminded Morgan. "No, I saved you some H-O-T D-O-G-S," she said. "I hope you weren't expecting anything fancy."

"No, we've been feasting in Seattle ever since Torrie got here," said Morgan. "S-A-L-M-O-N and S-U-S-H-I every day is too much even for me."

Astrid gave a half-hearted laugh and turned toward the kitchenette. She removed a package of wieners from the tiny refrigerator and looked out the small window as she extricated a dripping pan from the dish rack without disturbing the other dishes piled there.

Morgan helped herself to the dark bitter coffee that had sat too long in the pot on the counter. She poured it into a huge UW mug and sat at the table to talk to Astrid. Torrie sat on the carpet and started scratching Tasha between the ears. "Is she a border collie?" she asked.

"No, a sheltie—a miniature version of a collie. They're a working breed. If I don't keep her busy and give her jobs to do, she gets irritable and yappy. One day I heard a lot of quacking outside, and when I went out to check I discovered she had rounded up a bunch of ducks."

"What's this little box attached to her collar?" asked Torrie. "Does she rescue people lost in the mountains, like a Saint Bernard?"

Torrie thought she caught a look of alarm flash across Astrid's face before she answered. "No, that's her ID and medical records. If she gets lost while I'm up here, I want people to be able to find me locally."

Torrie nodded her head. "Some people don't even take care of their kids that well," she remarked, as she scratched Tasha behind the ears.

Astrid ran fingers distractedly through her own hair. "She'll be your friend for life," she said to Torrie who continued her ministrations to the pleased animal. "She loves to be scratched there."

Wearing overalls and a tie-died tee shirt, Astrid looked more hippie than graduate student—not an unusual sight in Washington, Torrie had observed. Astrid went to the refrigerator but returned empty-handed. After taking a rubber band from a drawer and twisting her long straight hair back into a bun, she returned to the refrigerator and opened the door again. "What was I looking for?"

"Condiments, maybe?" answered Morgan.

Astrid pulled small bottles of mustard and catsup and relish from the door and set them on the table, stopping first as she passed the window over the sink and peered out again into the dark.

After several unsuccessful attempts to engage her friend in conversation, Morgan put down her coffee cup. "Okay. What's really going on here?"

"Nothing, really," replied Astrid, absently fingering the pocket on the bib of her overalls.

"I know you better than that," said Morgan. "Your place is a mess, you have dirty dishes piled all over the counters, and you're eating hot . . . ," she turned to the living room where Torrie still entertained the contented pup. "D-O-G-S," she finished. "And what about all this stuff you asked me to bring? I know you would have had everything you needed for your research project. So why do you need all this other junk all of a sudden?" Morgan stared intently at her friend until Astrid looked away.

After checking out the window once again, Astrid poured out the thick black coffee and fixed a cup of steaming chai for herself and Torrie. "This is what you should be drinking in Washington," she told her guest.

Torrie took a tentative sip. "What's in this, anyway?"

"Tea with some interesting spices. I fix mine with soy milk."

"Not bad," said Torrie after a second sip. "Different, but not bad."

Astrid joined Morgan at the table. "Okay," she sighed. "I'll tell you what I know, but it's probably nothing. I'm sure I'm just overreacting."

She started by bringing Torrie up to date on her research. She was getting a master's degree in environmental issues at the University of Washington—known as U-Dub—and was spending the summer at Mount St. Helens doing field research.

"My area of specialization is ecological succession," she explained. "That's what happens after an environment undergoes a rapid, traumatic change, like a fire or a flood, and it begins to rebuild and repopulate. Mount St. Helens is a perfect laboratory, since it suffered such a severe natural disaster, and now the growth is returning."

"Yeah, I noticed," said Torrie. "I thought it was all going to be like the blast zone. I was really surprised to see all the trees and animals, and those beautiful purple flowers, the—what do they call them? Fire—something." Tasha had fallen asleep with her head on Torrie's lap and she was careful not to disturb the little sheltie.

"Oh, yes. Fireweed," responded Astrid, and Torrie thought she saw that same disturbed look cloud Astrid's countenance.

"Fireweed is what I have been focusing on," Astrid went on. "It is usually one of the first plants to inhabit a destroyed area. I'm most interested in the earliest developments in reclaiming the land," she explained. "I think that has the most implications for the whole Pacific Northwest right now. You've seen our clearcuts?"

"Yes," Torrie answered. "Morgan pointed some out to me. I didn't realize that they logged in national parks."

"Not the parks," corrected Astrid. "Just the national forests. 'Managed lands' has a completely different meaning to outsiders. They picture land being 'managed' for their recreational purposes. Anyway, I'm trying to discover the best way to handle the recovery process. The clear cuts are really damaging to the ecology and the habitat. If the land is too fragmented, some animals don't have enough area to hunt prey and propagate. Some creatures never recover."

"Can't they just get the lumberjacks to stop making the clearcuts?"

"You haven't met our Washington timbermen," interjected Morgan. "By the way, they're called 'loggers.' They've been doing it the same way for decades and they're not about to change."

"I always thought lumber—loggers went into the forest and cut the biggest trees and left the rest standing."

"They used to do that," explained Astrid. "But it's a much more difficult way to get the timber out—and more dangerous, too. Also the lumber companies discovered that it was economically more feasible to clearcut and replant all the trees the same size. That makes a section much easier to harvest when it's ready."

"So, in the meantime, we have an ugly scar in our scenery to look at for the next forty years," Morgan complained.

"Right. That's why I'm studying to best way to initiate that regrowth process. I'd like to propose a method that's more environmentally sound."

"Without losing profits for the lumber industry," guessed Torrie.

"Exactly. There's already an existing outdoor lab right here. I can observe the natural method in the monument area and compare the results with what's happened with the planned replanting done by the timber companies."

"It sounds like interesting research," said Torrie.

"But it still doesn't answer my question," put in Morgan. "What's so important that I had to come all the way up here with that pile of papers?" she asked, waving her hand in the direction of the overflowing box on the counter.

"I told you that I had been focusing on the Fireweed plant. Well, I've been charting its growth patterns and traced its spread over the past fifteen years . . ." She paused.

"And . . . ," prompted Morgan.

"Well, it seems that starting with the growing season this year, there has been a significant change from the established patterns." She stopped for a sip of her cooling drink.

"Go on, go on," urged Torrie.

Astrid put down her cup and adjusted the tangle of brown hair at the back of her head. "Well, if my records are accurate, this year it seems that the Fireweed is mutating."

Chapter 5

MUTANTS

"Mutating?" said the cousins in unison.

Torrie jumped up without warning and Tasha yelped and started running in frantic circles. "What kind of mutations?" she asked, joining the other two girls at the table. "What does that mean?"

"Is it dangerous?" asked Morgan.

"Calm down, you two," said Astrid, waving both hands downward as though the motion itself would literally calm them. "Like I said, it's probably not anything, really. Lots of mutations are actually improvements."

"Yeah, name *one*," challenged Morgan. "Mutations usually create changes that harm the species," she reminded her.

"I knew I shouldn't have told you."

"Why not?" snapped Morgan. "Do you think we can't understand it, or what?"

"It's just that non-scientists tend to overreact," Astrid said calmly. "Mutations are a perfectly normal part of the evolutionary process; it's nothing to get alarmed about," she said. "It's only in the movies that they're used for evil purposes and get out of hand."

Torrie and Morgan looked guiltily at each other. They had, in fact, gone to see *Jurassic Park* just after Torrie flew into Seattle. And Astrid was right: it hadn't been the mutations that caused the problems, it was the genetic tinkering by the greedy villains that had created all the havoc in the prehistoric theme park.

Astrid remembered the dinner just in time to rescue the hot dogs, which by now had boiled nearly to extinction. She set the haphazard meal in front of her guests and they went through the motions of eating. None of them was willing to broach the sensitive subject again.

After the meal, Astrid got out a map of the volcanic monument area. She laid it on the floor and they all gathered around as she showed them the area north of the volcano that had been set aside for scientific study. She traced an irregular line with her finger; it delineated a roughly pie-shaped area flaring out to the north and encompassing the crater, the pumice plains, and several canyons and lakes, including Spirit Lake which the girls had seen earlier on their way up to Windy Ridge. "All this shaded area is off-limits to outsiders," she explained. "This is an incredible outdoor laboratory. Where else would you get a chance to study the results of a natural disaster in an authentic situation like this. It would be a little difficult to get funding if you proposed blowing up a forest so you could study ecological succession."

"I see your point," said Torrie. "So what is it you're actually researching about this ecological . . ."

"Succession. It's the process that environmental systems go through in returning and re-establishing themselves in a damaged area—like after a fire or flood. Plants that help fix nutrients in the soil come back first, then they're followed by birds and small rodents, and others on up the food chain. That's why you see so few varieties of species now around the blast area. The delicate balance isn't ready to support more complex symbiotic interactions yet."

"Oh, yes. That's what that ranger was telling us about this morning."

"What that gorgeous ranger told us," interjected Morgan. "Have her tell you about her ranger, Astrid."

Torrie gave Morgan a withering look and Astrid got up from the floor and fixed herself another drink.

Morgan seemed to sense the change of mood in the small room and picked a new victim. "Who is this colleague of yours? Is he a researcher? It is a *he* isn't it?"

Astrid turned out the light in the kitchenette and moved to the living room. She sat heavily on the couch where her face was masked in shadows.

"His name is Eddie Martinez. Our research has overlapped in a couple areas," she said, her voice taking on a husky tone.

"What is he researching?" persisted Morgan.

"He's a geologist—he's been taking seismology readings on a ridge overlooking Coldwater Lake."

"Geology doesn't sound like it's related to your field. Are you sure he's just a friend?" asked Morgan.

"You can't ever leave it alone, can you Morgan?" Her tone was icy, but on the verge of cracking. "Can't you for once let it rest? He's been missing for two days." She broke off and lowered her face to the cup which she gripped desperately with both hands.

Both girls stared unbelievingly at the scientist and even Morgan seemed uncomfortable and stopped her line of questioning. She returned to a study of the map, leaving an awkward silence hanging in the room.

Not knowing what to say, Torrie changed the subject.

"What are the seismologists looking for? Do they think there might be another eruption?"

Astrid took a deep breath and another sip. It was a long time before she answered and Torrie wondered if she had done the right thing by trying to get her talking about something else.

At last she spoke. "They were concerned about it for the first few years—there were actually several eruptions after the big one in May of 1980."

"Really?" said Torrie. "Why didn't we hear about those?"

Astrid replied with a sniff. "Because our local celebrity Harry Truman was gone. Nobody was interested any more without all the hype of an old man who refused to leave his home."

"But they're sure it's not going to erupt any more?" asked Morgan, looking up from the map.

"Well, of course nobody knows for sure, but they're calling it a dead volcano. It's Mt. Rainier they're worried about now," she added, looking pointedly at Morgan.

"Thanks a lot. Guess I'll leave Seattle for the safety of California after all."

"And be swept out to sea when the 'big one' hits?" queried Torrie.

"Okay, you two. Enough of this. You watch too many disaster movies." She set down her coffee and resumed her explanation of the map.

"This is where Eddie has his equipment set up," she said, indicating an area north of Coldwater Lake. "He has to monitor the equipment constantly so he's able to keep an eye on things in that area. He's not too far from where I've been taking specimens of Fireweed in these canyons." She pointed out an area farther to the west.

* * *

Nestled in a remote canyon, a flourishing field of Fireweed is undergoing some startling changes. In the cool night air the normal heathery hue is taking on a shade that is decidedly more of a peach than the mauve characteristic of *Epilobium angustifolium*. Had any astute hikers been allowed in the area they might have noted the strange coloration, might even have surreptitiously removed a sample to be displayed in a vase, pressed in a book.

But no one is out on this moonlit night when the puzzling transformation takes place. No one is there to question why the purple Fireweed turns peach at night, or whether it is just a trick of the moonlight. No one is there except the unsuspecting colleagues of the plant once hailed as a hero. Unsuspecting gophers and bees and bats on the verge of experiencing something much more far-reaching than the devastating blast. Their hero is turning into a monster.

* * *

"You say his research overlaps with yours," said Torrie. "I don't understand what connection geology has with botany."
"Actually, we're both in the field of environmental studies. People are beginning to realize even more that what happens to one part of the environment has an impact on everything else. It's become so important that universities are offering specializations in the field now. Government and big business are paying good money for consultants to advise them on responsible management of resources—renewable resources are big now."
"Is that what you plan to do?" asked Torrie. "Become a consultant?"
Astrid laughed. "It's tempting," she said. "But I'll probably follow family tradition and be an underpaid teacher."
"Your mother's a teacher?"

"Mom and Dad both . . . were. They've been gone since I was a child."

"Sorry," said Torrie, and returned without further comment to her study of the map.

Astrid showed them some of the hiking trails around the mountain. "If you really want to appreciate the volcano, you'll have to do some hiking. Did you know that Mount St. Helens is the second most climbed mountain in the world? It has really gained in popularity since the blast."

"Really?" said Torrie. Then she ran her finger along a dotted line. "Is this a trail?"

"Yes," answered Astrid. "We have over 200 miles of trails in the region—mostly for hiking, and biking; but horses and even motorcycles are allowed in some areas."

"Isn't this one in a restricted area?" asked Torrie, still focused on the original dotted line she had located in the shaded area north of the crater.

"Actually some of the trails do go through restricted areas," explained Astrid. "Boundary Trail and Loowit are two that run for miles through the area. But you are strictly prohibited from leaving the trails. They're monitored pretty closely to control unauthorized activity. You really should plan to take a couple of hikes," she urged.

"I'd be up for that," said Torrie. "I haven't had a chance to use these seventy dollar hiking shoes yet."

"I hope they're broken in," said Astrid.

"Sure. I broke them in on all the mountains in East Texas."

"Not!" said Morgan, and all three laughed.

With the tension broken, they resumed making plans for the next few days.

Astrid was going to take a day off to show them around and after that they would be on their own. They told about their explorations and some of the intriguing things they had learned. Astrid decided they must be exhausted if they had driven all the way from Windy Ridge to Ape Cave in one day.

Torrie earned a scowl from her cousin when she said that if Morgan wasn't tired from driving, Torrie was worn out from being her passenger.

Astrid broke in and suggested they all get to bed because they had a long day ahead of them and should get started early. Soon Morgan and Torrie were nestled in their sleeping bags on the lumpy hide-a-bed and Astrid came to see if they needed anything before she retired.

Just as they were ready to settle in, they were startled by a loud knock at the door. Astrid answered it and slipped out on the steps to talk to her visitor. The girls strained to listen. Morgan mouthed Eddie's name, but they couldn't make out the gist of the conversation through the partly-closed door.

When Astrid came back in, they could tell, even in the moonlight, that her face had paled. She sat heavily in the chair by the door and after a few moments she spoke. "That was Eddie's boss," she said slowly. "They're officially declaring him missing."

Chapter 6

KILLER HONEY

The sleepy travelers awoke the next morning to a relatively sunny sky. Astrid said nothing about the news she had received the night before. She went about the breakfast preparations mechanically, and the girls didn't attempt to ask her any questions. She looked as though she hadn't slept all night.

Their hostess had decided to serve breakfast outside to take advantage of the rare treat of sunshine and they all went outside, balancing plates of scrambled eggs, bacon, and toast as well as steaming cups of coffee. Tasha was overjoyed and came wagging out of her doghouse under the trailer where she had been banished the night before. Astrid shooed her away and Tasha whimpered, looking quizzically at Torrie. Torrie slipped her a piece of bacon and scratched the dog with her foot where the animal cowered under the picnic table.

Several of the neighbors were also enjoying the clear morning and the little pond was ringed with fragrant fires. A cluster of semi-permanent housing flanked one end of the water, and tents and recreational vehicles filled in the remainder of the area. The entire compound was sheltered by a bank of tree-lined hills, with Tower Rock stretching toward the sky in the distance—the only visible rock outcropping in sight. On the opposite side of the pond was the manager's log home and office where the tourists could buy anything from firewood to fishing tackle. Frequent splashing attested to the well-stocked pond which lured the fisherman to the challenge, but no one was fishing this time of day.

Breakfast over, the young women loaded their day packs and squeezed into the cab of Astrid's little black Chevy S10 pickup. They put the rest of their provisions inside the topper on the truck bed. Torrie was relieved she wouldn't have to put up with Morgan's driving another day.

The only thing that Astrid had said to them that morning was that she planned to stop at Eddie's cabin before they started on their tour. She hoped to discover some clue connected to his disappearance.

They traveled south on the highway that cut through the heart of the surviving forest—the same way they had gone the day before on the way to Ape Cave. Astrid pointed out features of the landscape they hadn't noticed and named several species of plants and trees: the area was an example of a coniferous forest with alpine meadows, she explained, and the large lake they were passing was Swift Reservoir, a popular recreation area. In contrast to the dreary views of the water they had glimpsed yesterday, today they saw it glittering and dancing in the sunshine.

Astrid turned off on an inconspicuous secondary road and after a few winding turns they approached an isolated cabin hidden from view of the road. Blue facets sparkling through the spaces between trees revealed that Eddie's place was located not far from the shore. She pulled up beside the cabin and turned off the engine. Torrie watched Astrid swallow conspicuously before she opened the door and started up the path toward the front porch.

"Do you want us to come with you?" asked Torrie.

"Sure," replied Astrid, without even turning to look behind her.

"I'm not sure I want to . . ." began Morgan.

"Well, I'm going in," announced Torrie, and left her cousin sitting alone in the pickup. By the time Torrie's feet clumped onto the wooden porch, Astrid was just opening the door. She watched Astrid's cautious moves; the older girl appeared hesitant, as though not sure what to expect. A thin sliver of light sliced through the plainly furnished living area, swimming with dust motes. The cabin was simple, but cozy and remarkably neat for a guy's place, thought Torrie, then reprimanded herself for the stereotype. The place was permeated with the rich smell of pine.

"Do you see anything unusual?" she asked as Astrid began a slow sweep of the room.

Astrid didn't answer right away, didn't touch anything, then shook her head and slowly opened the door that led into the bedroom. Torrie was right behind her as she circled the bed and opened the closet door. An annoyed look crossed Astrid's face and she slammed the door closed again. "Why that jerk . . ." she stopped. "He went camping."

Torrie slipped around to the closet and opened the door a crack, but didn't see anything that gave her any indications of the owner's activities. "Are you sure?"

"Yes. That's where he keeps his camping gear," she said, indicating the closet. "It's all gone."

Torrie watched as her friend struggled to keep control of the emotions that surged behind her countenance: relief, anger, hurt.

"We were planning on hiking to the summit of the volcano this weekend. If he went without me . . ."

Torrie released her breath more loudly than she had

planned. She was sorry for Astrid's distress but relieved that her own worst fears had been unfounded: no dead body in the cabin. Had she really been expecting to find a body? Her imagination was definitely getting out of control. Better focus on the reality of the situation. Betrayal by a boyfriend she could deal with. All too well. Unauthorized bodies showing up in unexpected places—that was another matter altogether.

They walked back into the kitchen and Astrid poured them both a drink of fresh spring water from a jar in the refrigerator. They stood at the counter. "He must be pretty important to you," ventured Torrie.

"I thought so," Astrid admitted. "We've spent a lot of time together and I thought we had a lot more going for us than just the research. But apparently he doesn't think so."

"I know how that feels."

The slamming of the screen door cut the conversation short as Morgan breezed in. "Find out anything?" she asked, looking from one girl to the other.

"He's camping out."

"Really? Where?"

"I have no idea," answered Astrid, then she abruptly set her glass on the counter. "Wait. I may be able to figure out where he went." She crossed to a rustic roll top desk and opened it. The pigeon holes were all neatly stacked with letters and bills and other correspondence, with writing instruments neatly laid along one side. Astrid pulled a large ledger from one of the larger holes and took it to the small table in the kitchen area.

Both girls watched inquiringly as she opened it near the middle where a parchment bookmark with a wide navy blue ribbon marked the spot. She fingered it for a moment before she started reading. "I gave this to him."

"What is that book?" asked Morgan. "A diary?"

"Hardly a diary," said Astrid, clearly annoyed at the suggestion. "It's a journal of his research. It might mention some research he was planning or . . ." Her voice trailed off. "He gets a lot of ideas for his research by writing things down as they occur to him. But I can't imagine him doing something without telling me about it." The last comment was intended for herself rather than her listeners as she turned to her perusal of the book.

She continued to skim over the last few entries, then closed the book. "Nothing. He hasn't written anything for the last few days, and we'd already talked about the things he mentioned in the journal." Tenderly, Astrid replaced the bookmark and then returned the book to its place. As she did, her hand passed over a small silver box, and lingered there. Then she slowly opened it to reveal a vacant spot where something had rested on velvet padding. "This is where he keeps his new compass," she explained. "He's pretty proud of it. He said he could go anywhere in the world and find his way back. Let's hope it works for him this time."

"Let's go," she said abruptly. "If he went climbing, I may be able to find out where he went."

The girls piled back into the truck, and on the way to Ben's Trading Post Astrid explained that anyone who wanted to climb the volcano itself had to get a permit. It was possible to reserve a place in advance, but remaining spaces were assigned by lottery the night before at Ben's. It was a central location for campers and hikers to find out the latest news and check up on each other. And since hikers were required to register there, it was the place to start looking if someone came up missing.

Astrid's truck crunched in the gravel of the parking lot, which was fairly deserted at this time of day. She got out and walked swiftly over to a large board posted outside the main entrance of the shop. Torrie and Morgan were not far behind. After a few minutes, Astrid turned around and started walking slowly back towards the truck. "His name's not up there. He's not on the mountain today." She started to open the door of the Chevy.

"Wait a minute," said Morgan. "Why don't we get something to drink while we're here?"

Torrie readily agreed and Astrid reluctantly followed them into the cluttered interior of the shop, scanning the smattering of customers as she walked in. It was an outdoorsman's paradise with gear for every purpose, along with the typical Mount St. Helens' souvenirs—and a lot of mementos made from ash. To one side was a small café, nearly deserted now that the breakfast crowd had departed. Astrid went back to talk to the only employee on duty in the gift shop area. He was a small man with a goatee and seemed too slight to be carrying the bundles of firewood he was bringing in from the back. He seemed glad to interrupt his duties and answer her questions.

Meanwhile, the other two browsed the shop and Torrie picked out a few souvenirs of her trip: some earrings made of ash, a video of the eruption, and a stack of postcards. Then a small jar filled with a golden liquid caught her eye and she picked it up to read the label.

"Look at this," she said to Morgan. "This isn't something you could find just anywhere. It's Fireweed honey." She started to add it to her collection of treasures, then thought better of it. She didn't want to carry it home on the plane, and Morgan would never let her take it on their camping trip. Talk about baiting your tent.

* * *

A lone bee skims along the rim of a remote canyon. She is a worker, one of a team in charge of seeking out a new home. Something is wrong with their supply of honey.

The current hive lies cluttered with the dead bodies of hundreds of workers and drones. So many workers have been diverted to the job of mortuary duty that the supplies of nectar and honey are down. That means the precious larvae are in danger, and that creates a serious situation. The hive must make any sacrifice to protect its food supply and its young, and most of all, the queen. But something is wrong with the honey. Something beyond the realm of their understanding. Something that confuses and disorients them. Something that requires immediate, maybe unusual action.

She is a European bee. Unlike her notorious Africanized cousins, this strain is usually docile. In a good season, with ample supplies of flowers to build their stores, a foolhardy person, or a knowledgeable bear, might successfully make off with a pawful of the golden liquid without incurring undue harm—as long as the guard bees are not alarmed. But this season something is wrong with the honey. The worker does not comprehend the concept of toxins and mutations, but she does sense the seriousness of the situation and the need to take action to protect the hive. Meanwhile, a dozen of her companions work a grid in the re-emerging forest; soon they will report back to the queen with their recommendations.

Two hundred yards later the scout bee stops. Before her is a small square wooden building that seems deserted. In its door is carved a crescent moon.

Perfect. They can begin their prolonged swarm to safety right here. She turns and heads back to the dark recesses of the cave they have so long considered home. She is ready to reverse the action that brought her tribe to the cave many generations ago; she is going to return to the wild.

* * *

As Astrid finished her conversation with the firewood man, Morgan spotted a phone, so she talked the others into having their drink at one of the booths while she made a call home to check on her job status.

"Did you find out anything?" asked Torrie after she and Astrid had ordered drinks.

"No, Ben's not around this morning. Fred said he might be climbing today." She smirked. "It seems so unlikely to think of Ben in hiking gear."

"Why is that?"

"He just doesn't seem like the mountain man type. He looks more like an accountant with his wire rim glasses, and he always wears a dress shirt to work. People call him 'Gentle Ben.'" They really respect him, though. He has a lot of influence around here."

"But the other guy hadn't heard anything about Eddie?"

"Fred? No, he doesn't pay too much attention to what goes on around here. He just does his job and keeps to himself." She took a sip of her coffee. "I don't think he feels comfortable speaking English; he's got a pronounced accent. Even as long as I've known him, I still have trouble understanding him sometimes. He has a son or nephew or somebody that went to U-Dub, so he seems to think I should know who he is." She shrugged. "I guess he feels we have something in common. He's always seemed interested in my research, while is more than I can say for a lot of people around here."

They both found themselves checking their watches as Morgan's phone conversation dragged on and on.

Torrie guiltily started gossiping about her cousin. "She's changed our vacation plans twice. First we had to put our trip off because she got some unexpected job interviews. She's already been offered a good position with Microsoft, but she keeps holding out for something better, whatever that is." Torrie turned for another look at her cousin now in animated conversation. "She wants to live at home and pay off some college bills, which I can't blame her for. And she doesn't like the idea of the long commute from Ballard to Redmond."

Astrid nodded and murmured her understanding but wisely kept from offering her opinion.

Torrie continued her tirade, alternating between accusing and defending her cousin. "She switched her major three times in college," Torrie went on. "Of course, I'm one to talk—I started out in business, but now I'm not sure that's where I want to be."

"What do you do now?"

"I've been working at my dad's company. Since he doesn't have a son, I guess he decided he'd start grooming me for the business. But it didn't take me long to realize that I can't stand being cooped up in an office from nine to five. I'm doing bookkeeping right now. That's got to be the worst."

"Did you major in accounting?"

"No, Dad just thinks I should be familiar with all aspects of the industry while I 'work my way up.' Funny, I've always been closer to my dad, but when I try to follow in his footsteps it doesn't seem to be working out."

"How does he feel about that?"

"I don't think he realizes it yet. He just can't understand how tough it is being the boss's daughter. He's offered me a promotion when I get back, but I just can't see myself making a career in an electronics factory."

"I know an easy way for you to solve that."

"How?"

"Don't go back."

They laughed and Torrie realized how much she missed having someone to talk to about important things. Girl things. She hadn't realized until now how much of a void Myndi had left in her life. She shouldn't have let her crisis with Aaron destroy the closest friendship she'd ever had. Maybe when she got back home . . .

Astrid had asked a question and Torrie had to ask her to repeat it. She had said that if the girls really wanted to see the mountain, they could put their names in for the lottery tonight and climb it in the morning. Astrid didn't think she'd be able to accomplish much of her research tomorrow anyway with her mind on Eddie.

Before she could answer, Morgan came rushing up out of breath. "You'll never believe who I have an interview with— Pacific Coast Seafood."

"Is that good?" asked Torrie.

"Good? It's just the kind of job I've been hoping for. They have a couple of openings in areas I might be interested in, one as project manager and the other in marketing."

"What would you be doing, selling fish? You could do that at Pike Place Market," remarked Torrie. "Do they train you to throw them or is that a pre-requisite for the job?"

Morgan ignored the sarcasm and plunged into her account of benefits, opportunities for promotion, and the suite of offices overlooking Elliot Bay.

"Great," said Torrie when the torrent of words finally subsided. "Now you'll have something to look forward to when we get back from our trip."

"Trip? Forget about the trip. I have to be back for an interview tomorrow afternoon."

Chapter 7

SPIRIT LAKE

Torrie was livid. Morgan's capriciousness had already ruined most of her vacation and now she was planning on deserting Astrid when her friend most needed her. Rather than confront Morgan she turned sullen, just short of pouting. In the midst of her own distress, Astrid served as arbitrator and decided that they should go ahead with the plans for the day. Then the girls could leave early in the morning, in time to get to Seattle for Morgan's appointment the following afternoon.

Astrid planned to go check out the Climber's Bivouac that afternoon for any news about Eddie. Although the cousins' disagreement was settled—or at least simmering—neither of the girls was in a particularly jovial mood when they decided to stop for lunch at the Cougar diner. Morgan had taken a seat next to Astrid across from Torrie in the booth, and made a great show of ignoring her cousin as she studied the menu. They ordered and were eating in silence when the bell over the door announced new clients and Torrie glanced up. Coming in the door was their ranger and he was headed their way.

She cleared her throat conspicuously, but Morgan was in no mood to catch the usual secret cousin-communication. The ranger and his companion, apparently a sheriff's deputy, judging by the uniform, were nearing their table before either of the other girls noticed.

"Hi," Torrie greeted the ranger uncertainly.

"I see you're still here," he said. He held his hat in both hands and shifted restlessly from one foot to the other. "Notice we got you some better weather today," he said, and grinned broadly at her. He had prominent laugh lines at the corners of his eyes, a feature Torrie found appealing.

"Yes, I appreciate that," she replied, returning his smile.

Just then Morgan looked up and noticed the drama being played out. She spoke up. "Well, if it isn't our own private ranger. We were just talking about you." She reached out and put a hand on his arm as she talked. "Why don't you and your friend join us. We have plenty of room."

She patted the seat next to her and scooted over, forcing Astrid against the window side of the booth. The ranger eyed the space next to Morgan for a moment, then turned to Torrie. "I wouldn't want to crowd you. Mack, bring a chair over and put it at the end," he said to his friend and sat down next to Torrie.

She blushed as she moved over to make room for him, then looked up in time to see Morgan's unmistakable glare. Torrie had to confess she felt a power rush. It wasn't often she got the better of her cousin in the male department—Morgan tended to leave a string of broken hearts in her wake.

Torrie turned her attention back to the ranger, who had just introduced himself as Brad. His deputy friend was Mack. They were a totally mismatched pair: Mack was short and round with a dark shock of unruly hair. His dark-rimmed glasses gave him a bookish look that was heightened by a pale complexion. But he was pleasant and courteous and Torrie decided she shouldn't judge by appearances—after all, Brad seemed to like him.

Astrid immediately asked if he had any news of Eddie's disappearance. Mack brought her up to date on what the department knew—or what he was allowed to tell.

Brad unobtrusively changed the subject. "We've been having a little trouble with our pocket gopher population this summer," he began.

"You mean your heroes?" asked Torrie.

* * *

By the shores of Spirit Lake a young pocket gopher is behaving strangely. He has just finished a lunch of Fireweed roots and is shaking his head repeatedly to rid himself of the acrid taste. In the distance he hears a group of loud tourists approaching. The ever-present invaders of his domain. He's tired of running to his burrow to hide from this perennial pest. It's time to be proactive.

* * *

Brad went on to describe some of their erratic behavior. Usually reclusive by habit, several had exhibited behavior that could almost be described as aggressive. "That *is* off the record, though. We can't alarm the tourists."
Torrie watched to see how Astrid was taking this piece of information.

Fortunately, Mack turned the conversation to lighter fare. Torrie soon discovered why the ranger enjoyed his friend's company.

The deputy regaled them with tales from the eruption and the subsequent recovery period. The people had responded to the tragedy with courage and humor, evidenced by tee-shirts and novelty items with survival slogans. A volcano-shaped ashtray that actually smoked when a cigarette was inserted was a popular item, and altered dollar bills began showing up with President George Washington wearing a particle mask. Suggestions were made to change the name of the state to "Ashington" and the state motto to "The Evergray State."

But the humor masked the depth of the loss. Almost all the survivors had lost someone in the disaster. Others had experienced narrow escapes in damaged vehicles, raging rivers, and mud flows. Mack's father, a highway patrolman, had been killed in his efforts to rescue a young couple from a submerged vehicle. Torrie wondered what part that had played in his decision to go into law enforcement.

They were interrupted by the crackle of Mack's two-way radio. He replied to the garbled message that no one else at the table could understand and signed off. "Got to go investigate an accident at Spirit Lake," he announced. "Probably some fool tourist got off the trail again."

"Or your gopher got him," suggested Morgan.

"More likely the place is still haunted." said Mack.

Brad offered to go along with him and the two young men excused themselves. Brad tipped his hat to Torrie as they left the table. "Maybe I'll see you around. We have some awesome sights around here."

Torrie nodded in reply and stammered. "Maybe so."

Morgan began to berate her the minute the guys had walked out the door. "I can't believe you passed up that opportunity."

"What opportunity?" Torrie snapped.

"Obviously he wanted to see you again. You didn't even tell him where you were staying. How is he going to get in touch with you?"

"Don't worry about it, Morgan. I've got other things to

think about besides chasing some ranger all over the mountainside. Besides, we're not even going to be here after tomorrow, thanks to you."

"You're hopeless. No wonder you don't have a man."

"Excuse me," said Torrie rudely. "If you haven't forgotten, I *had* a man. It's not my fault I lost him to the Gulf War." She stood up and stormed out the door, leaving Morgan to pick up the ticket.

After a few brisk strides around the parking lot she reluctantly joined the others in the pickup. The ride up to the Climber's Bivouac was even quieter than their trip from Ben's store had been. The road winding its way up the mountain was as curvy as the one they had been on yesterday but today she could peer into the depths. This road was narrow and graveled and hugged the mountain, and they bounced and jolted over the uneven surface until Torrie was sure she was going to lose her lunch. She clamped her eyes shut each time they went around curves and the view gaped open to reveal the nothingness below.

They arrived finally at the camping area which was occupied by the support teams of the hardy hikers who had left for the summit as early as five in the morning. Astrid began her rounds of the assembled tents and RV's while Morgan and Torrie stood awkwardly outside the truck waiting.

Torrie spoke first. "Truce?"

"Sure. I've had this job on my mind . . ."

"I know. We used to do this when we were kids. I thought we'd outgrow it."

"Me, too." Morgan studied her feet. "That was cruel what I said about Aaron . . ."

"Forget it. Right now I'm more concerned about Astrid. She needs our support."

"You're right. Shall we go see if we can do anything?"

"Why not?"

They hugged briefly and went in search of the botanist.

The three split up and questioned everybody on the grounds, but their efforts didn't yield any information. Astrid was completely dejected on the return trip and the cousins could do nothing to cheer her up.

Finally Torrie asked her, "What was Mack saying about Spirit Lake? Is it supposed to be haunted or something?"

"There are some old native American legends," she said. "Even the early explorers wrote about some of them."

"Like what?" queried Torrie.

"Well, the explorers tried to get some native American guides to take them up to the mountain, but they were all afraid to go. They believed the lake was full of bear-faced fish and that there were cannibals or demons along the lake shores."

"And Big Foot," added Morgan.

Astrid nodded. "I think that legend started later." She continued her story.

"The most interesting thing is that several of the tribes in the Northwest have similar myths about Loowit—the smoking lady. According to the legend an old lady was given the task of guarding the fire that had been given to the tribes by one of the great chiefs. She was on a natural bridge that went over the Colombia River. She became famous and two young braves fell in love with her and started fighting over her."

"With the old lady?" asked Torrie.

"Oh, no" Astrid hastened to clarify. "As a reward for being the fire-keeper, she had been changed into a beautiful young woman."

"Oh, of course," said Torrie.

"Anyway, the lady couldn't decide between the two, and her suitors ended up destroying the villages and forests with fire. So the great chief punished all of them by turning them into mountains."

"Those are the three mountains you can see in this area," added Morgan.

"Mount Rainier, Mount St. Helens, and . . ." ventured Torrie.

"No," Morgan said. "Mount Hood, Mount Adams, and Mount St. Helens. The lady was changed into Mount St. Helens, so it's the prettiest mountain—at least it was until she blew her top."

"So the legends might be based on earlier volcanic eruptions," Torrie speculated.

"It seems so," agreed Astrid. There is evidence of volcanic activity during the time the native American tribes settled in this area. "It just seems ironic the lake that was believed to be so full of evil was such a popular resort area. That's where Harry Truman—not the president—had his lodge. He'd been there his entire life and refused to leave when everyone was being evacuated before the 1980 blast. Then everything was destroyed in a matter of minutes and the lake was covered with a raft of floating logs."

"That's what we saw yesterday," Torrie remembered. "Up by Windy Ridge. Where did all those logs come from?"

"Those are the trees that had been growing on the hills surrounding Spirit Lake," Astrid said sadly. "An avalanche came down the mountain after the eruption and hit the lake. It caused a huge tidal wave that went up the opposite side and just obliterated the forest. They estimate about a million trees were destroyed in a matter of minutes. Most of them ended up in Spirit Lake."

"So this Harry died?" asked Torrie.

Astrid nodded. "He was never found."

"That's horrible," Torrie responded. "I had no idea how quickly everything happened." She was silent a moment pondering the immense power that had instantly come into play in this great theater of nature. She was almost ready to believe there *was* some kind of evil associated with the lake.

Chapter 8

JOHNSTON RIDGE

At Astrid's urging, the girls awoke early the next morning and had a quick breakfast. She had convinced them that they should accompany her to Castle Rock and at least tour the visitors' center near there. It would be a shame for Torrie to come this far and not get a complete picture of the volcanic monument, and that center had the best displays to get an overview of the area. Astrid had already exchanged her signature overalls for more touristy clothes and looked very Washington with thick socks, leather hiking boots, and a black-and-white striped poncho for the inevitable shower. The cousins agreed to the plan, and Torrie had mimicked the appropriate gear as much as possible with what she had with her, but had to settle for her new sweatshirt tied around her waist in place of a poncho. Morgan, of course was a total fashion statement in spite of the fact she had been camping.

At the last minute Torrie jumped into the truck with Astrid, saying that she had a few more questions for her.

Morgan didn't have time to object, but she was obviously displeased.

When they passed through Randle, Torrie commented on the treatment they had gotten from the Bad Hair lady.

"So you've met Marge," Astrid said. "She's sweet on Eddie."

"That old hag?" asked Torrie in disbelief.

"Eddie is nice to everybody," she explained. "He used to stop by the ranger station quite often to get updates on the weather and road conditions. One day I went along with him. Needless to say, she wasn't too thrilled with me."

"That would explain why she clammed up when we told her we were looking for you," said Torrie.

Astrid nodded without comment.

After a long drive they arrived at the Mount St. Helens Visitor Center and Morgan pulled up beside them. Astrid directed them to the displays, then went to make a phone call. Torrie could see why their friend had urged them to see this particular center. It served as the perfect introduction to the area, and Torrie was pleased to see that it had an exhibit on ecology. In fact, she was enthralled with the displays and exhibits. It gave her a chance to piece together the history of the region: the massive destructive power of the eruption and the remarkable recovery, both of the human spirit and the natural world. She and Morgan were standing in front of a replica of the mountain when Torrie made a decision.

She turned to Morgan and announced, "I'm staying."

Puzzled, Morgan replied, "Staying? What do you mean you're staying?"

"I'm staying here, with Astrid. You can go back to Seattle without me."

"You can't do that. How will you get back and catch your plane?"

"I'll take a bus, hitchhike, whatever. I just don't think Astrid should be left alone right now."

Before Morgan could answer, Astrid walked up to them. "About ready to take off?" she asked.

Morgan opened her mouth but Torrie spoke before her cousin could. "She is, but I've decided to stay. If that's okay with you, that is."

Astrid looked from one girl to the other. "Morgan?"

"Sure, she'd like to stay. She's been wanting to get a story to take back for her little home town newspaper. She's still got a week left so she might as well be here as sitting in Seattle waiting for me to get back from job interviews. She might even make herself useful and do your dishes or something," she added, looking at Astrid.

"Of course, I'd be glad to have company," replied the botanist. To Torrie she said, "You could come with me while I check on my fireweed fields. That would be a good way to get research for your story. I think it's a great idea. I'd love to have you." The older girl looked away quickly. Torrie hoped it was to cover some emotion connected with Eddie and not a reluctance to have her stay.

Morgan hitched her purse strap higher on her shoulder. "Well, we'd better get your things out of the Porsche so I can be on my way. Astrid, why don't you just loan me your keys and we can go transfer the stuff."

"No, I'll come help," said Astrid. "It's no problem."

Leave it to Morgan—had to make it look like it was her idea. But Torrie was too euphoric to worry about who got the credit. She was going to stay in this intriguing place and unravel some of its mysteries. The idea of writing a story for the paper didn't sound half bad—she might even attempt to take some pictures. She followed the others out to the vehicles and the transfer was quickly made. Morgan insisted on leaving all the camping supplies with them, especially the rations, just in case they got "too busy to cook." At the last minute Torrie remembered to confiscate the three-day pass they had bought, and placed it on Astrid's windshield.

Once Morgan was on the road, Astrid and Torrie resumed their journey up the Memorial Highway, nibbling on the goodies that Morgan had left them. It was a wide, modern four-lane that stretched fifty miles from the interstate to the multi-million dollar facility at the top of the ridge claiming the closest view of the west side of the gaping crater. The area had drawn over 500,000 tourists a year for the past several years, ever since the modern facilities had been developed on this side of the monument.

Although it was early in the season, the parking lots of the visitor centers were choked with RV's and campers and vehicles of every description, many with license plates from far away states and Canada. Astrid told her there shouldn't be quite as many when they got to the top—a lot of tourists left their large vehicles halfway up and drove the small cars they were towing instead.

Torrie had her reporter's notebook out and was plying Astrid with questions. She had even purchased a disposable camera before they had left the visitors' center. She might as well give this journalism thing a fair shot—in spite of a lifetime aversion to it. Astrid pointed out some of the other centers as they drove by.

"You can borrow my truck while I'm working and come see the rest of these interpretive centers when you have more time. The monument is so spread out it's impossible to see it all in a weekend. I'm glad you decided to stay longer." She choked back a sob before continuing. "I'm glad for the company, too."

Torrie, nodded, even though she knew Astrid was too occupied with driving to see her.

As they passed the Forest Learning Center Astrid pointed. "Be sure to take my binoculars when you go, and stop by here. You can usually get a good view of the elk herds along the river. They should be returning from their winter pastures by now and heading back up into the mountains."

Torrie strained her neck to get a better view of the barren plains below. The highway followed the meanderings of the Toutle River Valley where immense mud flows had scoured the vegetation from one end of the valley to the other. The ashen landscape still looked extremely inhospitable. "You mean they can survive down there? What do they eat?"

"They thrive on grass and clover, and they love soaking in the river during the summer heat," she added. "The herds actually returned quite soon after the eruption. Once the colonizing plants took hold and spread, the elk were attracted back to the area.. This is the time of year they'll have a lot of newborn calves with them."

* * *

A young elk scrambles and stumbles in the high grass along the river bank. He is too young to be off with the mother cow in her pursuit of forage; he has been left with the female assigned as the "babysitter." He is recently weaned and has started sampling some of the tender grasses that serve as mealtime and playground as well as hiding place. He impatiently noses away some pesky little creatures from the colorful flowers growing there. They make annoying buzzing sounds and cause painful spots on his nose and eyelids. Besides, they're in the way of the fragrant plants he wants to sample. He succeeds in shooing them away and eagerly samples the strange new fare.

* * *

"You seem to know a lot about animals for a botanist," said Torrie.

Astrid laughed. "When you're studying an ecosystem, you have to look at all the life interactions, even humans.

Especially humans." She was silent for a moment as they crossed an immense bridge spanning a large body of water. She pointed off to the left. "That's Coldwater Lake. That's where Eddie and his crew are doing their research."

Torrie was momentarily dizzied by the high bridge and doubted that she'd be able to maneuver a strange vehicle over the heights on her own. She made a mental note not to come up this far by herself. Mountain roads were not her favorite venue for driving adventure. After they crossed she relaxed a little and responded to Astrid's last comment. "You're right. This is a long ways from your campground—or Eddie's cabin for that matter."

"It is. That's why a lot of the scientists set up a makeshift campsite near their area of research. They might stay for several days at a time to save commuting time."

"So it's possible that Eddie is camping out somewhere following up on some research."

"Let's hope," said Astrid somberly. "Let's hope."

They had reached their destination. The 16,000 square foot Johnston Ridge Observatory perched on a ridge at 4200 feet and offered a spectacular view into the heart of the crater. It was named for the volcanologist who had lost his life while monitoring volcanic activity from this very ridge. He was the one who had uttered the famous words, "*Vancouver! Vancouver! This is it!*"

Astrid explained the background while they walked from the truck to the entrance. Torrie was distracted from the other girl's lecture by the strange serenade surrounding them in stereo. As it became louder, she stopped at one of the retainer walls with its display of native flowers and listened intently.

"What's that noise?" she asked.

Astrid pointed. Hovering around the flowers were hundreds of insects, wings creating an incessant buzzing and clacking sound.

"What are they?" Torrie asked. The creatures were never still long enough for her to get a good look at them.

"Grasshoppers," her friend replied.

"Grasshoppers?" Torrie exclaimed. "I never knew they made noise like that."

"This species certainly does," she said. "They say that if you ever got lost out there on the hummock plains you'd be able to find your way back here with your eyes closed—just follow the sound."

They joined the crowd moving toward the entrance and were soon inside. Most of the people seemed to be assembled around a large exhibit, and Torrie followed until she could get a view of what was attracting so much attention. Directly in front of her was an enormous relief model with an aerial view of the eruption. As the narrated script explained the stages of the 1980 tragedy, thousands of fiber optic lights illuminated the display with color coded waves of light: first the ash-filled steam projectile hurtled across the landscape, then the avalanche, the pyroclastic flows, and finally, the river of mud.

Each new wave of destruction cut a deeper, wider, swath through the once-peaceful vacation paradise. Torrie shivered and pulled her sweatshirt up over her shoulders.

Astrid whispered, "Wait until you see the presentation in the theater."

They got a ticket for the next showing and joined the line that was being funneled through a long hallway leading to the entrance doors. Murals of pristine old growth forest lined the walls, and sounds of chirping birds accentuated the serenity.

At last they were admitted as the previous viewers streamed out the doors at the front of the large theater. Torrie and Astrid found seats about halfway down and settled in as the lights dimmed. The wide screen showed a continually changing collage of pre-eruption images and little by little built the suspense of the impending blast. Slow rumbles that Torrie first thought she imagined began the foreshadowing, and gradually built until the climactic moment when the full-blown eruption was shown visually, accompanied by the collective gasp from the audience, literally moved by the increasing vibrations in the theater.

Torrie inconspicuously reached for a tissue to dab her eyes, and as the lights slowly came back on, she realized she was not alone in experiencing the emotional impact. As the audience sat stunned, the huge velvet curtains began to open, and there before them was the mouth of the crater in real time, still sending up weak puffs of smoke.

The girls joined the silent crowd as it filed out the front of the room and entered the adjoining hallway. Here the walls contained the "after" mural—the counterpart of the tranquil scene they had passed through as they entered. The photographs portrayed absolute destruction. Brief swatches of color reminded Torrie she was not viewing pictures in black and white.

She studied the scenes of horror for only a few minutes before she turned to Astrid. "I can't deal with this. Can we leave?"

Astrid nodded silent assent and the girls left, images etched into Torrie's memory which she knew she could never erase.

They began the long descent back to the interstate and from there returned to the Gifford Pinchot Forest and the Tower Rock campground. Torrie used her sweatshirt as a pillow and was asleep with her head leaning against the passenger window by the time they arrived at the trailer. Torrie was exhausted and she was only the passenger. She wondered how Astrid had the energy to keep going.

As they prepared a quick snack before getting ready for bed, Tasha scurried to the door and began her special frantic bark. Just as Astrid attempted to shush her they were startled by a knock at the door.

Astrid quickly moved to the door and pulled back the curtain. She let it fall back and turned to Torrie, her face ashen. She slowly turned the knob and opened the metal door, then motioned for the caller to enter.

It was Mack, and his look mirrored Astrid's. He stood with his hat clutched in front of him with both hands as if hanging onto it for support.

"I'm afraid I have bad news," he said. "That accident we had to check out at Spirit Lake yesterday..." His voice trailed off and he looked at the ceiling. "It was Eddie."

PART TWO

VICTIMS & SUSPECTS

Chapter 9

THE DIVERS

"Is he . . ." Astrid stammered.

"He's dead." Mack said grimly. "I'm sorry, Astrid."

Astrid turned pale and Torrie rushed to her side. Tasha whimpered and scratched at her master's feet. Torrie led Astrid to the sofa and invited the deputy to sit down. She jotted down details of the tragedy that she knew Astrid was unable to absorb at the moment.

The body had been discovered at Spirit Lake by a scientific team doing research there. Eddie was trapped under the mat of logs that still floated on the lake. The department had been unable to determine how long he had been in the water or how long he had been dead. There was bruising that indicated a blow to the head, but that was not necessarily the cause of death. Mack would let her know what information he could as soon as possible.

In other words, thought Torrie, since Astrid wasn't a relative, she wasn't entitled to any particulars. Mack had probably come to see her just as a matter of courtesy; she allowed herself to hope that maybe he had come as a favor to Brad. She guessed that this was usually the sheriff's job.

Astrid nodded at the appropriate moments and continued staring straight ahead. Torrie took over as hostess and saw the deputy to the door.

"One more thing," he said to the distraught scientist. "His parents are coming up from California day after tomorrow. They asked if you would meet them at Eddie's cabin."

Torrie looked at Astrid for a response that didn't come. "She'll be there," Torrie promised and Mack replaced his hat and left in the patrol car.

Torrie fixed two cups of chai, but drank hers alone while Astrid's got cold.

Her hostess still sat on the couch, her fingers smoothing and ruffling Tasha's fur. Finally she stood. "I need to take a walk," she said, and started for the door followed by Tasha.

Torrie considered going with her, but Astrid seemed to anticipate her gesture. "I'll be okay," she said. "Tasha will go with me. She needs to keep busy," she added flatly.

Torrie paced the confined space and drank another cup of the soothing brew. She had almost decided to go out looking for her friend when she heard returning footsteps on the steps.

Astrid's eyes were red, but she seemed composed. "Are you ready to get up early again tomorrow?"

Torrie agreed.

"Good. We have a lot to do."

True to her word, Astrid had them on the road by 7:00 am. Torrie noticed she was wearing the same outfit as yesterday and wondered if she had slept in her clothes.

They headed north and Torrie thought they were going to Randle, but when they reached the intersection, Astrid took a left and took the road leading to the monument.

"Where are we going?" she asked.

"Spirit Lake. I have to see where he died."

When they reached the Harmony Falls scenic overlook near Spirit Lake, Astrid shouldered her day pack. "Ready for some hiking?"

Torrie shrugged. Not knowing what the botanist had had in mind for the day, she had only put on her fanny pack that morning and grabbed a couple of energy bars and a bottle of water. She grabbed the water bottle from the receptacle on the dash board and hurried to catch up to Astrid, who had already started down the steep path toward the log-covered lake. Torrie hoped it wouldn't be a long hike.

Astrid led the way down a steep path and then began walking along the shore of the lake itself. The place was nearly deserted except for a couple of distant hikers and a boat several hundred yards down the shore. The wind gently nudged the mat of logs into new positions. Astrid kept her eyes trained on the ground—looking for tracks or clues, Torrie guessed.

"I can't imagine what he was even doing by this lake," Astrid said. "It had no connection with his research and as you can see, it's not a particularly scenic place."

"Maybe somebody else talked him into coming here," Torrie suggested. "Did he have any other friends around here?"

"Everybody was Eddie's friend," she said. "But I can't believe he would have come here without telling me. We always did things like this together, or at least we let the other one know where we were going to be. This is a desolate place up here. Everybody operates on the buddy system."

They strolled further, not finding anything that Astrid considered of interest. Suddenly she stopped. "Why is that boat out there?"

"That one over there?"

"Yes. It hadn't occurred to me before, but there shouldn't be a boat here. This isn't a recreational lake."

"Didn't Mack say he was found by some divers?"

"Yes, but that's strange, too. Why would anybody dive here?" She hesitated a moment. "Let's go see what they're up to."

Torrie reluctantly followed. If people were dying around here she wasn't sure she wanted to go talk to some strangers on an isolated beach. Since her only other alternative was to climb the steep path back to the truck, she followed.

When they arrived at the boat no one was around. Astrid walked over to the lone craft and examined it. It was a small nondescript boat equipped with an outboard motor. The bottom was cluttered with equipment Torrie didn't recognize.

"It looks like they've been running sonar tests on the lake bottom," said Astrid. "That would explain what they're doing here. See that piece of metal shaped like a torpedo? They use that to take underwater readings."

Torrie breathed a sigh of relief. So they were merely scientists and not serial killers after all. "So, shall we go on back?"

"No, I want to wait and ask them some questions."

She sat down on a large rock and offered Torrie a handful of trail mix. Both sat eating and drinking from their water bottles until they heard the sound of splashing on the other side of the boat.

Two heads emerged from the steely gray water of the lake, masked and covered with rubber caps. The divers began slowly walking toward the shore, water dripping from their wet suits as the water became more and more shallow. The tall one on the left was clad in yellow, his shorter partner in blue. They waved in greeting and removed their alien-looking face masks.

Astrid introduced herself and Torrie and the two divers nodded in acknowledgment.

"I'm Blaine Matthews," said the taller one, "and this is my diving buddy, Dave. I'd offer to shake your hand, but . . ."

He shook his arms and the water cascaded off his suit. "Just sight-seeing?"

"No," said Astrid. "My friend was . . . discovered here yesterday. I just came to . . ." She left the sentence unfinished.

"I'm sorry," Blaine said. "I didn't know he had any friends around here." He was older and obviously the one in charge. With a thumb, he pointed to his buddy. "Dave is the one who found him."

Astrid's legs almost collapsed beneath her and the two dripping divers rushed to her side. They helped her back to the rock she had been sitting on earlier, and Dave helped her drink from her own bottle. He kneeled on the pumice-lined beach at her side.

"Are you okay?" Blaine asked.

She nodded and sat for a few minutes more, then began to ask them questions. Dave gave Blaine a questioning look and the older man nodded almost imperceptibly. They told her that they had been diving on the bottom and that the sun filtering through the logs above had revealed the body. It had evidently been snagged on one of the partly-submerged upright logs and could neither float to the surface or sink to the bottom. He probably never would have been discovered if the men hadn't been diving that week. Torrie was grateful they didn't offer any details about waterlogged bodies.

"What are you diving for?" asked Torrie while waiting for Astrid to gain her composure.

"We're doing research here, like everybody up here at the monument," answered Dave. "This is a ready-made laboratory."

"So I've heard. What exactly are you researching? There doesn't seem to be much life here."

"There's really more than most people are aware of," continued Dave. "But that's not what we're interested in. We've been studying the way the logs sink. They don't all end up horizontally on the bottom—it seems that a lot of them sink in an upright position. Blaine's testing a hypothesis he has."

"Really?" said Torrie, her interest piqued. "What's your hypothesis?" she asked the older man.

This time Blaine gave a slight shake of his head and scowled at Dave as the other man opened his mouth to speak. "I'm not at liberty to say at this point," Blaine said, answering the question himself. "Until we finish our research here, it's just a hypothesis." He turned and started back toward the boat. "If you'll excuse us, we need to take advantage of the daylight."

Astrid stood shakily to her feet, and Torrie sensed that their time had run out. She reached out a hand to steady Astrid. "Ready to head back?"

* * *

On the shores of Coldwater Lake a harried pocket gopher scurries back and forth from her den to her dinner. She starts to eat a Fireweed plant she had pulled into the den earlier. Curiously, as the blossoms begin to cool in the coolness of the burrow, they start glowing in the dark. Instead of their usual magenta hue they turn a light, fragrant peach color. Mother gopher feasts on her usual fare of Fireweed roots, but they are tangy and pithy, and her supper does not set well. She is irritable and out of sorts. She nips at the heels of her brood and sends them scurrying to the deep recesses of the burrow. She bares her teeth at her mate and he goes in search of a peace offering.

There are too many tourists around. Why don't they leave her in peace? With all these two-legged giants around, it's impossible to raise a family right. One of these days one of them is going to push her too far . . .

* * *

Back in the truck Torrie asked, "What did you make of that?"

"What? Their finding Eddie? Didn't you believe them?"

"I'm not sure. They seemed pretty secretive about what they were doing."

"That's not unusual. A lot of scientists are that way. They're afraid somebody is going to steal their theory and take it to the public before they get a chance to publish their findings."

"I guess so," said Torrie. "It just seems they were eager to get rid of us when I started asking about their research."

"They must have smelled a reporter," Astrid suggested.

"Am I that obvious?" Torrie felt almost smug. So she did come across as a reporter. Maybe she was more suited for that kind of job than she would have imagined.

"I have to go into Randle and check my mail," Astrid said. "Shall we eat out?"

Torrie agreed wholeheartedly. Another supper of H-O-T D-O-G-S did not have the least bit of appeal.

After stopping by the post office, they went to a local café. While they were enjoying their dinner a loud group of men entered. They were dressed in dirty plaid shirts and ragged pants held up with suspenders.

"Loggers," Astrid whispered. She looked down and pretended a fascination with her food. "Maybe they won't notice me."

Puzzled, Torrie informed her they were headed their way.

One of them stopped at their table. "Well if it ain't the tree hugger," he said loudly.

Torrie's eyes widened and Astrid looked up and pulled a strand of hair behind her ear, but didn't answer.

"Leave her alone, Vern" said another who had already found a table. "Haven't you heard what happened to her friend?"

"Yeah, I heard," he snarled. "Them city folks ain't got no

business up here in this country nohow." If the man wasn't drunk he was certainly doing a good impression.

A hard-faced waitress came and got in his face. "Go sit down, Vern. If you're going to make trouble Hank'll throw you out."

He started to answer, but her angry stare and one hand firmly planted on her hip showed she had no intention of backing down.

He scuffled off to join his two friends at a table against the back wall and Astrid mouthed a "thank you" to the waitress.

Without looking her way Vern said loudly, "All these scientists tromping around in the woods—they even got our wildlife riled up." The waitress gave him a hard look but he ignored her and studied the menu as though he might actually order something other than "the usual."

The girls finished up quickly and went to pay their bill. The tough little waitress took their money.

"What did he mean about the wildlife?" Astrid asked.

"Hadn't you heard?" she replied. "Some tourist got bit today by a pocket gopher up by Coldwater Lake."

Chapter 10

"RABIES"

By now Torrie had almost gotten accustomed to a six o'clock wake up call. Astrid wanted to go to the hospital in Kelso and see what she could find out about the bite victim. She was convinced that it couldn't be rabies, but she wouldn't tell Torrie why she thought so. Torrie didn't know if all this activity was to keep her mind off Eddie, or if she really thought the events might be connected somehow. Torrie had an uneasy feeling that Astrid wasn't telling her everything.

Astrid stopped at the first available phone to call Mack. Eddie's parents were expected in shortly after noon, so that would give her enough time. The hospital visit was, not surprisingly, a disappointment. Since she had no official connection with the case, she wasn't allowed to visit the patient, who was in serious condition. She did manage to corner a talkative nurse and at least find out what the symptoms were: high fever, head and muscle aches, disorientation, and swelling of the lymph nodes—pretty much generic symptoms for the onset of any number of diseases. Torrie had once again fallen into her semi-official position as scribe, and was inconspicuously—she hoped—taking notes as Astrid asked the questions.

When they finished, Astrid sent Torrie to the vending machines while she checked one more possible source of information. When they met in the parking lot, Astrid cheerfully waved a piece of paper in her hand.

"What's that?" asked Torrie.

"The name of the veterinarian who examined the gopher. What time is it?"

It was already past eleven but Astrid decided to take the time and go talk to the vet. She didn't seem too eager to face Eddie's parents.

They pulled up in front of a small brick building that served as a clinic. "*Dr. Hong Li, DVM,*" read the sign outside. The girls entered and told the receptionist what they wanted. Two people with pets in tow read magazines and waited.

Soon a small, trim Asian woman came into the waiting area. She appeared to be in her early thirties and wore her long sleek hair pulled back. She extended a hand and gave each girl a firm handshake. "I understand you want information about rabid gopher," she began.

"Yes," Astrid said. "I'm doing research at the volcanic monument, and I think this incident may be related to my studies."

"How interesting," replied the doctor. "Where do you study?"

"I'm at U-Dub—the University of Washington," she amended.

"Yes, they have very good program there. Please come into my office."

Torrie noticed Astrid hadn't mentioned that her area of study was botany.

The girls followed and sat in the chairs the doctor indicated. Dr. Li sat behind her large desk flanked with the requisite diplomas and pictures on a dark paneled wall. Many pictures were of the doctor with various small animals. The oversized chair seemed to swallow her up. She placed a hand on each arm of the chair and looked steadily at Astrid.

"Now, what you want to know about gopher? This is ordinary case of rabies."

"That's what I was wondering about," said Astrid. "Doesn't it seem unusual that a person would contract rabies from a pocket gopher? Isn't that pretty rare?"

The doctor's face darkened. "The gopher is rodent. Is not unusual for rodent to bite." She raised an eyebrow to emphasize her last statement.

Astrid refused to be dissuaded. "I took a course in diseases transmitted from animals to humans . . . ," she began.

"Ah, you take course," said the doctor, shaking her head slowly and meaningfully. "And this is three-hour course, perhaps? I study veterinary medicine five years. I diagnose many cases of rabies. The gopher is rabid." She stood up and put both hands firmly on the desk. "Now, if you have no more questions for your research, my patients wait."

Astrid pressed her luck. "Would it be possible to take a look at the gopher?"

Back in the car Torrie suggested, "Maybe you should have asked to see the gopher first."

Astrid laughed. "That was pretty naïve, I'll admit."

"So this was pretty much a wasted trip."

"Maybe, but I think her reluctance to show me the gopher may be significant."

"Do you think she's hiding something?"

"Possibly, but not necessarily," Astrid began. "If this case dealt with something she wasn't expecting, she might not notice any unusual symptoms that didn't fit the pattern and just assume it's a standard case of rabies."

"You seem pretty sure that it isn't rabies. Is this connected somehow to your study of mutations?"

"Think about it," replied Astrid. "What do pocket gophers eat?"

Torrie was puzzled, but given Astrid's frame of mind, she decided not to ask her about the rodents' culinary preferences.

It was mid-afternoon by the time they got to Eddie's cabin. A rental car was parked outside when Astrid pulled up and stopped the engine. "I don't really want to do this," she admitted.

"Do you know his folks?"

"I met them once. Eddie took me down to the California coast one weekend, but I stayed with his brother's girlfriend, so I didn't see that much of them."

"Do you want me to go in with you?"

Astrid hesitated. "Thanks, but it would probably be better if I went alone. I'm not sure how everyone is going to react. Including me."

Torrie nodded in agreement. "Don't worry about me. I'll just take a walk down by the water."

Astrid was silent. "Eddie loved to walk down there," she said. "We spent evenings just enjoying the peace and quiet." She seemed far away for a wistful moment, then snapped back to the present. "You don't have to hang around," she said. "Why don't you take my truck and go see some things on your own?" She held out the keys.

"You don't have to do that," said Torrie.

"No problem. Why don't you head back towards Ape Cave and go on to Lahar Canyon. That's a pretty place."

"You're sure?"

"Of course." She pressed the keys into Torrie's hand. "I'll get Eddie's parents to take me back to the trailer."

Torrie first checked the glove compartment to make sure she had a map of some kind. Then she studied the controls of the truck. Stick shift, she noticed—she hadn't driven one of those for awhile. Once again Grandma's foresight had paid off. She had insisted that all her grandchildren learn how to drive a manual transmission. She herself had driven an old Ford all over the country following Grandpa before he was shipped off to Europe during World War II. "You never know when you'll have to know how to drive one," she reasoned. Uncle Derek had taught her in Grandpa's old pickup on the backroads near the Madison's Iowa farm.

Torrie killed the engine a couple of times before she got backed out onto the road. She hoped the highway to Lahar wasn't as bad as the one to Windy Ridge—mountain driving had never been part of Grandma Minnie's training agenda. As she approached the turn-off to the canyon, she happened to remember to check the gas gauge. They had been driving all day and Astrid had been too distraught to think about it. She decided to detour to Cougar and fill up before losing herself in the forest somewhere with no fuel.

After she filled up she drove past the restaurant where they had eaten yesterday. Had it been just two days ago? Her world had been spinning since then. When she got almost past, she realized there was a green DNR truck parked out front. Could it be . . . ? She slowed. Probably not. It's not like Brad is the only ranger around here. Still, it resembled the truck the blond had picked him up in that first day they met. She was almost past the restaurant going too slowly when she stalled the engine. I take that as a sign, she thought. I'm going to stop. She started the truck again and threw gravel into the air as she entered the parking lot a little too quickly.

She checked her watch. A bit late for lunch. Coffee? That would be a good reason to stop. Come to think of it, she really hadn't had lunch. She took several deep breaths and walked in. Two rangers were sitting at the table. One, a man, had his back to the door; the other was the perky blond. Torrie almost regretted her decision and considered getting coffee to go.

The blond leaned over and said something to the other ranger and he turned and looked her way. It was him. She gave a tentative wave and started to sit down at the counter. Then he waved her over. She was glad she didn't have to embarrass herself by interrupting if he'd rather be with the blond. He greeted her enthusiastically and introduced her to Kirsten, his companion.

"Join us," he said and moved over to make room for her on the bench seat.

Another decision made for her. She wondered how Kirsten felt about it. No evident change in her cheerful expression—at least not yet. Torrie warily sat down.

Torrie mentioned the sad news and Brad asked how Astrid was coping. Both were sympathetic.

"I was with Mack when he went on that call," he reminded her. "But when he found out it was a fatality . . ." He couldn't finish. "Glad I didn't have to face that."

An uncomfortable silence followed as the three pondered the tragedy that had struck in their midst.

And Torrie pondered Kirsten. She had that clear pale skin that natural blondes were blessed with, Scandinavian probably. The hair that she had been wearing down the other day was twisted and hidden under her ranger hat. Besides being tall she was sturdily built with muscular legs—hiking legs.

Kirsten broke the silence by asking, "So, Torrie, what have you seen around here?" Her eyes glittered when she spoke and she seemed genuinely friendly. Maybe she and Brad were just friends, colleagues. And they did talk about things they did with some of the other summer rangers. Kirsten was definitely excited about her job. As Torrie recounted her sightseeing stops both the rangers interrupted from time to time with bits of wisdom and information about their favorite sites.

"Will you be able to see anything else?" asked Kirsten.

"Now that . . . things have changed?"

"I think so," Torrie answered. "Astrid offered to let me borrow her truck. And I think she'll be with Eddie's parents again tomorrow."

"Have you seen Coldwater Ridge?" asked Brad.

"We drove past it," she said. "But we pretty much drove straight up to Johnston Observatory. If 'straight' is the right word."

"Great place," said Kirsten. "It's my favorite place to work. I love to watch people coming out after they've been in the theater."

"It's impressive," agreed Torrie. "Awesome," she added, trying out Brad's word. "But I was a little edgy when I saw the smoke coming up from the dome."

"Oh, that," said Brad. "That's really just dust being kicked up from landslides. Nothing to worry about. Tell you what," he continued. "I'm working up at Coldwater tomorrow. Why don't you come up and meet me for lunch?"

Torrie was looking at Brad, but she checked her peripheral vision for any sign of a reaction from Kirsten. Things seemed calm enough on the other side of the table.

"I'd like that. What time?"

"Anytime between noon and two. I'll watch for you."

Before they parted, Kirsten encouraged her to go on to see Lahar Canyon, but when Torrie found out she would have to cross a deep gorge on a swinging bridge she changed her mind and went back to the trailer. She played a few rounds of Frisbee with Tasha, then fell into a deep sleep on the sofa. She hadn't realized how much of a toll the stress had taken on her.

When Astrid returned, she took her turn on the sofa. She lay with one foot on the floor, her arm resting on her forehead.

"Are you okay?" asked Torrie. "Can I get you anything?"

"I'll be all right. Well, maybe some chai. Yes, that sounds good. Do you mind?"

"Of course not."

"You probably don't even know where to find it." Astrid started to get up.

"Of course I do. You got me hooked on it, remember?" Astrid smiled for the first time that evening.

Later the girls sat with their tea in the tiny living room. Astrid told about her day with Eddie's parents. They were still in shock and going through the motions—the real grief would hit after all the necessary arrangements had been made.

Mrs. Martinez had spent the afternoon doing motherly things: packing up his dishes, doing laundry, fretting about what to do with his clothes.

Astrid told Torrie what the sheriff's office had found out, at least what they were willing to reveal. They had towed Eddie's jeep into Kelso. It had been found near the trail head at Sheep Canyon. They wouldn't know what to do with it until they had talked to his parents.

"I still can't figure out what he was looking for," continued Astrid. "I know he had found out something but he wouldn't tell me what it was—or where."

"Did he think you might be in danger?"

Astrid hesitated. "There was that possibility. The work we've been doing isn't exactly popular with everybody."

"Protecting the environment? I thought everybody would be behind that."

"Not really. At least not everyone can agree on how it should be done. The timber industry wants to manage resources and the environmentalists want to save the spotted owls and their habitat in the old growth forests. And of course you've already noticed how the loggers feel about any outside interference. The Mount St. Helens crisis saved a lot of them from financial ruin—the industry almost shut down in several parts of the Northwest."

"Really? I hadn't realized it had been that bad."

"Things have calmed down a lot in the last few years. Back when some of the more radical groups like Green Heart were out here things got really nasty. Protesters were chaining themselves to trees and even burying their feet in concrete to save the forest."

"In concrete! You've got to be kidding. Why did they do that?"

"To stop logging in sensitive areas. It worked for a while, too."

"How did they get out of the concrete? They did get them out, didn't they?" Torrie was horrified.

"Oh, yes. They had to break up the concrete blocks so they could take them to jail."

"Pretty severe." Torrie shook her head. She sipped her chai without speaking.

After a while Astrid spoke. "Actually it's kind of incongruous." Her eyes were beginning to show signs of the grief she had borne the last few days.

"What is?"

"Eddie and I don't approve of those extremist movements. Didn't." She glanced uncomfortably at Torrie before going on. "We felt that a lot of the views held were too bio-centric."

"Bio-what?" asked Torrie. "What does that mean?"

"It's the philosophy that attempts to save animal and plant species at all costs. Everybody has been pouring billions of dollars into these research projects that so many times result in people losing their jobs. Sort of a reverse discrimination in the animal kingdom.

Torrie was stunned. "I'd never heard that side of it." She scratched her head. "But what does that have to do with you and Eddie?"

"Eddie and I made a lot of enemies. Researchers' ideas aren't always welcomed, because their discovery may threaten someone else's livelihood. I think Eddie must have discovered something that was upsetting to someone."

"Well, does that mean you think someone intentionally—hurt him?"

For the first time, Torrie began to realize the implications of the situation she was in. She wondered if Astrid was keeping things from her for the same reasons Eddie hadn't told Astrid everything he knew. Maybe her friend thought Torrie was in danger. Or maybe the stress of losing her boyfriend and colleague were just causing Astrid to overreact.

Before Astrid could answer, Tasha scrambled to her feet and scurried to the door, barking all the way.

Torrie felt a shiver ripple down her spine. Just how desperate were these nameless, faceless enemies?

Chapter 11

TIMBER

Astrid followed Tasha to the door, where the sheltie waited, whimpering and wagging her tail and looking expectantly at her master.

"Do you think someone's out there?" asked Torrie.

"Oh, no," Astrid assured her. That's the way she asks to be let out. You'd *know* if a stranger was out there."

"Right. I remember. She sounded like a whole pack of dogs the night Morgan and I got here."

Astrid opened the door and a grateful Tasha rushed out.

"Do you just let her out like that without a leash?" asked Torrie.

"If she's just going out to do her duty, she'll be right back."

As predicted, Tasha soon returned and the girls began readying themselves for bed and making plans for the next day. Once Astrid fell back into her usual nightly routine, she seemed to relax and began to tell Torrie what the deputies had found out. Torrie added the notes to her already overflowing notebook. She made a star in the margin by something she needed to tell Brad—something that might convince him to help her check some things out.

Then, since Astrid seemed to be in the mood to talk, Torrie decided to pursue the matter of the gopher. "You never told me what connection the gopher has with your own research," she said.

Astrid took a deep breath and answered. "You're already in the middle of this, so you might as well know," she said. The Fireweed in one of the plots I've been studying has undergone some puzzling changes. Remember I mentioned the mutations?"

Torrie nodded.

"Well, I sent some samples back to the lab at U-Dub to have it analyzed," she continued. "I got a very stern message back from my prof insisting that I stick with the hypothesis I had originally formulated. Nothing unusual about that. In fact that would be a pretty typical response from a thesis advisor, and I wouldn't have thought any more about it, except that a former student that had been in my class while I was a graduate assistant was working in the lab at that time. He got in touch with me and told me that the tests had been done, but the results had mysteriously disappeared. My student had been there when the tests were performed and he knew they indicated some unusual chemical properties. He just couldn't remember what they were because it didn't seem significant at the time."

Torrie sat wide-eyed, listening.

"He also said that some of the substance had been injected into lab rats."

"And what happened?"

"Their behavior became very erratic and they became agressive."

"Like the pocket gopher."

"Exactly."

With that final thought just before bedtime, Torrie spent an extremely restless night. Astrid was up early, however, readying herself for another day with Eddie's parents.

She was meeting Mr. and Mrs. Martinez in Kelso so they could make final arrangements about Eddie and meet with the sheriff again. Torrie would drop her off there and have the use of the pickup again. The bad news was that she would be driving up the mountain highway that led up to Johnston Observatory. She had a vivid recollection of the chasms on both sides, so even though it was a wide modern road, she was uneasy at the prospect. She was, however, a little more excited about having lunch with Brad than she cared to admit. Even so, she was determined to keep her emotions out of it—she had some important questions to ask him.

Torrie's apprehension about driving the mountainous highway soon dissipated as she took in the breathtaking scenery. Astrid had given her some final tips before they departed in Kelso and Torrie felt more confident about her solo outing. The day promised to be clear, and with Astrid's binoculars she might be able to spot the herds of elk.

She saw the sign for the Forest Learning Center and pulled off and looked for a parking space in the spacious paved lot. It was filled with recreational vehicles and she had to park at the far end. She was surprised to notice that some of them had very small windows. I guess some people like their privacy, she concluded. She walked up the path toward the viewing area which was equipped with mounted binoculars overlooking the Toutle River far below. Evidently "viewing" the elk wasn't going to be as close up as she had expected. With some advice from a family at the viewing area, she found out where to look for the elusive animals.

After several false "sightings" of what turned out to be vegetation, she finally located the animals with the binoculars. The herd of elk was little more than a smattering of small dots on the wide sandy bank of the narrow winding river, and she soon lost interest. She tried to locate the area where Astrid was researching. According to the maps the botanist had shown her, it should be on this side of the mountain near the rocky canyons. She clearly saw the large hummocks on the plains that had once been chunks of the volcano. She thought she saw a helicopter in the vicinity of what looked like a waterfall. Probably one of those tours out of Randle, she thought.

From this vantage point she could clearly see the mud flow area that she had seen delineated on the maps of the area. The Toutle had served as a natural channel for the insane rush of the volcano's innards gushing from the crater. The peaceful scene today was in sharp contrast to the stories she had heard of rushing torrents that had swept along houses and vehicles, scores of upright trees, and even bridges.

Torrie finally located a cluster of females gathered with a few calves. The aloof male was nowhere to be seen. The animals were resting, some submerged in the shallow water, and Torrie soon decided she was not going to get much of a look at their lifestyle.

* * *

The clover doesn't taste right this season, but the young elk doesn't know the difference. He continues nibbling at this newly discovered treat until nibbling turns to gorging. He eats until his wobbling legs betray him. His immature digestive system is not developed enough to ward off the toxin that is soon surging through his veins. He crumples into a high stand of grass and lays his head listlessly on a cool patch of ground, waiting for his babysitter to come and urge him to move on.

The appointed caregiver comes looking for her lost

charge and nudges him. She keeps nudging until his mother returns and begins her woeful bawling.

* * *

After a few minutes Torrie walked back down the hill. She looked at her watch. Ten thirty. Still plenty of time before she had to meet Brad. Might as well take a look at the center while she was here. It would be a while before she unraveled all the mysteries of the volcanic monument.

As soon as she entered she realized that the sponsor was the Weyerhauser Company, one of the large timber interests in the Northwest. The enemy? Or co-laborer in the re-establishment of the ecosystem? Torrie decided to find out.

She entered the airy, modern building that housed several displays showing the daily work of—what did Morgan say they were called? Loggers. The mannequins were busy with various stages of the harvesting process while captions described the processes in great detail.

On another wall was a series of displays that explained the experiments the company had undertaken in the task of determining the best way to repopulate the destroyed timberland. One of the illustrations showed various planting depths: "*in the ash, below the ash, with the ash removed*", said the captions. *"The young seedlings thrive best in the soil with the ash removed,"* was the conclusion of the experiment. Duh. Torrie wondered what government grant had funded that discovery. They could have just called up her Grandpa Madison and he could have given them the information in five minutes. Saved them millions of dollars.

But what did she really know about the timber industry?

A final scene emphasized the clothing the workers wore and pointed out the safety advances that had been made over the past few decades: safety boots and goggles and leather gloves, to name a few. Logging was a dangerous profession.

As Torrie studied the flannel-clad mannequins with their suspenders and boots, she realized they were all dressed like Vern and his buddies. Loggers could be dangerous, too.

At the last station, Torrie watched a video describing the responsible management of renewable resources. The narrator reiterated some of the statements made in the displays: the forests were a crop, to be managed and harvested responsibly, just as any other agricultural product. It demonstrated the ecosystem-friendly new equipment that was used to carefully select the trees ready to harvest without upsetting the delicate balance of the forest habitat.

Good method, thought Torrie. Or was this just propaganda? She had seen the stands of young trees in the monument itself that were being allowed to propagate naturally. She wondered which ones were doing better.

She picked up a few brochures and started across the parking lot. Just about the right time to meet Brad—not so early that she'd seem overeager, but not late enough to miss his lunch hour.

Just as she unlocked the door of the pickup and started to open it, a shadowy form appeared out of nowhere. The door slammed shut before she could get in, and a tall, wiry man blocked her escape with one hand on top of the pickup.

"What do you think you're doing?" he demanded.

"Let me in my truck," Torrie countered, taking what she hoped was a menacing step toward him.

"This isn't your truck." His dark eyes narrowed. "Where's Astrid?"

"Who are you?" She wavered between relief that he knew Astrid and a continued wariness.

"You haven't answered my question."

"You haven't answered mine, either. Who are you?" she repeated. "Do you know Astrid?"

"You'd better believe I know her. And I know she doesn't let anybody drive her truck."

"Well she let *me* drive it. She didn't need it today. She's ... busy."

The menacing stranger sneered. "Busy, huh? Probably going through all the loot her boyfriend left. She must have made a pretty good haul. I was smart to get away when I did." He took a step back. "Go ahead. Drive your precious pickup. She won't need it now that she has her Spanish boy's jeep."

Torrie hesitated and he took another step back.

"Go on," he said. "But watch your back. That woman's dangerous."

Torrie got in, but he grabbed the door before she could close it. "Just take a message to her for me. Ask her why that little elk calf died. If she's so smart, how come she and her friends are up here messing up the environment." His mood turned dark again and Torrie started the engine.

He moved closer and took her chin in his hand. "Just tell her if she knows what's good for her she'll get off this mountain."

Torrie doubled up her fist and knocked his hand away from her face. "Leave me alone," she yelled at him, and popped the truck into gear. Unprepared for her action, he lost his hold and she careened across the parking lot with the door flying wildly. She stopped abruptly at the exit leading back to the highway and the door slammed shut. She locked it and looked back. He was still standing where she had left him, waving his fists and screaming at her. She was glad she couldn't understand what he was saying.

With trembling hands, she put the truck into gear and resumed her journey up to Coldwater Ridge.

To her relief, Torrie found Brad on the interpretive trail, just where he said he would be. He was pointing out Coldwater Lake, explaining that it had formed after the volcano. He flashed her a smile when he saw her, emphasizing his attractive laugh lines. He pointed at his watch and gave her a "ten-more-minutes" signal. She wandered into the building and tried to focus on the exhibits.

He soon joined her. "Ready to eat?" he asked.

"I'm famished." She patted her stomach with a still-trembling hand.

He took her hand between both of his. "What's the matter? You're shaking."

"Why don't I tell you after we eat."

He shrugged, then ushered her to a table with a view and they ordered. "So how do you rate this extended vacation?" he asked. She explained her current job crisis and how it tied in with her relationship with her parents. She told him how so many of her decisions had been made in rebellion against her mother: she took French in high school and college because her mother was so enamored of Latin America. Torrie had made many family trips to Mexico against her will, and in spite of herself picked up some survival Spanish skills, but her true love was Europe. She had made a class trip there during college, and was determined to go back some day. "Unfortunately," she said, "I haven't found a way to make my French pay off—not too many jobs in Texas looking for that kind of bilingualism."

He nodded sympathetically and she realized she had probably been babbling. But it was a good way to keep her recent encounter from crowding into her thoughts. She chattered on about insignificant things until she felt calm enough to tell him about her ordeal.

"What do you know about that dead elk?" she asked.

His expression turned serious. "You know about that?"

"Yes. Why? Is it supposed to be a secret?"

"Not exactly," he began slowly. "But we try not to let information like that get out to the tourists. It tends to unsettle them."

"I don't find that nearly as unsettling as being accosted in the parking lot of a visitor center."

"Someone attacked you? When did that happen? Where were you?"

Torrie raised a hand. "Whoa. One question at a time." I was down at the Weyerhauser exhibit." She pushed her remaining food around on her plate, trying not to look at him. "This guy recognized Astrid's pickup. Thought I'd stolen it or something."

"What did he do? Did he hurt you?" He held her gaze with his piercing blue eyes.

"No, no. I'm okay. Just rattled." She went on to tell him about the rest of the incident.

"And he's the one who told you about the elk calf?"

Torrie nodded.

"I'll let Mack know. He can be keeping an eye on you."

"Like that's going to help if I'm out in the forest somewhere."

"Well, don't go into the forest." He was beginning to sound impatient.

"I may have to," she said. "In the line of duty."

"What duty would that be?" He gave her an amused look.

"It appears I'm in the middle of a murder investigation. I may have to go into the forest to dig up clues."

His eyes darkened. "Why are you calling it a murder investigation? It was an accident."

"Astrid is convinced . . ."

"Astrid. She's just . . ."

"What?" snapped Torrie. "A hysterical woman?"

"No. I was going to say she's too emotionally involved. The sheriff's department doesn't see any reason to consider foul play."

"Well I happen to believe Astrid. She's an accomplished scientist. She's trained to observe and question."

He finished up his fries before he answered. "But even the best scientist can lose their objectivity when they're too close to the problem."

Torrie decided to drop it before she became irrevocably angry and lost her chance to recruit him in her investigations. She wondered if Morgan would accuse her of using him. He had picked up the bill and started to stand up. "Speaking of scientists," she began. "What do you know about the guys up at Spirit Lake—the ones who found him?"

"The divers?" he asked as they walked toward the cashier. She nodded.

"Not much," he said. They were outside by now and Torrie was afraid he was going to bolt at any minute and go back to work. But he continued to tell her what he knew about the divers. "They've been up at the monument a few times. They started coming up soon after the eruption to do some kind of research. They usually stay over at the Cispus Learning Center—over near where Astrid is—and sometimes they bring groups and give tours. We haven't had any dealings with them because they're pretty law abiding. They clean up after themselves, don't break any park rules . . ."

Now was the time to hit him with the interesting bit of information she had learned from Astrid last night This could be her only chance to enlist his help. He was staring idly out into the emptiness of the landscape and probably thinking about getting back to his own tours. "Did you know they discovered some fibers under Eddie's fingernails?"

"What kind of fibers?" He asked without turning to look at her.

"Kevlar."

He whistled loudly and turned to face her. "You mean, as in diving suits?"

"Exactly."

Torrie watched as he worked his jaw back and forth and pushed his hat back on his head with his thumb. She studied his eyes as he digested the information. At last he readjusted his hat.

"Is Astrid still staying in that little trailer at Tower Rock?"
She nodded.
"I'll meet you there after dark tonight. I've got an idea."

Chapter 12

CISPUS

Torrie got to the trailer before Astrid and had started supper before her hostess arrived.

"Smells good," Astrid said as she entered, and stooped to greet the eager Tasha. She dropped onto the couch. "What did you find to cook?"

"My specialty—tuna casserole. Except I couldn't find any onion rings so I had to improvise."

Astrid nodded absently. The sparkle had gone from her eyes.

"Hard day?" asked Torrie.

"Yeah." She patted Tasha. "I'll tell you about it later."

Over the meal the girls exchanged stories. Astrid had been with Eddie's parents during the entire grueling process of talking to the sheriff and the coroner and making arrangements to ship the body back to California.

"I got to look at the contents of his backpack" she said.

Torrie looked at her expectantly.

"There was no topo map and his new compass wasn't in there. There's no way Eddie would have gone on a hike without them. And you saw they weren't where he usually keeps them."

"Where did they find his backpack?"

"It was in the back of his jeep."

"And the map and compass weren't in the jeep, either?"

Astrid shook her head.

"What do you think happened?"

"I'm not sure. Someone could have lured him to the monument. Maybe on the pretext of an emergency. But he always carried everything he needed in a day pack. He could have grabbed that if he was going into the wilderness. Or maybe someone invited him out to dinner—or somewhere else he didn't need his gear. Then while they were out they decided to go to the lake. But I don't understand why anyone would go to Spirit Lake anyway—there's nothing there. Maybe someone overpowered him and took him there against his will. I just can't see him going out there by himself at night."

"What makes you think it was at night?"

"The time—the time of death . . ." Astrid let out a gasping sob before continuing. "It was about midnight. And I saw him that afternoon. They can't find anyone else who saw him that evening."

Torrie pondered the options, then grew alarmed. "So you were probably the last person to see him alive. Does that make you a suspect?"

Astrid shook her head vigorously. "They don't have any suspects because they're still calling it an accident."

They finished the meal and Astrid insisted on doing the dishes.

Torrie looked at her watch. "Brad is coming over this evening."

Astrid raised an eyebrow.

"It's business."

"Business? That's a new one. What kind of business could you possibly be doing after dark?"

"It's not business, exactly. It's about Eddie."

Astrid turned and faced Torrie, her hands still soapy. "What about Eddie?" she asked sharply.

Torrie wasn't sure how much to say. She began cautiously. "Brad has thought of a way to investigate some leads."

"What leads?"

"Just some suspicions we have?"

"We? You mean this isn't an official park investigation?"

"Well . . ." began Torrie.

Astrid was visibly agitated. She shook the soap from her hands, grabbed a towel, and faced Torrie squarely. "Those suspicions aren't about me, are they? Is that why you asked if I was a suspect?"

Torrie was dumbfounded. She hadn't expected this reaction.

"Well, am I right, or not?" She didn't wait for Torrie's answer. She threw the towel on the table and brushed past Torrie. "C'mon, Tasha," she said and took the eager dog outside.

Torrie didn't know what to do next. She hoped Brad arrived before Astrid returned. She finished up the dishes and turned on a burner to fix the drink that by now had become routine. Before it was hot she heard footsteps on the front steps.

When Astrid came in, Torrie could see she had been crying.

"I'm sorry, Astrid. I didn't mean to imply . . ."

Astrid waved off her apology with an impatient gesture. "Don't worry about it. I'm just stressed. I know you didn't mean anything." She sat on the couch, pulled up an afghan, and rested her head on her knees.

Torrie brought her a cup of chai and sat at the opposite end of the couch facing her. They sipped in silence for awhile. Torrie checked her watch again. "Almost 8:15. I would have thought he'd be the punctual kind." Then she remembered the incident at the Forest Learning Center and told Astrid about it.

Astrid asked her what the guy looked like. When Torrie told her, she said. "It must have been Jimmy. He would have recognized my truck."

"Jimmy?"

"My ex-boyfriend. Jimmy Dimarco. He's Italian. Very romantic." She smiled a wistful smile, then became serious again. "But extremely jealous. He just couldn't tolerate me working long hours in the field. Especially when I started teaming up with Eddie. So I had to break up with him. We had a really nasty scene in a restaurant."

They were interrupted by Tasha's visitor bark. "It must be Brad," Torrie surmised, and got up to let him in. He was carrying a dry cleaner's bag over his arm and a duffel in the other hand. He was wearing a mischievous grin.

"Official gear for our investigative work," he said, indicating the bags.

Torrie looked curiously at him.

He set the duffel on the chair by the door, and held up the plastic-covered garment for Torrie to see. Official ranger uniform, complete with hat. "Compliments of Kirsten," he explained. He produced the hat and plopped it squarely on Torrie's head.

She tentatively took the brim in both hands and adjusted the hat. "Is this legal? I don't want to get arrested for impersonating a forest ranger."

He looked at his watch. "It's going to be dark soon. Nobody's going to see you anyway. Besides, would you rather get arrested for trespassing?"

"I take that to mean it *is* illegal for me to wear this."

Astrid interrupted. "What *are* you two up to, anyway. Torrie, you still haven't told me what this is all about."

Brad explained their plan to check out the divers' story over at Cispus.

"I don't want you to get in trouble on my account," said Astrid. She gave Brad a look Torrie couldn't quite interpret.

"I think you two may be right about Eddie's death," he said. "It's in the park's interest to find out what really happened."

"Do you have the authority to investigate?" asked Torrie.

"Well, not exactly," he said. "I would if it was an official murder investigation, but let's just say I have friends in the right places." He turned to Torrie. "Do you still want to go through with this?"

Torrie looked back and forth between her two new friends; then Tasha gave a challenging bark and ran back and forth from Torrie to the door. "You're right, Tasha. I need to do this." She picked up both bags and started for the small bedroom. "I'll be right back."

In a few minutes, Torrie returned in a uniform with pants a little too long and top a little too big, but convincing enough to make her look like an authentic ranger—especially with her hiking boots.

After some final words of caution from Astrid, they were on their way.

The Cispus Learning Center where the divers were based was only a few minutes away from the Tower Rock campground. When they arrived, Brad turned his little car onto the road giving access to the grounds. Torrie's legs were shaking so badly she could barely get out of his car and she tripped as they started along the roadway.

"Are you all right?" he asked.

"I'm fine," she whispered.

"Don't whisper," he whispered. "We need to act like we're here officially."

"Okay, lead the way," she replied in a voice she hoped

sounded confident. She was glad it was dark—she didn't feel the least bit official.

When they reached the entrance to the center, they discovered that the bar blocking the way in was padlocked. They walked around the end.

"This doesn't look like it would keep anybody out," she said.

"It's just to limit vehicle traffic at night," he explained. "Let's walk on over there toward the main lecture hall. It looks like they might be in a class right now."

"At night?" she asked.

"Yes, that's what most groups do. They go out for field studies during the day, then come back at night for classes."

"This way," he said, taking her elbow and guiding her toward a long wooden building. The lights were dimmed and the windows were too high to see the audience inside. Torrie could just make out the top of the speaker's head as he moved back and forth. He seemed to be showing slides; the top of what appeared to be a screen was visible and the lighting changed with an irregular rhythm as the pictures flashed.

"What is this place?" she asked. She remembered not to whisper about halfway through and "this place" seemed to boom in her ears.

"Groups can rent it for conferences," he explained. "I checked out our diver friends; they've been taking their group on hikes around the area."

"What kind of classes are they giving?"

"I guess there's one way to find out," he said, and moved closer to the building. The windows were open to let in the cool night air, so they didn't have any difficulty hearing.

"The volcano was still active for several years after the initial eruption," the voice inside was saying. "One of the post-eruption events was an immense mud flow. It followed the path of the Toutle River and demolished the entire valley in a matter of minutes. Then over the next few months the volcanic forces continued to work beneath the mass of solid mud and ash and sent up steam vents. Some of those were so forceful that they formed complete canyons. That's where we've been doing a good deal of research."

He paused as a muffled voice in the audience evidently asked a question.

"No, unfortunately, we can't take you back into those areas. The canyons are in the area that is reserved exclusively for scientific research. But you're right, we have discovered that the strata that were formed resemble those in the Grand Canyon. And we know for a fact that these were formed in a matter of hours, not billions of years."

Torrie and Brad heard a rustle of comments among the audience.

"We *will* be able to get a closer look at the canyons tomorrow when we go up to Johnston Observatory," the speaker continued. "And tomorrow night we'll have a video on our findings in the one they call 'Little Grand Canyon.'"

Then the screen went dark and the lights went up. "Before we take our break," continued the speaker," we'll hear a word from Dr. Matthews. He's found some exciting things at the bottom of Spirit Lake—some things that may make the Petrified Forest National Park change its interpretive signs."

Brad gave Torrie a startled look.

"He's the one Astrid and I talked to at the lake," she said. He has some kind of theory about why the logs sink standing up. It didn't make the least bit of sense to me."

"Tell me about it later," he said. "If they're going to take a break pretty soon, we'd better check out the other buildings while we have a chance."

She nodded, and they moved silently from one building to another, Brad shining his flashlight into the windows. He instructed her to keep checking the ground.

She obediently shone her light in front of her as she walked, then asked, "What exactly am I looking for?"

"Footprints."

Before she could ask for a clarification, they reached the third building and he called out, "Bingo!"

She rushed to his side at the doorway. The door was locked, but he was aiming his long black flashlight into the dark recesses.

A row of wet suits hung neatly along the wall, probably five or six. They seemed to be in different colors corresponding to their sizes. There were the blue and yellow ones like the divers had been wearing when Torrie and Astrid talked to them, and a smaller green one that looked to be about the right size for a woman.

They heard random voices coming from the large hall. The students must be on break. Torrie was sure Brad must be able to hear her heart beating. She prepared to make a break and run toward the car, but to her surprise, he headed toward the meeting room. "What are you doing?" she croaked in a voice that threatened to fail her.

"Follow me," he said. "And keep checking the ground."

"What kind of footprints am I supposed to be looking for?"

"Cat tracks."

Torrie scrambled to keep up with his long strides.

As they approached the building, a man with a name tag came out of the building carrying a stack of booklets and large manila envelopes. He carried himself with the air of one in charge.

Brad approached him. "Good evening," he said.

"Evening." The man returned the greeting and nodded at Torrie. "What can we do for you?"

"We're investigating a cougar sighting in the area. Has anyone in your group seen any sign of one?"

Torrie quickly looked down so the man wouldn't see the

look of surprise on her face. Following her beam of light to Brad's side, she came to a stop beside him.

"Any luck?" Brad asked her.

"Haven't seen anything yet," she said, grateful she didn't have to lie.

The man asked a few questions which Brad answered expertly. As Brad turned to leave, the man suggested that they come in and announce their warning to the group.

Torrie gave Brad a panicky look, then followed the two into the building. The room was filled with groups of people milling about talking and looking at books on the display tables that lined the walls. Their guide invited them to help themselves to some brochures and excused himself. He went across the room and talked to a man with gently graying hair.

Torrie and Brad were occupied with stuffing their pockets with the literature from the table, when Torrie glanced up. Approaching them were their helpful guide and one of the divers she and Astrid had talked to yesterday! He was sure to recognize her and know she wasn't a ranger. With her back to the two men she said loudly to Brad, signaling him with her eyes and swinging her flashlight for emphasis. "I'll go out and take another look around. Meet you back at the car."

Breathlessly she rushed back to the car, abandoning the pretense of looking for tracks. She was still breathing noisily when Brad returned.

She explained her hasty exit and he told her about standing up authoritatively, warning people not to go out alone after dark and to keep a close eye on their kids until the cougar sightings were confirmed.

Back in the car he sighed, "When this gets back to my boss, it'll probably be the *last* summer I work for the Parks Department.

"If the things we overheard tonight are true," she replied, "you may not *want* to."

Chapter 13

VICTIMS

Brad and Torrie rode in silence back to the trailer and went inside. Astrid wasn't back yet and Tasha was nowhere to be found. "That's unusual," said Torrie. "She usually leaves her in the trailer while she's gone."

"Maybe she came back and took her along."

"I don't know whether Eddie's folks are dog people or not. They might not want a mutt in the car."

Brad shrugged. "While we're waiting for her, why don't we look at these brochures we picked up."

"Oh, I had forgotten all about them," she admitted. "I've never been so scared in my entire life."

"But you did a great job of coming up with an excuse to get out of there before the doc came over."

"You think so? I thought it was pretty clumsy myself."

"Nah. You're a natural."

Torrie sat next to him on the sofa where they could look at the literature together. She picked up one brochure that showed a picture of Blaine and Dave lecturing to a group on a hike. "These are the divers we met," she said. "Oh," she remarked in surprise as she continued reading. "They're both doctors. Neither one of them mentioned it when we were talking to them. You'd think they'd be pushing their theories more. Isn't it pretty important professionally to discover some new bit of knowledge you can write a book about?"

Brad shrugged. "Maybe that's why they're not talking about it. They don't want anyone else to find out about their idea until they can break the news in the media."

"Look at this," he said, indicating a map of the area. "See this area with the cross-hatching? That marks the same canyon where Astrid has been doing her research."

Torrie leaned close to see the place he indicated.

"What was it they were saying about their research in the canyons?" she asked.

"Some kind of connection with the Grand Canyon," he replied. "I didn't get all of it."

Maybe he didn't *want* to get it, she thought.

"This is where the dead elk calf was found," he was saying. He took out a pen and marked an "X" on the area. "And here," he said as he placed a second mark, "is the site of the pocket gopher incident."

Torrie studied his markings—all concentrated within a relatively small area.

"Where was Eddie's research?" she asked.

He pointed to an area near the center of the map. "Not too close, but in the same general area. If he did as much hiking and camping as Astrid says, he might have stumbled onto something in this region." He drew an irregular circle around all the suspect points. "This is all within a five square mile area," he said, tapping the spot with his pen and massaging his chin with his left hand. "Close enough to be suspicious."

Torrie was momentarily distracted from their discussion

by the soft scratching sound of his hand on his beard. The dark shadow of his emerging beard emphasized the determined square jaw. Not a guy who would easily be sidetracked, she decided.

He turned and caught her staring at him.

"What?" he asked.

"Nothing," Torrie lied as she picked up a handful of brochures.

"Has anyone ever told you you have beautiful eyes?" he asked.

She blushed.

"Now tell me what you were thinking," he said. "I've seen women get that look before and it's never good." He narrowed his eyes and mimicked her stare.

"What's that supposed to mean?" she asked. They continued with their gazes locked until Brad took the brochures from her and placed them on the end table.

"Nothing," he echoed. Then he stood up and offered her his hand. "We're getting too stressed out over this, let's go outside for a little walk."

Torrie hesitated, then stood. "Probably not a bad idea," she said. But she wondered whether they were stressed over the situation they were in—or each other. "Let me go change." She returned in shorts and hooded sweatshirt and they went outside.

A full moon was peeking from behind the hillside overlooking the camp grounds. They strolled around the pond and listened to the fish splashing in the water and to the quiet hum of forest sounds.

"It's so peaceful up here," he said. "I've been coming up here since I was a kid. I think this forest is my favorite place in the world."

"Did you ever come before the blast?"

"My folks might have brought me, but I was too young to remember what it was like then. My memories are of the blast zone. My brother and I used to pretend we were hiking on the moon. We loved the wildness and barrenness of it. I've watched it all grow back, little by little since then."

"Is that what made you decide to be a summer ranger?"

He nodded.

"It sounds like a fun summer job. I'll bet you make a lot of friends that way."

He agreed. "Some of these people have been coming up here and working for years."

"Are you and Kristen pretty close?" she asked, pretending not to be interested in his answer.

He smiled. "Just friends. We're the only rangers who don't like to stay up late and party. We just hang out and rent videos."

Deciding to change the subject before he thought the subject mattered, she asked, "Is it just you and your brother?" she asked.

"Yeah, Trevor. He's two years older than I am."

"What does he do?"

"He studied Business Management at Western Washington."

"Western Washington," she repeated. "What do they call it? Dub Dub?"

He gave her an indignant look.

"That's a big difference from a forest ranger," said Torrie, trying to retrieve the conversation she had almost derailed with her impertinence." He must not be into the outdoors as much as you are."

"Everybody in Washington is into the outdoors," he said. "Especially in the summer when the rain lets up a little. We have everything: mountains, ocean, islands, whales, old growth forests—anything you could possibly want. In fact, in Bellingham every year we have a marathon race that begins with skiing on Mount Baker and ends up with swimming in

Bellingham Bay. We have five different events like mountain biking, kayaking, and swimming."

"Sounds like fun," she said. "Do you compete?"

"You mean in the race? No, I leave that to Trevor. I learned long ago not to compete with my older brother."

"That sounds like there's a story in it."

"Not one I like to tell," he admitted. "What about you? What do you like to do?"

"I grew up playing cowboys and Indians with my cousins," she said. "I guess that's not politically correct anymore. But I always wanted to be a cowgirl."

He laughed. "Quite a career switch, cowgirl to factory-manager-in-training."

"Not as much as you'd think," she said. "Remember, I live in Texas. In fact, my best friend Myndi lives on a ranch. I used to do a lot of horseback riding with her and her . . ." She stopped.

"Go on," he prompted.

"Never mind," she said.

"A story you don't like to tell?"

"I guess you could say that." She stooped and picked up a rock and started turning it over and over."

"Actually it's a story I probably should tell," she said. "Maybe I can make it go away." They had circled the entire campgrounds and were back by the small lake again.

He led her to a bench under a tree. "Want to sit down?" he asked. "I'm a good listener."

Slowly, she began telling him about Aaron, her high school sweetheart. When her family had moved to Texas while she was in middle school, she was traumatized. Myndi and her older brother Aaron were the only ones who hadn't taunted her with "Yankee-go-home," and the three had become close friends. Then in high school she and Aaron had started dating steadily and everybody assumed they would be married. Until the Gulf War. Aaron, already graduated and in the reserves, had been called to Desert Storm.

Torrie stopped, the lump in her throat making it impossible to talk.

"It's okay," Brad said. "You don't have to finish."

Still clutching the small stone, she turned away so he wouldn't see the glistening in her eyes, then swallowed and went on, still turned away from him. "He came back from the war, but he had been . . . wounded. He decided it wasn't fair to me to date 'half a man' so he broke it off. He wouldn't even see me again. He wanted me to remember him the way he was." She took a tissue from her pocket and dabbed at her eyes.

"How did it happen?"

"Victim of 'friendly fire,' I guess. Nobody in his family will talk about it."

"How serious were his . . . injuries?"

"I don't know. Nobody will tell me. Aaron made everybody promise not to tell me. It's just not fair. He made the decision without me. It was my life too. He should have told me, he should have . . ." She trailed off. "I think the worst part was feeling like I'd lost Myndi and his family, too. I've hardly talked to them since he came back. It's just too awkward when they all have this terrible secret and everyone's afraid they're going to let it slip." She gave in to a noisy sob.

Brad gently put his arm around her. "It's all right," he said and patted her shoulder.

"I haven't dated anybody since then. I just couldn't bring myself to . . . to put myself through that again."

He stroked her hair. "I know. It's not easy to lose someone."

Torrie nodded and they sat in silence for some time. Then Brad took her chin and turned her face toward him. "It may take some time, but time heals." He ran his hand across her cheek and she placed her own hand on his.

"I know, I know. Thanks for listening." She leaned her head on his chest and he embraced her warmly. Torrie breathed in the tranquillity of the scene, feeling a glimmer of promise that she could move toward overcoming her pain. The moment was interrupted by a scuffling in the forest behind them.

They awkwardly disengaged from the spontaneous embrace and turned in the direction of the sound. It was Tasha. She was wet and bedraggled and looked like someone had drug her through a mud puddle. The dog went down on her belly and wriggled toward Torrie.

"Is she hurt?" asked Brad.

"I can't tell. Do you have a flashlight?"

He produced one from the pocket of his jacket and they examined her.

"She seems to be okay," said Torrie after her initial examination. I wonder where on earth she's been. And how she got out?"

"Was the door locked when we got back?"

"I'm sure it was. But then I guess I'm not totally sure. I just used the key without trying the door. I expected it to be locked. But I'm sure I would have noticed if it had been ajar. I don't think she's learned to open the door yet, have you, girl?" She patted the matted fur. "Poor thing. Let's go wash her off."

"Do you think you should wash her at night like this? She might get too cold and get sick."

"Maybe so. I don't know what I'd wash her in anyway. But I know where Astrid keeps her brush. We could at least clean her up a little bit tonight." They started back towards the trailer. "Come on girl," Torrie said, and patted her thigh to get the dog's attention.

Tasha whined and followed a few steps, then stopped and looked over her shoulder toward the woods.

"Come on, Tasha. Come on, girl," Torrie repeated.

Brad whistled. Still the dog refused to come.

"I've never seen her act this way," said Torrie. "I'll go get her food. That should work." As Torrie started towards the trailer, Tasha turned and started running towards the steep hill where the bright moon was still barely visible in the thick foliage.

After several attempts they were still unable to get the dog to respond; she kept turning and heading up the trail that led to Tower Rock. Torrie said, "It's almost like she wants us to follow her."

Brad studied the dog for a few moments. "You may be right," he said. The two looked at each other.

Torrie shivered and pulled her hood tight around her face. "We probably should."

Brad went first, illuminating the way with his flashlight, and the dog's mood brightened distinctly. Torrie struggled to keep up and had to keep dodging branches in her face and hazardous obstacles on the mostly unused trail. Finally they reached the outcropping of rock, dark against the moon's backlit glimmer. Tasha had arrived ahead of them and was running in circles around the area. Brad suddenly stopped and held out an arm to halt Torrie's progress.

"What? What is it?" she asked.

"Don't look," he warned her, but she stubbornly pushed past his restraining arm into the clearing. There at the base of the rock lay the crumpled body of Astrid.

Torrie stifled a scream and turned away from the scene. She dropped to the ground and covered her face with her hands, moaning softly. "Oh, God, no. No, no, no. Not this. This can't be happening."

Brad strode to Astrid's pale body and knelt over her. He felt for the carotid artery, then shook his head grimly. He searched for a thin wrist, but both arms were beneath her; he couldn't reach them without moving the body.

Tasha abandoned her futile attempts to rouse her master

and went to Torrie and began licking her face. "Oh, Tasha, Tasha," she said. "What happened? I wish you could tell us." She reluctantly stood and turned again to face Brad. "Is she . . . ?

His jaw tightened. "Yes. She's gone. Probably been a while."

"You're sure? You don't think we should try to revive her? Oh, yes. She might still be alive." Energized by the thought, she jumped up and rushed toward the body.

Brad grabbed her before she could reach her intended goal. "No, Torrie. It's too late. There's nothing we can do. We can't disturb the scene."

She crumpled against him with uncontrollable sobs and he held her for the second time that evening.

"We need to call the sheriff," he told her gently.

Within the hour the area was swarming with uniformed officials. Brad had roused the owner and borrowed his phone to call in the accident. Even Tasha had been convinced to return to the trailer with them, and Torrie put her leash on.

The investigating deputy confirmed Brad's guess that she had been dead for some time before they discovered the body. After what seemed like endless questioning, Torrie was advised not to leave the area since they would need to make a more thorough investigation if it was judged that the death was not accidental.

"I can't believe this," she said when she was alone with Brad again. "I was the only one who believed that Eddie's death wasn't an accident, and now I'm a suspect in Astrid's death."

"You're not a suspect," he assured her.

"But they won't let me leave town."

"That's just routine," he said. "We discovered the body so we may be able to remember something significant about what happened."

By the time the investigators left, it was three in the morning. The two returned wearily to the trailer. Torrie started up the step with a subdued Tasha in tow.

"Do you want me to stay?" Brad asked.

"No, I'll be fine," she told him without much conviction.

"I won't come in," he said. "I can sleep in my car."

"You don't have to do that. I'll be okay. Really. And I've got Tasha." She sat down on the steps facing him and scratched Tasha's matted fur. "I was feeling so sorry for myself earlier," she said. "Right now my problems don't look so big."

Brad knelt in front in her and picked up both her hands. "Torrie, I don't mean to scare you, but you could be in serious danger right now."

"What do you mean?"

"You're still pretty sure Eddie had discovered something that led to his death?"

She nodded.

"And Astrid probably knew what he knew—at least some of it."

"Yes, but . . ."

"Listen," he said. "If the same people who did away with Eddie are the ones who killed Astrid . . ." He paused and took her face in his hands. "You could be next."

Chapter 14

SUSPECTS

Brad spent the night on the couch. Torrie had slept in the stuffed chair wrapped in Astrid's afghan with Tasha at her feet. At least she spent the night in the chair—she wasn't sure she had actually gotten any sleep. She had expected Brad to kiss her the night before on the steps, but she was glad he hadn't. Or maybe she wished he had. She wasn't sure what she was feeling right now. Too many unfamiliar emotions raged within her. Too many horrible things were happening to her.

She was relieved when the first tentative rays of the sun eased through the windows and stirred up dust motes in the little living room. Now she could start doing something constructive. The first was to clean up poor Tasha, whose mud bath was now coarse and caked. Quietly she begin murmuring reassurances to the disconsolate pup.

She thought she remembered seeing a plastic tub under the trailer with Tasha's things. Noiselessly she let herself out with Tasha at her heels. Sure enough a tub was there, along with some doggie soap. The process of heating water and finding old towels took a while, but Torrie was glad to have something to do to keep her occupied. By the time Brad woke up, she had a fresh, clean, well-fed dog, and had even had time to shower herself. She had fixed herself a cup of chai, but when she held the mug in her hands, she realized she couldn't bear to drink it.

She was relieved when he suggested they go for breakfast at Randle after he showered. She wanted to get away from the place, and she was pretty sure she had exhausted the meager food supply in the trailer.

Torrie was distressed that they ended up at the same little restaurant where she and Astrid had eaten such a short time ago. Vern and his buddies were there again. She wondered if they had heard about Astrid, or even if they might be the ones responsible. After she and Brad ordered she noticed that the loggers were getting ready to leave. If she was going to find out what they knew, this would be her only chance.

"Morning, Vern," she said loudly as the men approached her booth.

Several restaurant patrons eyed her with curiosity. Brad's expression registered alarm and concern.

"Well aren't we up bright and early this morning," Vern returned even more loudly; then he focused his gaze on Brad. "Or maybe you've been out all night."

He guffawed loudly and punched his companion, Big Joe, in the ribs.

Torrie was momentarily flustered at the innuendo and searched for a revealing question.

"Maybe *you're* the one who's been out all night," she rejoined.

He hesitated, as though confused by the question, then countered, "Not me, I have to work for a living. Not like your little tree-hugging friend. Suppose she's missed you yet?"

Big Joe was attempting to move his friend toward the cash register, but Vern turned for one last comment. "You'd better hurry home before she wakes up. You wouldn't want her to know you'd been out all night with that ranger." He gave her an exaggerated wink.

"What was that all about?" asked Brad after they had gone. "Do you know those guys?"

Torrie explained about their earlier encounter with the men.

"And I suppose you think they might have hurt Astrid."

"Yes. I was trying to find out if they knew she was . . . gone."

"Well, you didn't find out anything, did you?" He sounded angry. "Torrie, you're going to have to leave this investigation to people who are trained to do it."

She answered evenly, "You seemed willing enough to let me help out with your investigations at Cispus."

"That was different." Then his anger turned to concern. "Beside, if these guys *were* responsible and they thought you suspected something, you'd be putting yourself in danger."

She looked at him unwaveringly. "Brad, I'm already in danger. You said so yourself," she reminded him. "And I don't intend to sit around doing nothing while a killer goes free."

Brad had refused to let her spend the day alone, so he had called another ranger to cover for him on the trails. He planned to help Torrie follow up on leads, which at this point only amounted to their suspicions. They started at the Randle Ranger station where Marge was on duty. Brad told her about the accident and asked if she had heard anything suspicious.

"I'm not the one that spends time in the forest," she replied coolly. "You need to start with your little partying ranger friends. Unless they're too drunk to notice." She turned to Torrie. "Eddie didn't deserve to die. He was one of the good ones. But that wench you call your friend was always meddling in things that didn't concern her. She got what she had coming to her."

Brad put a warning hand on Torrie's arm and gave Marge a hard look. "Just keep your ears open," he said. "This thing isn't over yet and *nobody's* going to be safe until the people responsible are caught."

Torrie was trembling when they left, and she was glad Brad was doing the driving. It was going to be a long day. They planned to get some specifics about the loss of the elk calf and then go to Kelso. Brad's aunt was a friend of the veterinarian and she might be able to learn more about the alleged rabid pocket gopher than Astrid had been able to find out. Then Brad was going to talk to Mack and find out what he could "off the record."

The events of the previous night finally caught up with Torrie and she slept all the way from Randle to their first stop. She sleepily opened her eyes when the soothing hum of the engine stopped.

"Where are we?" she asked.

"Forest Learning Center," he replied. "I'm going to see what I can find out about the elk calf. You can just wait here," he said as he opened the car door.

Torrie adjusted the jacket she was using as a pillow and lay her head against the window again. Then suddenly she was wide awake. "Wait," she said. "I forgot to tell you. That guy that accosted me here . . . he's Astrid's ex-boyfriend—Jimmy de . . . something. He works here."

"Thanks for the warning," he said. "I'll watch my step. Just stay here," he added and locked the car doors.

Torrie attempted to sleep, but was too uneasy. She thought about joining Brad but decided he might get straighter answers if he wasn't encumbered with a "tourist."

She had finally dozed off again when he returned.

"Bingo," he said. "Our friend Jimmy didn't show up for work today."

"Does anybody know where he is?"

"No. He didn't call in. But I got his address." He patted his shirt pocket. "Looks like we've got another errand to run in Kelso."

Once in Kelso Brad again decided he could investigate better on his own and he left Torrie at the Kelso visitor center. They have a great relief map of the area, he had told her. She could study the canyons that everyone seemed to be so interested in. She had been a little put off initially, but decided she'd use the time to call Morgan. It hadn't even occurred to her yet that someone at the university should be notified of their graduate student's death. In fact, with no family, she wondered who the sheriff's department had called.

Morgan was bubbling with news. She had accepted the job. It was ideal. She could stay with her parents, just for a while of course, and could commute downtown on the bus. It was only fifteen minutes away and she wouldn't have to worry about parking. She loved her coworkers and her boss was actually willing to listen to some of her suggestions.

"Morgan," she had said three times before she could get her cousin to stop and listen. "Morgan, I have some really bad news."

"What is it? Are you all right? I knew I shouldn't have gone off and left you down there."

"I'm fine," said Torrie. "It's Astrid."

"Oh, poor Astrid. She must be taking Eddie's death really hard. Is there anything I can do?"

"Morgan," Torrie repeated. "Astrid's dead."

The line was silent.

"Are you still there? Morgan?"

"Did you say . . . ?"

"Yes, she apparently fell from Tower Rock?"

"Apparently," began her cousin. "What do you mean 'apparently'?"

Torrie went on to tell her about the sheriff's office investigations and of her and Brad's suspicions. Morgan agreed to call Astrid's department head to find out who should be notified. She made Torrie promise to be careful and said she would be down that weekend. Morgan ended the conversation with an insinuation about Brad. Always Morgan.

Torrie was intently studying the relief map when Brad returned. Jimmy's roommate didn't know where he was either and hadn't seen him for three days.

"Convenient," said Torrie.

"He got a little hostile when I tried to get more information out of him."

"Do you think he's covering something up?"

"No, I think he was high on something. I try to stay clear of people like that. You never know what they might do. I did get a new lead, though. I ran into Mack and got a little out of him about Astrid's accident."

"What did you find out?"

"For one thing, the time of death was about nine o'clock. So she was dead before we ever got back to the campgrounds. There's nothing we could have done to prevent it."

Torrie shuddered. It must have happened soon after she and Brad left for Cispus. If they hadn't gone off on their little jaunt, Astrid might not have been killed. Or maybe she'd be lying out there at the bottom of that rock along with her. Brad was tender, as though he sensed the guilt she had been feeling. "What else?" she asked weakly.

"He said that she was clutching a piece of paper in her hand. They think it was something she might have tried to write after she fell . . . or whatever happened."

"What did it say?"

"She didn't get a chance to write much. It just said B-E and then trailed off."

"That's all? Just B-E-? Be careful, maybe? A warning to me?"

"The sheriff's office has no idea. It's not much to go on."

"Be there. Be at . . . someplace. Be sure." Torrie played with several phrases then got a notebook out of her pack and started writing things down. "Could it be the beginning of a word?" she wondered aloud. "Beat, beware, before, behind, beside, been, beverage . . . ?"

"None of that makes any sense."

"Not right now, but I've learned never to reject any possibility."

It was getting late and they had one more stop to make. They pulled into Ben's just before the crowd began to gather for the lottery to see who would get climbing passes for the next day. Torrie remembered with a pang that Astrid had invited her to climb to the summit with her. Now she'd never have the chance. Not that she'd relished the idea of actually reaching the top—it was a long way down from the rim of the crater.

She was relieved to be among the crowd and have a moment of distraction from the heaviness she had been carrying for the last twenty-four hours. Had it been that long already? This was the most dreadful thing that had ever happened to her.

Brad interrupted her reverie. He had been circulating among the crowd trying to pick up clues, but most of the crowd consisted of tourists that seemed bent only on getting a chance at conquering the imposing summit. "Guess who else isn't around?" he said when he returned to her side. "Ben. According to Fred, he hasn't been around all day."

"Ben. B-E-," Torrie said. She felt a crawling sensation in the middle of her back. "Do you think that's what she started to write?"

"It's possible," Brad said hesitantly. "Fred told me that Ben has been obsessed with the idea of opening the crater itself to hikers. He thinks it would increase his business here. He's secretly been circulating a petition."

"Why secretly?"

"Because the scientific community would fight it. They want to keep the restricted areas for their research. Opening it to the general public would destroy a lot of the pristine outdoor laboratory the scientists have valued so much the past fifteen years."

"So if Astrid had found out about his petition . . ."

"Exactly. I think we can add him to our list of suspects. You have started a list, haven't you?"

"No," admitted Torrie. "But I see an empty booth over there. I think I could start it over supper."

For the third time that day they sat and ordered a meal together. Lunch had been a quick burger at Kelso and she was ready for something more substantial. She got out her notebook again and wrote a separate name on each page. Okay, let's see what we have on each of these. Don't the police look for motive and opportunity and—what was the third thing? Weapon?"

"Means," he answered.

Together they compiled a list. When they finished, Torrie read off the results:

JIMMY: Threatened Torrie and unhappy with Astrid. Missing from work and apartment since before A's death; hasn't called in, nobody knows where he is (suspicious roommate)

BEN: Also missing; Motive=A. represented opposition to his plan to open up crater and disturb research. Bottom line: he stands to increase his tourist business. Also A's note says B-E-

DR. LI: Withheld information about gopher; Motive?? (none evident)

MARGE: Has been hostile since Torrie arrived. May have had a crush on Eddie and clearly disliked A. (Is that a strong enough motive? Brad doesn't think so. She's *always* been unpleasant)
VERN & FRIENDS: Verbally abusive to Astrid about her work. Even though her work or her philosophy doesn't threaten the timber industry, V. doesn't know that. (Even Brad wasn't aware of A. & E.'s views on bio-centrism, and was sure the loggers wouldn't have understood the implications)
THE DIVERS: Ones who found body & may have been the last to see him. Seemed reluctant to talk about their research. Plenty of *opportunity* and a perfect alibi to be in the area. (T—Could professionals in the scientific community actually stoop to murder? Brad—of course they could if their research was threatened.)

"Did we miss anybody?" she asked as she finished reading.

"Not that I can think of," he said.

She snapped the notebook shut. "I guess that's all we can get done today."

"Where are you going to spend the night?" he asked. "I have to go back to Kelso tonight so I can go to work first thing in the morning. But I'm sure my aunt would be glad to let you stay with us."

"No, I'll be fine," she said. "Morgan is coming down in a few days and I kind of feel responsible to look after Tasha."

He shrugged, but she could see the worry he tried to mask behind those clear blue eyes.

"I'll take you back, then. You'll still be using Astrid's truck?"

"As long as it's not impounded."

"I don't think it will be. They would have taken it by now if they thought it contained any evidence. But since you had it all that day..."

"Right. And since I'm a suspect, they're more apt to impound *me.*" She smiled for the first time since their tragic discovery.

Brad sadly returned her smile but repeated his former assertion that she was not regarded as a suspect. She wondered how much Mack had told him that he wasn't passing on to her.

Later in the trailer she began packing her things. After tonight she might decide to stay at Brad's aunt and uncle's after all. She had forgotten how solitude could turn to loneliness and the gentle forest noises turn threatening. She felt somewhat comforted by Tasha's presence but remembered that the dog hadn't been able to protect her own master.

As tired as she was, she decided to go over the notes she and Brad had made on suspects and see if she got any new ideas. As she looked over the list she thought about the papers Morgan had brought to Astrid. Those might provide some critical clues. If Astrid thought it was important enough for Morgan to make a special trip down here, they were surely connected to the suspicions she and Eddie had. And hadn't Morgan commented that Astrid would have brought everything she had needed for her original research? So these notes might help Torrie figure out what was really going on.

She got up and went to the niche Astrid described as her "office." She looked at the counter where Morgan had placed the box, but it wasn't there any more. "I'm sure it was here yesterday," she said aloud. Maybe Astrid had put the stuff in her portfolio, she thought, and went to the place where she always left it on the floor. It was too bulging to leave on top of the desk; it would have fallen off. Relieved that it was in its place, Torrie reached for it, but realized that it wasn't bulging any more. Alarmed, she unzipped it and found that all but a few loose scraps of paper had been removed.

Who would have taken this stuff? she asked herself. Did the deputies take anything last night? Were they even in the trailer? She struggled to remember, but much of that horrid scenario was obscured by a mist of confusion and horror. They took all of Eddie's stuff—even his jeep. But they'd had to retrieve it from the "scene of the crime." What made this different? Because his "accident" happened in an isolated place away from his cabin? But that didn't make sense either. Come to think of it, they didn't even believe that Eddie's death was an accident so why would they impound his jeep? Was someone trying to keep some incriminating evidence from getting out? If so, that might mean someone in the sheriff's department was behind this. And if they suspected foul play in Astrid's case, wouldn't they have searched her trailer? Or maybe they did and she just didn't recall. Or maybe she really was a suspect and they were just waiting . . . for what? For her to do something suspicious? To lead them to her co-conspirators? Maybe they were even trying to frame her.

She shook her head. This was getting wild beyond belief. She went back to the bedroom and forced herself to think calmly. She took out the notebook again and tried to write down all the questions that had come to her. She'd run them by Brad the next day. Maybe he could make sense out of them. Then there was the matter of the portfolio. If the deputies thought it contained evidence, wouldn't they have just taken the whole thing instead of just the papers that were in it?

Then she felt a cold chill run down her backbone. Maybe it wasn't the law after all. Maybe someone else had come back here yesterday while she was gone and taken the papers. She may have even left the door unlocked when she and Brad went for a walk. And she still wasn't sure if it had been locked when she and Brad got back from Cispus. Anyone could have come in and ransacked the trailer. But they must have known what they were looking for, because nothing else seemed to be disturbed. . . . No, it was only confusing her to be thinking this way. She'd try to get some sleep and think about it tomorrow when the comforting sunlight had chased away all those dark shadows.

She decided to sleep fully clothed, and searched the trailer for some kind of weapon. She settled for a large butcher knife from the kitchen—it would fit into the side pocket of her daypack. She didn't plan to go anywhere without it until whoever had murdered Eddie and Astrid was safely in jail.

She started to fill Tasha's bowl, but only a few crumbs fell from the old Tupperware container Astrid kept filled with dog food. "Well, let's check your storage bin, girl, and see if there's any extra food there."

She went outside with the empty container in one hand and the knife in the other. She was followed by an eager sheltie, who knew exactly where they were headed. Torrie pulled out the large plastic bin under the trailer where Tasha's other things were kept, and opened it up. Sure enough, a partially-used twenty-five pound bag of food was in there. Torrie unrolled the top of the bag and pulled out the scoop. She started to refill the plastic container when the scoop met with an unexpected resistance. She jabbed again and this time uncovered a zippered plastic bag. "Looks like we've got some coupons for your next bag," she said to the dog, who was salivating in anticipation.

Torrie removed the bag, but to her surprise it contained not coupons, but a thick stack of papers—the college notes Morgan had brought from Seattle.

"Hurray," she exclaimed, then looked around furtively before saying more quietly, "It looks like Astrid was one step ahead of those creeps after all."

After getting Tasha fed, she followed up on her original plan and took the butcher knife into the bedroom. She also pulled a chair in from the kitchen and lay it in front of the door. Since the sliding door didn't have a knob she could prop it under, she decided that if anyone tried to get in, they would have to trip over the dog and the chair first.

Once settled in bed, she carefully removed the contents of the plastic bag and began reading.

Most of it was about diseases that could be transferred from animals to humans. Astrid had already told them about that. There were several pages copied from the Internet about genetically modified plants. Torrie studied the URL; the Internet address looked like it was from some university in Delaware. The rest were pages ripped out of a notebook and written in what was probably Astrid's handwriting, although from what she knew about the scientist, ripping pages out didn't seem to be her style. Unless she had been in a hurry. The notes were on her scientific studies and Torrie couldn't make much sense out of them. Another project to undertake in the daylight, after a good night's sleep. Or maybe Brad would know somebody who could figure out what they meant.

Then it occurred to her to look for words beginning with B-E-in Astrid's handwriting. She scanned the handwritten notes but didn't find anything that seemed significant to her. Then she came across the word "Brand names," followed by a list of companies or scientific products that were totally unfamiliar to her. She wondered if the letters in Astrid's hastily scribbled message had been written in capitals or lower case. That could make a difference. She scribbled in the margin: B-E-, B-e-, then b-e-, printing first, then writing in cursive. Then she stopped, horrified. The B-e-she had written looked just like Astrid's "B-r" in "Brand names." Maybe it wasn't a B-E-after all. Maybe it was B-R-.

Maybe it was Brad.

Chapter 15

EXPLOSION

Torrie decided she would leave the trailer first thing in the morning. She wasn't waiting for Morgan; she certainly wasn't waiting for Brad. Things had gotten entirely too quirky. She got out of bed, finished packing up her things, and carried them out to the truck. Now I'll probably be a car thief as well, she thought; then she remembered she wasn't supposed to leave town. Or was it the county? The forest? She'd just go get a room somewhere and call Morgan and maybe Mack—unless he was in on this, too. He seemed pretty willing to give information to Brad, whom she now had serious doubts about as well.

She placed her daypack beside the bed, loaded with Astrid's notes, snack bars, flashlight, weapon—everything she might possibly need tomorrow, wherever she ended up. She gathered up a few of Astrid's valuables; surprisingly, her purse was still on the kitchen counter where she usually left it. It would bear searching for clues.

After several hours of fitful sleeping she was awakened by Tasha's yipping—a sound she hadn't heard her use before. The dog was throwing herself against the outside door with an alarming determination.

Groggily she half raised up on one elbow and started to slip the knife from the backpack. Then as she gradually became more alert she noticed something else was assaulting her senses—a smell. What was that smell? Propane? Had she turned the stove off? Had she checked the pilot light?

Before she could find the knife she heard unfamiliar sounds outside. Maybe scuffling feet, or voices, or both. In a panic she was jolted awake. She grabbed her daypack and her shoes and tried to open the door. With her hands full she could barely get the sliding door open. Then she tripped over the chair she had left to foil whatever danger she had imagined she might be able to foil.

When she entered the main living area she was aware of a loud hissing sound. It must be a gas leak. Tasha was still jumping at the door when Torrie reached it and fumbled to turn the bolt lock. She had barely gotten the door open and the two of them had started to scramble down the steps when a loud explosion and an intense heat rushed her from behind. The impact sent her sprawling on top of the dog several feet from the bottom of the stairs.

Lights were coming on in neighboring campers and tents, and half-clad campers were stumbling from their interrupted sleep. Help would soon be on the way. Torrie didn't wait for the helpful neighbors, or the sirens, or the friendly face in the crowd that might be a killer. She motioned to Tasha and leapt into the truck with her daypack, still carrying her shoes in one hand.

Now she was probably wanted for arson.

She headed up the road that by now was familiar, and had to pull over to let the volunteer fire engine go by. In the dark she wasn't sure of the turns; she just wanted to get enough distance between her and her attempted killer. Knowing that tourists would soon be filling all the sites around the volcano, she headed deeper into the forest.

She saw what appeared to be an abandoned logging road and pulled off. Fortunately it hadn't rained for the last couple of days, so she wouldn't leave any obvious tracks. She turned off the lights and the engine and took a deep breath. Where now? She needed to find a more secure place to hide out until she could get word to Morgan. But where?

She pulled out the flashlight and started pawing through Astrid's purse, which she must have grabbed when she made her terror-filled departure. She pulled out an address book and looked for local numbers. No luck. Most of them had Seattle area codes. Her next fishing expedition yielded a key ring. She browsed through them: two keys to the truck, one for the trailer, and a small one that looked like a mail box key. That's right. She remembered that Astrid had stopped and checked her post office box in Randle. Now, if she could just find a letter with her box number on it—there didn't seem to be one marked on the key. That would be worth checking out. Two keys left, one smaller one and the other the size of a house or apartment. Eddie's cabin? Of course. Unless she had given the key to his parents, this was probably to his cabin. And Astrid may not have wanted his family to know she had a key to his place.

She could stay there! Excitedly, she started the engine again and began to back out. Then she hesitated. Whoever had killed Eddie surely knew where he lived. It might not be such a safe place to stay after all. But she could at least search it herself. She might find something that everybody else had overlooked.

Right, Torrie, she told herself. All these experts have missed the evidence and you expect to waltz in there and find the missing piece of the puzzle? Oh well, she could always hope for beginner's luck. Besides, she had long ago learned it was worth the effort to check things out, even if it was something she had no understanding of. She had learned that lesson one time when she had borrowed Uncle Derek's old junker car to go job hunting. The engine had started to smoke, but since she didn't know anything about cars she decided her only option was to drive to a gas station and let a mechanic check it. As it turned out, fuel was spurting all over the motor. Lucky for her she hadn't driven it any further or it may have blown up. But she realized later that if she had just opened the hood, even she would have known it wasn't smart to drive with flammable liquid all over the hot engine. From then on she always made it a policy to investigate. Even an amateur can observe the obvious.

So if she was going to search the cabin she wanted to do it before it got light—less chance of someone happening by.

She amazed herself by finding the turnoff to the secluded cabin on the first try. The place was beautiful at night: the moon was still nearly full and it illuminated the entire clearing and sparkled on the patchwork of water visible behind it.

Torrie thought about how her last peaceful scene had exploded around her and waited a few minutes in the truck before getting out and crunching up the gravel path and thumping across the wooden porch.

Tasha did her doggy duties before joining Torrie on the porch. She waited expectantly to be let in. "Is this the right key, girl?" she asked.

Tasha wagged and Torrie tried the house-sized key. It worked. She got out her flashlight and moved stealthily around the moonlit room. The smell of pine replenished her spirits. The place gleamed, even in the dim light; Mrs. Martinez must have scrubbed every inch of it in tribute to her son. Not that it had been that dirty before, she remembered. It was amazing how much she knew about a man she had never met.

Torrie moved to the desk that had drawn Astrid on their

previous visit. The silver box was gone; the desk was empty except for a wooden desk set that must have come with the cabin—or else the Martinezes had decided to leave it for the next residents.

A search of the rest of the place turned up the same results. Everything was shined, and spotless, and empty. A futile trip.

Tasha must have sensed her uneasiness and seemed restless and eager to leave. At least she wasn't barking her there's-a-stranger-outside-the-door bark.

As Torrie turned to go, she noticed a pile of things next to the lamp table by the door. She hadn't noticed them when she came in; they were hidden behind the door. She walked over closer to inspect the dark bulk. It appeared to be a large backpack—the kind that serious hikers wear. Eddie's? What would it be doing here? She shined her flashlight on it and discovered an envelope lying on top.

She picked it up and read the writing on the front: *ASTRID*. With shaking hands she opened it. It was a note from Eddie's mom.

"*Astrid Dear,*" it began. "*You have been such a strength and encouragement to us these last few days. It has been a delight to know you and I am so grieved that you will never be part of our family. You meant so much to our Eddie. Please take his camping things and pass them on to someone who can use them. Maybe somebody can carry on his work.*" It was signed "*Rosalinda Mtz.*"

Torrie slipped the letter back into the envelope and shouldered the backpack. "I'll do my best, Eddie. I'll certainly do my best."

With backpack in hand, it didn't take Torrie long to figure out where she was going to hole up until Morgan came to her rescue. Safety in numbers, she decided. Why hadn't she thought about that before?

As they started out the door, Torrie was startled to see headlights coming down the road. Heart racing, she rushed back through the cabin with Tasha at her heels. Had someone followed her here? Or guessed that this was where she might come for refuge? She'd have to slip out the back door and make a break for the woods. She and the dog just barely got out the back door when the lights flashed by. The vehicle slowed but didn't stop. It headed on down the road past the cabin and disappeared. En route to a cabin further down the road? Or doubling back to the cabin in the dark?

For a few moments, Torrie was afraid to move. When she was sure the vehicle was not coming back, she decided to take her chances and return to the safety of the truck. First she had better lock the back door. She shined the flashlight on it, trying to determine how it locked. Then she noticed a large gouge opposite the door handle. This door had been jimmied, and recently—the fresh, clean cuts in the wood attested to that. She wondered if anyone in the sheriff's department had discovered it. Or if they would report it if they had.

She pulled out on the highway near dawn and headed west past the sparkling waters of the reservoir lake. She gassed up in Cougar just as the station opened, and hoped Brad wouldn't be around this early, or that no one would recognize the truck and point out which way she had gone—to whomever might be pursuing her.

She grabbed a few candy bars and soda pop and a donut for good measure. Then thinking that Eddie's backpack might have a camp stove, she picked up beans and canned stew. Might as well live "in style," she decided. Besides, she'd need the energy. In her unaccustomed role as dog owner she almost forgot to buy dog food. She started to get coffee, then realized that what she most needed after food was sleep. She was going to spend the first day in her campsite sleeping, if Tasha didn't lick her to death.

The sun had finally topped the distant mountain ranges when Torrie reached her goal—the Climber's Bivouac for the Mount St. Helens climb. As she suspected, the early risers had already begun the ascent and had disappeared onto the Ptarmigan trail head. The sluggards were just now finishing breakfast and would be heading out soon, leaving the support crew to play cards and tell stories until the adventurers returned scraped, bruised, and exhausted at the end of the day.

Torrie chose a spot at the opposite end of the camping area and found a secluded spot among the trees. She hoped no one would notice she was setting up her tent at the crack of dawn instead of at night. Thank goodness she had helped Morgan set it up that first night in the forest. It seemed eons ago. It seemed a simple matter—it was a dome tent with flexible metal poles supporting it. No need to even pound stakes into the ground. After Tasha had sniff-tested everything and Torrie had figured out how to expand the poles and slip them through the right slots on the tent, she was ready to go.

She didn't think anyone had paid any attention to her as she set up camp, so now she was just one of the many campers waiting for hikers to return. The only problem was the truck. She drove it as far as she could down a brush-covered path and propped a folding lawn chair she found in the truck in front of the license plate. From now on she'd just have to hope for the best. If anyone was looking for her, she was at least going to make it that much harder on them.

Yawning, she finished her donut and gave Tasha some dog food and water. She checked the daypack again for the knife, then removed it from the pack and put it under her pillow. *I can't imagine what I'll do if I ever have to use this,* she thought.

She called the dog inside the tent and told her to lie down and go to sleep. Fortunately the canine was as tired as she was and both were soon sound asleep.

Torrie didn't know how long they had been asleep when she heard voices outside the tent. This time she was instantly awake. Her chest constricted and she stopped breathing. Silently she reached for the knife. Tasha was still asleep. Some watchdog.

Afraid to move, Torrie listened to the voices and the crunch of footsteps on the path outside. Then she heard the voices get quieter and the footsteps faded down the path. Campers. Probably just kids, from the sound of the voices.

Torrie sheepishly put the knife back in its place and resumed breathing. Her heart was still racing in her temples and Tasha's head jolted up. "It's okay, girl," she said, patting the dog on the head. "Torrie is here to protect you."

When Torrie awoke again, she checked her watch. Four o'clock. Time for hikers to start straggling down: the quitters who didn't make it all the way or the extremely fit who had made the ascent and descent without pausing to catch their breath. She decided it would be best to use the bathrooms while she could blend in with the increased foot traffic. Weary hikers straggling in with their offerings in plastic bags were not likely to notice another disheveled face.

She peered out the tent flap before crawling out. Tasha followed and both of them took care of their important business. When Torrie returned to her campsite she dug into Eddie's backpack again. She found some bars that looked a little more nutritious than her chocolate bar, so she had a late lunch and decided to start a campfire after it got dark and she ran less risk of being observed.

She retreated to the protection of the tent and took out Astrid's notes again. It would be easier to read these while it was still light, even if it was terribly uncomfortable trying to sit on the sleeping bag and read. She almost wished she had decided to stay in the cabin. It was comfortable and well-lit and she would be able to see people coming. Too late to worry about it now. She had a lot to do while the light held.

She started with the Internet article from the university in Delaware. It was about phenotypes and mutagenicity. Great, she thought. I have a snowball's chance of understanding this. She waded through and finally came to the Mendelian laws which she vaguely recalled from college biology. At least she knew it had something to do with how traits were passed from one generation to another. That knowledge had always made her feel a little better about her amber-colored eyes, since no one else in the immediate family had them. A recessive trait, she had told herself back then, and came away with the reassurance that she probably belonged to her family after all.

She read on, looking for bold-faced terms that might give her clues as to what the article was even about: mutants, mutations (okay so far), modifications, photomorphogenesis. That one was underlined in blue. She wished she were reading this on the Internet so she could click on it. Break it down, she thought: *photo, morpho, genesis.* Light, change, and beginning. Great, she thought. I understand all the parts but I still don't have a clue what it means.

Temperature-sensitive was next; she thought she stood a better chance with this one so she read the paragraph. It described a kind of mutation observable in the case of the flower known as *Primula sinensis* that is red at room temperature and white at increased temperatures. *Primula sinensis.* Torrie was sure that wasn't Fireweed. The botanical name for Fireweed had *lobium*, or something like that, in it, for the lobes of the flower.

So why was Astrid so eager to get this research? What did this have to do with Fireweed and pocket gophers and geologists? And people getting killed?

She was relieved to note an underlined section at the end: very seldom does a mutant receive "optimized characters or an increased life span." Not totally relieved however; it only said in very rare cases. "Very rare cases" was highlighted—in neon green. Did that mean Astrid had also been relieved when she got to this part, or had she discovered one of those rare cases?

Next she went to work on the animal to people diseases. Hanta virus, rabies, and lyme disease were the subjects covered; Torrie turned to the section on rabies. So had Astrid, because several parts were highlighted with the same florescent color that she found on the last paper. Assuming, of course, that all these notes had been added since Morgan had brought them to her.

She saw that symptoms were highlighted. Most were typical of a number of diseases, but the last sentence had lime green exclamation points in the margin. After reading it, Torrie recalled why rabies was called "hydrophobia." In the last stages, patients demonstrate an intense fear of water, and can even experience violent spasms. Certainly didn't match the symptoms of the alleged rabies victim in the hospital. "Alleged?" She was beginning to sound like a detective.

All this seemed to point to Dr. Li as a suspect. Why was she so insistent that the gopher she had examined had rabies? Professional pride? Something more sinister? Or had she just never observed a patient in the last stages, since modern medicine has developed a cure and most cases don't proceed that far? She was beginning to think like Astrid—excusing the eccentricities of colleagues. But, unlike Astrid, Torrie knew that one of them was a murderer. Come to think of it, Brad had been willing to excuse the doctor/divers. Torrie didn't dare excuse any of them.

She wondered what Brad or his aunt had found out from the veterinarian. Then she realized she wouldn't be finding out. She was hiding from Brad. And other person or persons unknown.

On the next page Torrie found a picture of a pocket gopher—and a bright green star in the margin. "No pocket gophers have been implicated as reservoirs of any human diseases. That was the point Astrid had made to the vet, so these lime green markings must be from her recent findings. She hoped that meant whatever was turning plants red and white and making gophers sick wasn't transmittable to humans. But what about the elk? What had Brad found out? Come to think of it, Brad hadn't told her much of anything that he had found out. Trying to protect her? Or himself? Come to think of it, why had he insisted on doing all the investigating himself? Was there something he didn't want her to know?

Then a memory triggered a smile. She had been amused years ago when she discovered that the word for "research" in Spanish was *investigar*—investigate. Right now she seemed to be in the middle of both.

The light was fading fast and she had one more article. This one was on bio-diversity and terminator genes. She wasn't sure she wanted to know about them. The argument appeared to be that genetically altered plants pose a threat to the environment because the genes that make a commercial plant resistant to herbicide can actually be spread to neighboring weeds and they become superweeds that can't be killed. Torrie was getting a very tenuous understanding of just what Astrid had discovered.

The last highlighted remark was the one that disturbed her most: "once a mutated gene is released in the environment it can never be recalled."

Torrie lay in the darkness for awhile, trying to make sense of all she had learned in the past three hours. If this is as serious as it seems to be, what can be done about it? How much time do we have? And who is "we?" I'm all by myself on this mountain and I don't know whom to trust—or who is going to believe me if I go to them with this incredible theory. No wonder Eddie and Astrid had kept this to themselves. But they hadn't known that animals were going to start dying—and people.

By the time it was dark and Torrie finished cooking her supper and had retreated to the imagined safety of the tent, she had decided what she was going to do.

Before the sun came up Torrie opened her eyes in the dark. Something was wrong. The comforting doggy breathing was silent. Tasha was not in the tent. She began to reach for the knife, so slowly she could barely detect the movement herself. Something *was* breathing in the tent, and she was sure it wasn't her. Her sweat turned to ice on her forehead and she made one swift move toward the knife. Too late. A hand grabbed her wrist and another clapped over her mouth, capturing the scream that never escaped.

Torrie caught her breath through her nose and clamped her eyes tight. What she couldn't see couldn't hurt her. Or maybe it was a nightmare and she could will herself to wake up. But the foul breath on her face and the painful pinching of her wrist convinced her otherwise. This was real.

Chapter 16

BRAD

Torrie lay suspended in a death grip for she didn't know how long, but the attacks of fear were worse than the physical attack. In the dark she had no clue as to the identity of her attacker. Had he done something to Tasha? She should have barked. What did he plan to do to Torrie? And when? What was he waiting for? Worse yet, could it possibly be Brad, who had held her so tenderly just short days ago?

Suddenly her will to survive kicked in and drove out the fear. She refused to lie here and let herself be killed—or worse. Her eyes snapped open again and she saw a faint outline of her assailant. She relaxed and whimpered in a simulation of defeat, then swiftly, assuming her assailant was a man, she abruptly raised her knee in a defensive move her uncle had taught her.

The dark form groaned and she took the split second advantage and twisted with all her strength, getting out from under him. She made a futile grab in the dark for the knife, but came up with the keys instead. Never mind. They would have to do. She smashed at the faint form in the only area she could make out in the dark. The face. The groans were more serious this time and Torrie stumbled headlong for the tent flap and tried to get her legs under her and crawl out.

Before she succeeded the flap flew open and two bodies rushed into the melee. The flying ball of fur had to be Tasha, but she didn't know if the other shape was friend or foe. Tasha quickly attached herself to bare skin and the assailant-turned-victim was howling for mercy. The second shape turned a flashlight in the face of the would-be attacker and grasped him roughly by the collar.

He fired a stream of rapid-fire questions along with a good deal of cursing while the man pleaded with him to get the dog off. Torrie took her chance to stumble out of the tent and run toward the truck with the keys, which she still clutched numbly in her hand. When she reached it, she blindly felt in the back and found what she was looking for, and turned to run back toward the tent, stumbling in the dark as she ran. Poor Tasha. What would he do to her?

Before she could return to the tent, two forms exploded from the tent. A stranger running away with Tasha nipping at his heels. "Tasha, come back," she cried frantically. Then she stopped dead. Who was still in the tent? The attacker? Or her rescuer? If he was indeed her rescuer. Would she find him lying in wait to finish what he had started, or injured and in need of help?

She approached the tent cautiously, her newly-acquired weapon raised over her head. To her relief, Tasha came dashing back. Tasha was a good judge of character—let her decide. She knelt to embrace the wriggling animal. "Good dog, good dog. Now who's in the tent?"

As if she understood the question, Tasha ran straight to the tent and went in. She did the whimpering back and forth routine she had done the night she had led her and Brad to Astrid's body.

"Oh, please, God, no," she pleaded. "Not another body." She found it unsettling that it took such dire circumstances to force her to appeal to her deity after neglecting Him for so long. Evidently, her grandmother's many years of taking her to church hadn't entirely been in vain. Right now she wished for a very real flesh-and-blood savior.

Tentatively she approached the tent and pulled back the flap, weapon again raised defensively.

"Torrie," came the voice from inside. "Is he gone?"

Confused Torrie responded haltingly. "Yes. Tasha chased him off."

"Help me. I'm hurt."

Torrie recognized the voice at last. "Brad?"

"Yes. Hurry. I think I'm bleeding."

Fears and suspicions temporarily put aside, Torrie dropped to her knees and entered the tent. Brad was doubled over in the corner. The sun was just coming up, but it was still too dark to see well in the tent.

"What happened? Where are you hurt?"

He turned slowly to face her, and she still faced a moment of doubt. Was he her attacker or her rescuer?

When he turned all the way he smiled weakly. "Well, are you going to help me, or are you going to hit me with that tire iron?"

Forgetting she was still armed, she returned his smile and lowered the improvised weapon. "I'll let you know as soon as I decide who the enemy is," she replied.

"After the beating I took from that guy, I hope I'm still the good guy," he answered, then gasped in pain.

Then she could see the blood streaming down his face. "Oh, Brad, I'm so sorry. What do you need?" she asked.

"A rag. Something to stop this bleeding," he said.

She reached into the large backpack and pulled out

one of Eddie's clean T-shirts and applied it to Brad's head. A stream of blood flowed from his hairline. He grasped the shirt with both hands and held it in place. "Do you have a first-aid kit?" he asked. "Something for infection. He used my own flashlight on me."

After the first few fumbling minutes Torrie had him pretty well patched up and he assured her that it wasn't as bad as it looked—head wounds always bled like that.

As she started gathering things up she tried to reconstruct the events of the night. She wondered how badly the attacker had been hurt and if he would he be back. Or was Brad actually the attacker and had chased off her would-be rescuer? She struggled to remember what she had done in the dark—whether she had caused the gash on his head.

Once again she fumbled through her brain in an attempt to reconstruct the events. It was all a blur of confusion. Now it was almost daylight and she would have to decide how to carry out her plan. Soon, the day's lottery winners would begin streaming up the mountain and she would have to make a move.

Brad made the decision for her. He decided they both needed sleep and this would be as safe a place as any. With all the hiker support staying in base camp it would be difficult for the intruder to make a move until dark. By that time they would be gone. In the meantime, Brad enshrined Torrie inside the tent, armed with mace and his heavy-duty flashlight, and unknown to him, the sharp blade that had become her constant companion. He pulled his sleeping bag up right outside her tent flap. To protect her? Or to keep her from escaping him? Torrie was too tired to decide which; she sank into a deep, uncomplicated sleep.

When she awoke the sun was filtering through the opposite side of the tent. In the distance she could hear the normal camp chatter and clatter. She wondered if Brad was still outside. Silently she raised up and moved on all fours to the tent flat, pausing to listen. No sounds of breathing. Very slowly she began to unzip the bottom flap—a noisy process. She stopped, then not hearing anything she began again.

This time she heard a sudden scramble and an uncontrolled something hit the tent flap. She fell back and reached for the knife, which she realized she should have kept with her even while she undertook this simple maneuver. Before she could reach it, she recognized the ecstatic panting: Tasha. With relief, she quickly unzipped the tent the rest of the way, and the pup rushed into her arms.

"I should have known you'd be out there protecting me," she said to the wriggling mass that was alternately licking her and turning mad circles inside the tent, knocking over everything in reach. "Take it easy, girl," she said, patting her. "It's going to be okay." She wished she believed that.

She cautiously stuck her head out and took in the fresh air and the crisp smell of bacon and coffee. Brad was working at a grill nearby, preparing what appeared to be breakfast. Had she slept that long?

"Hungry?" he asked.

"I could eat a bear," she replied, then looked in the direction of the woods. "I don't mean that literally," she called in the direction of the woods in an apologetic tone.

"Don't worry. There aren't any around here," he said. "Not any cougars, either."

Torrie managed a weak grin.

"How are you?" he asked, serious once again.

She stood to her feet. "Well, I can stand up. That's a good sign. How about you?"

He touched the bandages on his forehead. "Sore, but I guess I'll live. Coffee?"

"Absolutely." She approached him with care and took the metal cup he offered her.

"Careful, it's hot."

She nodded.

"Breakfast will be ready in a minute. If you don't mind eating breakfast at three in the afternoon."

"No problem," she answered, seating herself on a camp stool.

When the meal was ready, she ate ravenously and downed three more cups of coffee. They ate in silence. Neither spoke until Brad had cleaned up the dishes and packed things away.

"I have an idea," he said.

"I'm listening," said she.

Torrie was again clad in the borrowed ranger's uniform retrieved from the pickup, this time wearing her own shorts, and was uncomfortable in the large-brimmed hat. Brad had assured her she'd be grateful for it in the sunshine (and rain), and they would be less likely to arouse suspicion if they looked like they were on official business. She wondered how he would explain the blood stains on his shirt, although he had evidently made an effort to remove them while she slept—there was a large moist spot where the blood had been.

Within an hour Torrie was carrying a bulging daypack and trudging down a trail leading away from the Climber's Bivouac in the direction of the barren wilderness that both frightened and intrigued her, threatened her and offered refuge. Brad was the unknown. His plan had essentially been the same as hers, but he was infinitely better prepared to carry it out. Tasha had been the deciding factor, and the point of contention between them. The dog was unswervingly loyal to the man even though he had initially refused to take her along. It was illegal and unsafe to take pets into a national monument, he had said. Torrie had finally decided to trust him, provisionally, after he had relented and said Tasha could go along. And she still had the knife.

They had started noisily on the trail to the east, leaving subtle, but clearly visible evidence of their passing. Then they had quietly doubled back through the forest and picked up the Ptarmigan Trail where it continued west on the path that skirted the mountain. Before they had struggled up the steep trail for fifteen minutes, Torrie had fallen and scraped her knee. It was going to be a long walk, but Brad assured her it was only steep for a short ways.

As he had warned, the hike was long and tedious. They were rapidly losing the sun, but were planning to forge along in the twilight as long as possible. They would stop for supper after it became too dark to proceed, then wait for moonrise. Brad estimated that the trek would take about twelve hours. Easy for him to say. He hiked steadily several feet ahead of her, Eddie's well-stocked pack riding easily on his broad shoulders. In one hand he carried a branch he had fashioned for a walking stick. Only the memory of the terrors she had experienced the last few days gave her the energy to carry out this plan.

But the niggling doubts about Brad kept fraying at the edges of her determination. What did he stand to gain from this little venture? Maybe he was just trying to find out how much she knew, or maybe he was going to take her out in this deserted place and lose her, permanently. She had made sure she had plenty of food and water in her pack, and she had kept a couple of Astrid's maps and Eddie's old compass—his new one had never turned up. Not that they would do her any good. She had hoped to observe Brad when he stopped to use his compass, but this was his stomping grounds. He seemed to know all these trails by heart, so she compensated by noting in her notebook each landmark they passed. She felt like a modern day Gretel and wondered if some mythic birds would come and snatch away the crumbs from her notebook, leaving her abandoned in the wilderness.

By sundown Torrie was exhausted and her feet were sore. Her discomfort caused them to make an unscheduled stop, and Brad produced some Mole Skin for her to put on her blisters. They sat on a fallen log and watched a fabulously beautiful sunset as they ate an energy bar. Tasha had to eat her dog food from the ground, since neither of them wanted to pack in her dog food bowl.

Brad tapped her on the arm. "Do you see that old dead tree over there?"

She nodded.

"There's an abandoned bees' nest in it."

Torrie strained to see. Finally she spotted the dried, lumpy form that was almost the same color as the blast-devastated tree. "Oh, yeah. I think I see it."

"That's pretty unusual," he said.

"You mean for bees to build a nest up here where there aren't any flowers?"

"No, to even see bees' nests in the wild. Mostly you only find them in commercial hives these days. But sometimes a queen will escape and they'll move on to greener pastures."

"So to speak," responded Torrie wryly.

"At least pastures with plenty of flowers," he said.

Keeping them on schedule, Brad prepared their cold supper and they attempted to sleep while waiting for the moon to illuminate their path. So far the weather was holding and the faint glow where the moon would emerge was already visible.

She must have dozed, curled up on her side with Eddie's jacket as a make-shift pillow, because she stirred when she heard the shrill beeping of Brad's wrist watch alarm. Time to move on.

In the dark he was more cautious and she was able to keep pace with him more easily. He kept his stick in one hand and his flashlight in the other. At one point he stopped, and probed thoroughly with the walking stick.

"What is it?" she whispered.

"Mud holes. I think these have all hardened by now, but they used to be pretty dangerous."

"Dangerous?"

"Yes. For years after the eruption these were all around the area. They acted just like quicksand, but they would broil you instantly."

Torrie shuddered.

"But you're sure they're all dried up now?"

"They'd have to be," he said. "Unless they were in some sort of protected area. These have all been exposed to the elements and they're totally hardened." He gave the area several more jabs and they moved on.

Torrie noticed that Tasha gave the area a wide berth.

By the time the moon had deserted them, they were close to their destination. Now they would get out the sleeping bags and attempt a real sleep. They planned to wake up early and be ready to move on as soon as they had first light, and hopefully before anyone else who might be out working or hiking in the remote canyons would be stirring.

Torrie had slept well in the downy mummy sleeping bag Brad had insisted she use. It was warm and almost comfortable and she awoke feeling better than she had for days.

The sun arose brilliantly as they broke camp. She should have been cheered by the glowing sunrise, but to the recesses of her mind came the saying: "Red in the morning—sailors take warning."

They were nearing the canyon area and Brad had taken out Astrid's map along with the divers' brochures and had laid them side by side.

"This is where it gets dangerous," he said.

"You mean it hasn't been so far?"

He ignored her. "Neither of these markings show a precise location, and we're going to have to get off the path. Which by the way, is illegal."

"Any more illegal than bringing a dog or impersonating a forest ranger?" she asked.

He threw his head back and made a disparaging sound. "The point is to figure out what's going on here," he said. "We'll work out the legality issues when we come to them."

"So how are we going to find whatever it is we're looking for?" she asked.

"See that opening in the rocks below?" He pointed straight ahead. "That's close to where both maps are marked. We'll head down that way and look for anything unusual."

"How will we know what's unusual?"

"Just keep your eyes open and watch Tasha. She's usually the first one to notice when something's not right."

Torrie raised an eyebrow. Maybe he had just pretended not to want Tasha along. Maybe he knew what he was looking for and hoped Tasha would be able to locate it for him. She patted the pocket in her daypack for the reassuring hard presence of steel.

Several hours later the sunrise's red warning came true and they were picking their way along the trail-less range in their plastic rain ponchos. It was only an annoying drizzle, but the moisture made the walking treacherous. Only Tasha was her usual unbridled enthusiastic self, checking out promising side paths and behind every suspicious boulder.

Torrie had begun to think the entire plan was futile and they were going to lose themselves up here in this wild place while the culprits went free. She stumbled again and decided she had better focus on every step or she wouldn't need Brad or anybody else to do away with her—she'd do it herself, plunging to the distant canyon bottom barely visible below. She remembered the rainbow she and Morgan had seen on their first trip up to Windy Ridge and knew somehow that even on this dreary, miserable day there was a rainbow glowing somewhere. She took heart in that and tried harder to find the mysterious something they were looking for.

Suddenly Tasha yelped.

Brad and Torrie both looked up from their ground-focused vigil and tried to locate the canine in the waning light.

"Tasha?" Torrie called.

Brad shushed her. "No. Let's go find her."

He started off in the direction of the barking, with Torrie right behind him. When they found the distracted fur ball she was making her signature mad circles, but was deviating from time to time to sniff at the source of her dismay. Brad raised his stick and approached cautiously, Torrie right behind him.

They soon saw what Tasha was so annoyed about. She had discovered a steam vent.

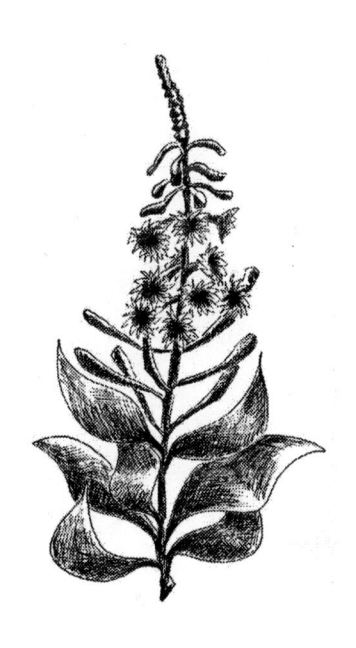

Part Three

HEROES

Chapter 17

BAT CAVE

"This is it," Brad whooped.

"What is it?"

"It's a steam vent."

"How is that going to help us?" Torrie asked.

"If there's a steam vent, it means there should be an opening around here somewhere."

"An opening to what?"

"Some kind of cave, probably," Brad replied. "Remember we overheard the speaker at Cispus talking about doing research in some canyons that were formed by steam vents. And that would explain why Astrid was so interested in Eddie's research. He had done a lot of exploring in this area near her plot of Fireweed."

"How do you know that?" asked Torrie warily.

"Mack told me," he said. "The sheriff's office went through his things and a lot of research pointed to this area."

"Were you going to tell me about it?" Torrie asked coldly.

"I'm not at liberty to discuss ongoing investigations," he said, turning his back on her and starting to make wide circles in the area of the escaping steam.

"But you are at liberty to bring me all the way out here, illegally," she shouted at his back.

"Let's not argue about it now," he said. "We don't know how much time we have, and we have to find that opening."

He seemed very sure that there *was* an opening, Torrie thought. But he was right about one thing. They probably didn't have much time to locate whatever it was they were looking for. She joined in his search.

Again it was Tasha who made the discovery. This time it was a small cleft in the rock big enough for a person to slip through. A lava tube. Like the one known as Ape Cave. Only this one still had its original inhabitants.

This time they agreed what to do about Tasha; she would have to be tethered at the entrance to the cave. Her presence would be too disturbing to the bats, and vice versa. Brad had hidden his pack behind a pile of dead logs, but Torrie refused to leave her daypack behind.

It was only after considerable urging from Brad that she got up the courage to enter. Bats do not really try to nest in your hair, he had explained. They would not be carrying rabies this far from civilization, and they did not suck your blood (the ones in this area were not the vampire kind). These were the rapid-fire facts he had given her in his mini-lesson on bats. Now they moved slowly so as not to disturb the nocturnal creatures.

Following Brad's example, Torrie stooped and entered the narrow opening. She traversed the undeveloped interior of the cave with trembling knees. Suffocatingly dark and damp, it was even more intimidating than she feared. As she misstepped and caught her balance with one hand on the wall, the words of their Ape Cave guide came back to her. She remembered that the walls were slimed with living creatures. She wiped her hand on her shorts and went on.

Brad had stopped in front of her and was shining his flashlight in large arcs.

"What is it?" she whispered into the dark expanse.

"This seems to be a larger cavern," he said, illustrating with the thin finger of light.

Without his telling her, Torrie could tell that the teeming blackness of the cavern roof was alive. The overpowering smell of guano and the eerie sense of living beings spoke in his silence.

"Was this formed by the steam vents?" she asked, to get her mind off their overwhelming presence.

"Probably not. Judging from the looks of the walls I'd say it's a lava tube."

"Formed by the latest eruption," Torrie surmised.

"Exactly. So nobody would know it was here."

"Except our villains," she said. And their victims, she thought, and hoped she wasn't going to become one of them.

They managed to slip quietly enough through the bats' domain so that they remained undisturbed. As they continued through the gently winding path of the newest lava tube, Torrie began to notice a change. She wasn't sure at first what it was, but the place began to seem less primitive, less forbidding. Little by little she began to isolate and identify the messages her senses were bringing her: the air seemed fresher; the pathway cleaner—almost as though it had been swept. It brought back a memory that refused to surface completely. Then it struck her. It reminded her of the tunnel of love at Disneyland. The thought was so ludicrous she laughed aloud.

"What is it?" Brad asked, stopping suddenly.

"Nothing," she answered. "I was just thinking this place reminds me of Disneyland."

"Some Disneyland," he replied. Then he held up his hand for her to stop and turned off the flashlight.

They both stood breathlessly in the unmitigated velvety dark. At first she didn't understand why he had stopped her. Then she heard it. From deep in the impenetrable recesses of their living tomb came unmistakable sounds. Human voices. At first she thought she imagined it, but the longer she concentrated the more she became certain of it. They were not alone in this dreadful place.

Fearing to move even a muscle, Torrie stood like a child playing the game of Statues. After the voices had subsided Brad whispered, "Let's go."

She willingly turned and had already taken a step back in the direction they had come before Brad turned the flashlight back on.

"No, this way," he said, and started leading her in the direction of the disembodied voices.

Reluctantly, Torrie returned to their search.

Slowly picking their way along the passage seemed to take forever. They were getting farther away from Tasha—and safety. Finally it seemed their fruitless task had dead-ended. In an obscure crevice Brad found a surface that was much too smooth and rectangular to be a natural formation. It looked like a door. But a door to what?

Torrie was ready to head back and report their find to the authorities, but Brad would not hear of it. His suggestion was to open the door.

"If it's a door, it's probably locked," she reasoned.

"To keep out what?" he countered. "The bats?"

"We don't know what we're going to find on the other side," she said. "Whoever belonged to those voices may be coming back."

He had already removed his pocket knife and handed her the flashlight. He was testing the edges of the supposed door. Torrie stepped back a few feet with the light, hardly daring to breathe. He pushed and prodded and poked with no success.

"See, I told you we wouldn't be able to get it open," she said in a hoarse voice. "Let's go, Brad. I don't want to be down here any more."

She took a few steps back and almost tripped over a protuberance on the floor.

She heard a clicking sound and Brad's triumphant "yes!" She recovered her balance and turned in his direction. Then she saw what had caused his outburst. Slowly and steadily the large door was sliding open and a thin sliver of light was growing from behind it.

"Good girl," he said. "I think you tripped the trigger."

"Literally," said Torrie glumly.

Relieved but apprehensive, Torrie left the dank, smelly lava tube and followed Brad into the clean lighted area. The tube resembled the one they had just left, but this one was obviously occupied by two-legged inhabitants: lighting was installed every few feet with a panel for electrical connections, and straight ahead, in the middle of the passageway, someone had installed a gleaming new metal door.

Brad and Torrie cautiously made their way toward the imposing door; Torrie knew what his next suggestion would be.

Reaching the door, he put his hand on the large handle. It slid easily. Then he turned and wordlessly asked Torrie the question she expected: "Ready?" She nodded her assent, then he slowly opened the door a crack and peered in. They heard a gurgling sound like a fountain and exchanged puzzled shrugs. Apparently satisfied it was safe, he opened the door further and searched the interior with his gaze, then opened it just wide enough to slip through, motioning Torrie to follow.

She entered right behind him and had to stifle a gasp at what she saw: inside was a fully equipped laboratory, complete with sparkling whitewashed walls, bubbling cultures, and a row of lab coats on a rack near a door on the opposite side.

Brad held out his arm to keep her from entering, and made another visual search. He then whispered, "I don't see any surveillance cameras."

"What is this place?" she whispered back.

"I don't know." He motioned to the left. "You go that way, I'll go over here and we'll see if we can figure it out."

Torrie crept alongside a counter in awe of the equipment she saw. She recognized beakers and flasks, an autoclave, and a centrifuge from high school biology class, but the rest seemed to be computerized equipment. How could they tell what kind of work was being done here, and by whom? She wondered if Eddie had discovered the lab, or only the lava tube itself. She shuddered. If he *had* been murdered for his discovery . . . She couldn't bring herself to finish the thought, and forced herself to study the equipment that lined the polished counter space. One item was a large black box that resembled an old-fashioned camera, but with a handle protruding from the top section of it; another was obviously a scale of some sort. On the floor near the end of one counter was a brightly colored container clearly marked for hazardous waste. Against the wall was a large stainless steel unit with glass front doors, resembling a refrigerated unit in a grocery store. She approached it and looked through the glass. Bright lights went all along the top section and the shelves below were lined with petri dishes. The thermometer just inside the glass read eighty degrees. Definitely not a refrigerator.

She turned the corner and was startled when she glimpsed Brad's shadowy form at the opposite end of the long counter. She jumped and sent a pair of tongs clattering loudly to the floor. He put a finger to his lips, and pointed to the source of the gurgling noises they had heard when they entered. A glass-encased box containing several flasks was in continual motion, stirring the fluid contained in the flasks. Brad moved away from the agitator and pointed at a large machine on the counter.

"FAX?" she whispered.

He shook his head and they both approached it. They leaned over to read the digital display on the front; their heads were so close together their hat brims touched and their breath mingled. The machine was evidently turned on and performing some inscrutable function. Torrie squinted at the display: it looked like a mathematical formula set on a series of stepped lines. Brad's face was also wrinkled up in puzzlement.

Torrie pointed to the name on the front: *GeneAmp PCR System*. "Remember that," she whispered, tapping her forehead. She moved along the counter, picked up a slide tray and studied it, wondering if it would do her any good to look for a microscope. Probably not. Identifying minuscule creatures had never been her forte—even when she knew what she was looking for.

He nodded. Then his demeanor changed. Without warning the expression on his face turned menacing. He began striding toward her purposefully, and Torrie was frozen to the spot.

Chapter 18

RED SUITS

Torrie gasped and dropped the slide tray she had just picked up. Brad unexpectedly grabbed her and clapped a strong hand over her mouth. For an instant she suspected the betrayal she had feared, then she felt his voice in her ear. "Get down," he said in a nearly inaudible whisper, lowering them both slowly to the floor as he spoke, and turning her head toward the glass doors of the unit she had originally thought was a refrigerator. The passageway that gave access to the lab from the opposite side was clearly reflected and from their vantage point crouched behind the counters Torrie saw what had caused Brad's sudden reflex: coming their way were two red-suited men in heavy black boots, armed with guns in holsters at their sides.

The men approached the pile of crates and began speaking in a foreign language. Torrie struggled to fight down the panic that was rising from her stomach into her throat. In a conscious effort she took deep, quiet breaths and strained for familiar words in the muffled conversation. She turned to Brad and he mouthed, "French?" She shook her head and they edged back, out of line of the reflected surface which would reveal their presence if the workers turned around.

Judging from the sounds of scraping and grunting, it appeared that they were loading crates onto a hand truck. Then, more unintelligible conversation, sprinkled with an occasional phrase of English—usually slang or cursing—then a squeaky wheel indicated their progress down the opposite corridor. They were moving away from the frightened trespassers.

Just as Torrie planned to resume normal breathing a large black form swooshed from the light fixtures above and landed on her head. Instinctively she raised a hand in defense and hit the brim of the awkward hat, sending it skimming along the floor of the lab—along with a dazed bat. Brad pulled her protectively into his arms and they listened breathlessly. The squeaky wheel had stopped and she heard a quick scuffle, then silence.

They heard a brusque "*Achtung*!", then silence.

She pictured the Red Suits with guns drawn; one of them, probably the leader, would be motioning the other to move around behind them and they would be surrounded, escape routes cut off. Astrid had been right, she watched too many adventure movies. Funny the things you think about when your life is in danger. If she were the heroine she would leap into the air with a shrieking karate call and kick both of them in the jugular before they knew what had happened. In real life she cowered in hiding; tears of fright flooded her eyes and her throat constricted.

Behind her, she felt Brad tense, sinewy muscles poised for action. No, he was moving slowly away from her—some hero he turned out to be. With the protective warmth of his body gone, she felt even more the chill of this subterranean place and an isolation more chilling than the physical cold.

Then she felt his warmth beside her again, and sensed a smooth shapeless movement in her peripheral vision: Brad was edging the bat away from them with the tongs. He slid it along the floor, closer and closer to the corner of the counter. Then, with a deft flip of the wrist he sent it catapulting in the direction of their would-be captors.

Heavy boots approached as Torrie once again went into hypo-ventilation.

"Who is that?" asked a harsh voice in thick English.

The steps moved closer and Torrie could almost hear the adrenaline rushing through her system. Or maybe it was Brad's adrenaline she heard, so close was he now.

Another muffled movement just inches from them, around the protective corner of the counter and a guttural laugh. "A darn bat."

The other voice mirthlessly gave a foreign command which must have been, "get rid of it and let's get this job done," because that's what the underling proceeded to do.

Light-headed with relief, Torrie could barely get to her feet when the two men were out of sight. Brad half-pushed, half-carried her toward the now welcoming environment of the dank lava tube. Turning on her flashlight again, Torrie turned, expecting Brad to be right behind her. Instead, he was standing indecisively at the entrance to the lab. "Let's go," she pleaded. "They're going to come back."

As if her pleading helped him decide, he turned in determination. "One more thing."

She waited as he darted back into the glaring, sterile white of the laboratory. In a moment he was back, zipping up his jacket pocket as he joined her in their precipitous rush to gain fresh air and freedom. As they tiptoed through the bats' bed chamber, Torrie missed the protection of the awkward hat.

"My hat!" she remembered. "I left it in the lab. Is that

what you went back for?" She turned around. "I've got to go get it. They'll know we've been here."

Brad grabbed her arm. "Don't risk it. Let's get out of here."

Their eyes locked in a challenge and she hovered in indecision. Finally she gave in. "Okay, let's get out of here."

At the entrance they took welcome gulps of the cool night air and collected Brad's backpack and a distraught Tasha. They decided to put some distance between them and the Red Suits, so Brad led them down the hill away from the crevice where they had entered the nightmare. As they neared the edge of a steep embankment, both stopped in disbelief. Before them stretched an enormous field of Fireweed, larger than any patch Torrie had seen before. Even in the dim light of dawn she could tell it was only Fireweed. No pearly everlasting or false dandelion or prairie lupines.

"Awesome," said Brad.

He led her, slipping and sliding, down the steep incline until they were standing knee deep in flowers. Torrie took a deep breath and inhaled the delicate fragrance. As she leaned over to get a closer look, Brad suddenly took her arm.

"Wait a minute," he said. "Something's wrong."

"What? What's the matter?"

"Look at it closely," he said. "Don't you see?"

Torrie stared for a moment, then she noticed it, too. "It's a different color. It's peach, or orangish. I can't tell in the dark." She stared at the field in wonder. Then she noticed something else. "It's glowing in the dark."

He looked again. "You're right," he said. Then a look of utter amazement flitted across his face. "Oh my gosh," he exclaimed, and began unzipping his pocket. He produced the small flask he had confiscated from the agitator in the underground lab and held it in front of her.

It was glowing pale peach in the dark.

After another night huddled in sleeping bags Torrie

was weary beyond words, but they still had a long way to go before she could relax—either her physical efforts or her mental vigil. On the trail the next morning she watched Brad's broad shoulders as he took firm, steady steps in front of her. Funny how being in a crisis with someone changes the dynamics. She knew that not everything she had felt back in that lab had been adrenaline, especially when he was holding her so close his scent mingled with her own. But it was foolish to think about it. Their lives were too different, their perspective and goals too distant. And the memories of Aaron still too painfully etched in her soul.

Besides, she still wasn't convinced he wasn't the enemy.

In the approaching daylight she could tell that he was leading her down into the hummocky valley on the north side of the mountain. It was nearer to civilization that way, he had told her. They had stopped at a stream and filled their water bottles because the path they were taking would be dry. They were some distance from the legal trail and Torrie was still unsure as to his intentions.

She kept alert to any indication that he meant to harm her, and she formulated an escape plan in her mind as they walked. She felt somewhat reassured when he pointed out the Johnston Observatory at the top of the mountain in the direction they were heading. Hadn't someone told her she could find her way back to civilization if she got lost, just by keeping that prominent landmark in sight. In fact, she could even find it in the dark, she remembered, by listening for the clicking grasshoppers. Her enthusiasm waned, however, when she thought about how long it would take to reach it; it took long enough driving.

She wanted to ask Brad what his plan was, but, as usual, he remained several strides ahead of her. She noticed the distance between them stayed the same, so what was the point in walking ahead of her? She began to think he was more competitive than he was willing to admit. Besides, she needed to save her precious breath for the long walk that lay ahead of them, and continually watch her step as she crunched the loose pumice beneath her feet. And keep continually on the alert—just in case.

After several weary hours they reached an established trail, and Brad had commandeered an ATV from a group of teenagers who were driving *illegally* in the area. With an emphasis on "illegally" he had persuaded them to surrender one of their vehicles to the disheveled rangers. When they reached the trail head, Brad put in a call to Mack who retrieved them from Coldwater Ridge. The two excitedly spilled out their story and Mack had taken them back to town. This time Torrie did not turn down Brad's offer to stay at his Uncle Gene and Aunt Melanie's house. A warm shower in a real house would be a well-deserved luxury, and would give her the first sense of safety she had felt for days.

Torrie fell asleep in the guest room with a towel still wrapped around her wet head. Bird songs and breakfast smells awakened her and she scuffled into the bathroom. She hoped the face looking back at her from the mirror wasn't really her. It took a few minutes of intense staring at the sunburned, flaking skin before she was convinced it was truly Torrie in the reflection. Her eyes were swollen with dark circles under them and she had scratches on her face she couldn't even remember getting. She did remember that makeup was not among the vital items she had placed in her daypack. She removed the towel and discovered her hair hopelessly snarled and standing up on one side. She appropriated someone's gel and made the best of it. Satisfied that she was presentable enough for a spelunker, she made her way to the kitchen—and coffee.

Brad sat with his aunt Melanie at a table on a sunny patio drinking coffee and speaking in low tones. Mel, as she asked to be called, was a trim, perennially cheery woman of about fifty. She wore her graying hair well and her eyes had laugh lines in a much more advanced state than Brad's. She greeted Torrie enthusiastically and jumped up to prepare her a hot, steaming breakfast.

"Brad's been telling me about your adventure," she said. "I can't believe you went into that lava tube. I would have been scared to death."

"I was," admitted Torrie.

"You poor thing," she continued. "Are you sure you're all right? Do you need anything?"

"No, I feel much better after the sleep. Thanks. Thanks for everything. I feel like I'm imposing."

"No, not at all. I'm glad to help out. Brad has been telling me all about it. How terrible for you."

Before she could reply, Brad excused himself. His uncle was going to drop him off at the sheriff's office and he would get a ride back with Mack.

When he had gone, Torrie picked up the conversation with Mel while her hostess busied herself at the stove. "This has certainly not been the kind of vacation I was expecting," replied Torrie wearily.

"Of course not. Well, you're welcome to stay here as long as you need to. Tasha, too. She's not a bit of trouble. You can tell she's been well-trained."

They were interrupted by the phone and Mel asked her to pick it up. It was Mack for Brad.

"You just missed him," Torrie said, and informed him of Brad's plans.

"If you hear from him again, let him know I'll be detained for awhile—I'm at the place where the jeep is impounded doing another inspection."

"I can hardly hear you," Torrie said. "There's some kind of interference on the line."

He repeated more loudly and she hung up and gave Mel the message.

"I'll tell him if he calls back," she said. "Now, Torrie, if there's anything you need, I'd be more than glad to help. Don't hesitate to let me know."

"No, I don't need anything," said Torrie, although she was tempted to ask for a hair dryer. Then she looked at Mel and recalled what Brad had told her about his aunt. "As a matter of fact," she said, "there is something."

That afternoon, Torrie pulled up in front of a now-familiar long brick building in Aunt Mel's car. Brad's aunt had been more than happy to arrange an interview with her veterinarian friend.

Torrie entered and shook the doctor's hand. "It was so nice of you to see me again, Dr. Li," she said.

"No problem. Call me Hong." She ushered Torrie into her dark but comfortable office and instructed the receptionist to hold her calls.

"Some things have happened since I talked to you last," began Torrie, not sure how much to disclose.

"Yes," nodded the doctor. "I hear about your friend. So sorry."

Torrie acknowledged the condolences and continued. "Are you familiar with the newest computerized laboratory equipment?"

"I do recent research in the development of vaccines," answered the doctor.

"I've been looking at some equipment that I couldn't identify and I wondered if you could give me an idea what it was used for."

"What lab it in?" asked Hong, her face expressionless.

"I can't tell you any more than that," said Torrie. "I could literally be putting your life in danger."

The veterinarian cocked her head either in surprise or disbelief. "What is this equipment you have interest in?"

Torrie began to describe the equipment as well as she could remember. The large black box actually *was* a camera, Dr. Li thought—one that was used to take pictures of culture samples after they had been stained with a dye. The large heated unit was probably an incubator for tissue culture, with a timer set to simulate day and night conditions. The enclosed counter with the long loop and needle that Brad had found in his search would be where lab workers could do aseptic work for sterile transfers.

Torrie could hardly contain her excitement; Dr. Li seemed to have answers for all her questions. "So what kind of work do you think is being done there?" Torrie asked.

Hong leaned forward and steepled her fingers. She seemed to be in intense concentration and it was a few moments before she spoke. "I can't tell. This equipment is common in many kinds of laboratories."

Then Torrie remembered the large machine she and Brad had studied. "There was one more thing," she added, and described it.

"You say there are numbers like a formula on the screen?" queried the doctor.

She attempted to sketch a rough diagram of what she remembered, but the doctor was still puzzled. Torrie wished she'd had the presence of mind to take pictures. All that time they were in the lab she had totally forgotten that she had a disposable camera with her.

"Oh, and it had a label or brand name on the front," Torrie remembered. "There were some initials and something about genes. Gene Trap, Gene Acts . . . Gene Amps. That was it. Gene Amps.

Hong looked up wide-eyed from the diagram she had been studying. "GeneAmp. Did it say PCR System?"

"PCR? Maybe. That sounds right."

"It's a thermal cycler," said the doctor grimly. "used to copy molecular data—to generate mutations. This lab you describe—they do DNA research. I think they do bio genetic gene splicing."

"What does that mean? What are they doing?"

"I think they produce new species of animal or plant."

Torrie whistled, trying to absorb what the veterinarian had told her, then decided to reveal her final clue. She pulled the small bottle from her daypack and shook it before placing it on the desk in front of the doctor. "It glows in the dark."

The doctor immediately picked it up and studied it, then stood and walked to a closet behind her. She opened the door and stepped inside with the bottle in her hand.

"Interesting. Most interesting," she said when she returned to her place at the desk.

"What is it?" asked Torrie.

"I never see anything like this," the doctor replied. "May I send sample to friend with lab?"

Torrie hesitated. "How much do you need?" she asked.

"I need all. He need large sample to test."

With mixed feelings, Torrie turned the vial over to Dr. Li and left with the uneasy feeling that she may have entrusted her secret to the wrong person. And she had given away their only piece of real evidence.

Chapter 19

BEES

Torrie was supposed to meet Brad back at his aunt's house, but she was reluctant to let him know that she had let the hard-won sample get out of their hands. She was eager to learn what he had found out from Mack, but he wasn't there when she got back to Mel's house. Just as well—she could put off his inevitable accusations.

Aunt Mel was in the back yard cutting some flowers to take into the house and Tasha was in pursuit of a rabbit. There seemed to be plenty to keep a conscientious sheltie hard at work. Mel greeted Torrie cheerily. "You had a call," she informed her guest.

"Brad?"

"No, I haven't heard from him yet."

Torrie was evasive when Mel asked her how things went with Hong. Mel didn't push it; she went on telling about the doctor's family and how they had escaped from Viet Nam during those terrible war years. She told Torrie that Hong meant "rose" in Vietnamese.

Torrie hoped that wasn't a sign. "I haven't had very good luck with flowers lately," she muttered.

"I hope you're not allergic," said Mel sympathetically. She indicated the rockery she was working on. "They're so beautiful."

Torrie distractedly agreed with her and Mel led the way into the house with an armful of freshly-cut flowers. "Oh, I almost forgot; that call I mentioned—it was somebody looking for that 'Ranger Girl.' They didn't leave a message."

Torrie pondered the information. Who would know she was staying here but wouldn't know her by name? As much as she was curious about the unidentified caller, after the harrowing experience she had just been through it seemed she didn't have the mental capacity left to process the information. But in spite of her ordeal, Torrie felt physically invigorated, restless. There was more to be done and she sensed that it needed to be done soon. Even though they didn't understand everything that was going on, they knew for sure that nature was out of control and they would have to do something soon to control the rampaging Fireweed and the burgeoning chain reaction it had set off. But what? All she could do now was wait.

Then she remembered the post office box key. That's one thing she *could* check on. Astrid may have had someone mail her some information that would shed some light on her research. She'd do that as soon as she got the truck back— and she just thought of where she could find Astrid's post office box number. She'd do a little *private* investigation of her own, and maybe she wouldn't even tell Brad about it. She went out into the backyard to spend some mutually consoling moments with Tasha.

She returned to the guest room and started rearranging her daypack, anything to keep her hands occupied until she could launch into her plan. What plan? She didn't have one.

The last plan she had almost resulted in disaster for both her and Brad. Of course it had been his plan as well as hers—she couldn't shoulder all the guilt on that one. And she still needed to find out what he had learned from Mack, if he'd tell her, and they would have to wait who knew how long to see what Dr. Li had found out—if the doctor did indeed plan to send the sample off and get it analyzed. Another variable. Torrie refused to berate herself any more over that *faux pas*. Plenty of time for Brad to do that later.

As though her thoughts had summoned him, she heard the hum of Mack's patrol car in the driveway as he dropped him off—they must have made contact—then the voice of Mel as she greeted him. She was weeding now in the front yard and from the stray words Torrie could catch of the conversation she decided they were talking about the yard. A slam of the door indicated that someone had entered, and she heard Brad excitedly call her name. Suddenly she realized what the background noise was she had heard when Mack called—it was grasshoppers. Mack hadn't been inspecting the jeep, he had been up at the observatory. Why had he lied?

Mel had treated all three of them to a latte with her state-of-the-art espresso machine and an array of flavored syrups. Torrie had chosen macadamia nut and was not disappointed. They sat on the patio which today offered a view of the mountain: it was still sunny—almost too good to be true.

"Well, what did you find out?" Brad asked as he gently blew on the hot liquid.

"You first," Torrie offered.

Eddie's parents had insisted on an autopsy, and the water in his lungs indicated that he probably didn't drown in Spirit Lake—the chemical makeup of the water there is quite different than what is found in other bodies of water.

"Wow," said Torrie. "So that pretty much proves that he was killed somewhere else."

"Not necessarily," he said. "The department hasn't found

anything that suggests foul play."

Mel echoed Torrie's suspicions when she suggested that someone in the department could be involved.

"Impossible," said Brad. "Oh, speaking of the department..."

He put down his frothy cup, stood up, and left the room.

Torrie turned to Mel with a questioning glance.

"You'll see," whispered Mel.

Brad soon returned proudly with a tool box.

"What's this?" she asked. Did he have some new strategy in mind?

"It's Eddie's tool box," he explained. "It was in his jeep."

"So..." Torrie began uncertainly. "What are you doing with it?"

"Long story."

"I'm not going anywhere," she said.

He explained that since the death was not officially classified as a murder, there was no need to keep Eddie's belongings as evidence. And since Eddie's parents had left his things with Astrid, Mack decided that Torrie was next in line—at least for the time being. She wondered if "for the time being" meant until they arrested her. She tried to refuse but he reminded her that using Eddie's backpack had probably saved their lives earlier.

She reached over and fingered the shiny, bright red metal box. "Maybe you're right." It almost seemed as if Eddie were reaching back from the grave and helping in the investigation into his own murder. Then a thought went through her with the impact of an electric shock. "There might be a clue in here," she said and began fumbling with the latch.

"Don't waste your time," he said. "The investigators have already been through it—thoroughly."

"Oh, yeah, I forgot," she said, abandoning her original intention and returning to the comforting warmth of the flavored coffee. "And of course none of them would withhold any information relating to the case," she added caustically.

Brad worked his jaw before responding. "What about you?" he asked. "What did you find out?"

"Not as much as I'd hoped," she began.

They were interrupted by the shrill ring of the phone. Mel answered and handed it to Torrie. "For the 'Ranger Girl,'" she announced.

Torrie picked up the receiver and greeted the caller.

"You must leave," said a hoarse voice.

"Leave what?" asked Torrie.

"You leave the mountain."

"The mountain?" she asked, straining to understand the muffled and heavily accented voice.

"You leave the mountain Saint Helen. You die."

"Die?" Torrie turned ashen. "What are you talking about. I can't hear you."

Brad was at her side. Without a word he snatched the phone from her. "Who is this?" he demanded angrily into the mouthpiece, then turned helplessly and faced Torrie. "They hung up."

Torrie slumped back into the chair.

"What was that about?" he asked.

"I don't know," she confessed. "Something about dying and leaving Mount St. Helens. I couldn't really understand it all. Whoever it was talked so soft I could hardly hear." She ran her fingers distractedly through her tousled hair. "And had some kind of accent."

"Asian?" he asked. He studied her with narrowed eyes. He and Mel sat motionless, awaiting her answer.

"No, I don't think so." Her listeners visibly relaxed. Had they also suspected Mel's friend, or were they worried that she was getting too close to their scheme? *Their* scheme? Was she actually thinking that Mel—generous, hospitable Mel—could be involved in this? "It sounded more harsh," she continued, her voice wavering. Or maybe it was just that the person sounded hoarse."

"German?" suggested Mel. "Or Russian?"

"Was it a man or a woman?" asked Brad.

She looked from one to the other, deciding whose question to answer first. "Man, I think. I don't really know for sure." To Mel she said, "It could have been German. I don't know any German people. I'm not sure I'd recognize the accent. Like I said, it was hard to tell."

"Did he threaten you?" asked Brad. He was clenching and unclenching his teeth and his brows were drawn together. "Was it that Jimmy guy, Astrid's ex?"

"It could have been. I'm not sure, but it didn't seem like a threat. Maybe a warning," she responded.

The three fell silent and returned to their coffees. None was able to come up with a logical explanation for the call—or were unwilling to voice the obvious. Torrie felt a chill in spite of the brightness of the day and the warmth of her drink.

After a few moments, Brad resumed his report from the Sheriff's office. "I asked Mack about the Kevlar," he said.

"Kevlar?" asked Mel.

"Yes," said Brad. "They found traces of it under Eddie's fingernails."

"And they're still treating this as an accident?" she asked.

Brad shrugged. "I guess they think he would be in contact with it in his work."

"Oh, yes. I'd forgotten about that," said Torrie. She wrinkled her brow wondering what would contain Kevlar in his work. "What did they find out?" she asked.

"They identified the color."

"And?" she prompted him.

"It was red."

"Red, red," she repeated, searching her memory for confirmation. "Did we see a red diving suit at Cispus?"

"Didn't you take notes when we went there?" he asked.

"Yes, of course." She jumped up. "I'll be right back."

She retrieved her reporter's notebook and pen from her pack in the guest room and was already leafing through it as she returned to the table. "Friday, Thursday . . . when was that? Oh, Sunday. Here it is. Has it really been that long?"

"What did you find?"

She began reading: "*3 suits large, yellow; 2 blue, medium; 1 green, small.*"

"That's it?" he asked. "No red ones?"

"That's all."

"You're sure you got it down right?"

"Of course I'm sure," she snapped. "I'm a reporter."

He held up both hands in a defensive pose. "Sorry. I just thought I remembered a red one."

"I know what you mean," she said. She absently scratched her head with the pen. "I was so sure we had located our suspects."

"Did any of them speak with an accent?" asked Mel.

Torrie looked up suddenly. "Now that you mention it, I don't think they did. I know the head of the organization and the main diver were American, from Arizona, I think." She turned to Brad. "What about that guy we ran into outside? The super-organized one."

Brad twisted his mouth in an effort to remember. "I just don't remember for sure. He was pretty hyper, but I can't think . . ." He blew out a breath noisily between his lips. "I just don't know. Let's put him down anyway."

Torrie began a new list in her notebook: *Foreign Accents*. She underlined it vigorously with three lines. "Who do we know with accents?"

"Jimmy Whatshisname," said Brad without hesitation. He pointed at her notebook. "Put a couple of stars after his name."

"Has anybody heard from him yet?" Torrie asked.

"Mack has some people checking, but no, nothing yet."

Torrie starred his name.

"What about Eddie's parents?" asked Mel.

"His parents?" chorused Brad and Torrie simultaneously.

"Oh, no, no," Mel gestured negatively. "I don't mean *they* would threaten you," she explained. "I just thought that if they had an accent, maybe some of his friends might, too."

"No, I would recognize a Spanish accent," said Torrie. "I've spent enough time in Texas to be familiar with it. No, it definitely wasn't a Spanish-speaking person." She thought carefully about how she was going to word her next suggestion. "I don't think we can rule out the veterinarian at this point, either."

A mysterious look passed between aunt and nephew.

"I know she's your friend . . ." Torrie trailed off without finishing and doodled nervously on the margins of her pad before adding Hong Li's name.

They brainstormed for another hour, listing everyone they could think of that would qualify as a suspect. Not a very long list. As annoying as the loggers were, they had to admit that none of them had what could be described as a foreign accent, although Brad added that Big Joe might be from Canada, eh?

Mel gave him a disapproving look.

Brad pointed a thumb in his aunt's direction. "She feels like she needs to take over for my mother when I stay here."

Mel gave him a tired smile and they continued with their pursuit of clues. In addition to Jimmy, the assistant at Cispus, and the veterinarian, they had only succeeded in adding Fred at Ben's store, and Sonia, one of the summer Rangers. She was from some eastern European country, Brad had said, maybe even one of the former soviet block nations, but he considered her a very unlikely candidate. He adamantly refused to add Kirsten to the list, but Torrie surreptitiously added a "K" to her "Rangers" category.

She hadn't decided whether Brad was naïve or overly

trusting, or, worst-case-scenario, protecting someone. She'd have to find out if he knew Mack had been up at the observatory, and why. Just as she was thinking that he still hadn't asked her how her visit with the vet went, he exclaimed, "Oh, I almost forgot."

For a moment she expected to be put on the spot, and mentally fumbled for a way to minimize the implications of her indiscretion in giving away their specimen.

But instead, he patted his pocket. "Bonus from Mack," he said as he removed a piece of paper and began unfolding it. Mel and Torrie watched him intently as he revealed a sheet of paper, evidently from a copy machine. He smoothed it slowly and carefully as if savoring the suspense. "It pays to have friends in the right places," he said with an uplifted eyebrow.

"Stop acting like a spoiled brat and tell us what it is," ordered his aunt.

He continued with his charade, ignoring the mounting frustration of the two women. Finally he placed the white slip on the glass patio table and pointed to the one word—or fragment of a word—swimming in the vast white space of the paper before them. He tapped it with a long finger. "Astrid's final note."

Torrie snatched it from the table and held it up to the light. "B-e; B-u;" she started spelling, trying different combinations. What a break to have the actual copy in Astrid's handwriting. "It could still be Ben, or Burt," she decided. "Do you know anybody named Burt?" she asked. "Maybe one of the loggers with Vern. I don't know all of their names."

"Too bad she didn't get to finish it," lamented Brad.

Torrie handed the sheet to Mel who studied it for several minutes, turning it this way and that. Then she spoke. "Look at this," she said. "This upswing on the end where it looks like she didn't finish. I think that might be an 'S.'"

Torrie leaned over and studied the letter in question. "I

think you may be right," she agreed. "So it could be 'Ben's,' or 'Bus,' or . . ."

Mel interrupted. *"Bees,"* she said with a finality that startled both Brad and Torrie. "It says '*Bees.*'"

After studying the document again, this time with a magnifying glass, the three agreed that Mel's interpretation was correct. "I wonder if any of Eddie's things would show a connection with bees." With renewed fervor, Torrie searched Eddie's tool kit, but the only thing she could find that was even remotely relevant to their quest was a bee sting kit. Significant maybe, but useless as far as the missing piece of information they sought.

Brad proposed that Mel drive them up to the Climber's Bivouac to retrieve their vehicles. Torrie placed her newly-acquired toolbox on the floor of the back seat of Mel's car. It would make a good addition to her newly-inherited pickup truck. She felt an uneasiness at the gains she was making at such great cost to others, then remembered that she might still be considered a suspect in Astrid's death. Would all these acquisitions cast more suspicion on her—make it look like she had something to gain? Jimmy had implied something along those lines about Astrid. Would the investigators actually think that meant she had something to do with this? She must find out what was going on—and find proof, before the authorities came and locked her up. She started to get in the back seat, but Brad insisted that she sit up front with Mel.

They got behind a row of three RV's heading toward Cougar. They must have been traveling together because they all had identical markings: lightning bolts in red and black.

"I don't know how they can stand traveling in that kind with the little windows," Mel commented.

"Yeah, I noticed some of those the other day," Torrie added.

"Something else that's strange," said Mel, "is that none of them have any bikes or lawn chairs fastened to the back."

"You're right," Torrie agreed. "I guess they came up here determined not to have any fun. So did I, come to think of it."

"And look what happened to you," said Mel.

Torrie grimaced. "At least I've made some good friends in the process."

They spent the rest of the trip pouring over their suspect list and Torrie pulled her notebook from her daypack and started adding notes. She turned in her seat so she could see both Mel and Brad as they talked.

Torrie started a new page entitled "*Bees*," and they recapped what they already know about the Fireweed and bee connection. Mel asked if the mutations in the Fireweed could be passed to the bees, but Torrie didn't think so, based on what she had been able to decipher from Astrid's notes. Brad wondered if the Fireweed might be poisonous and if the elk calf could have died from eating some of it, but Mel thought they ate mostly grass and clover, and she couldn't even remember seeing any Fireweed along the branch of the Toutle where the elk hung out. Torrie mentioned the deserted bee hive they had passed on their way to the cave, but Brad was sure it had been abandoned long before any of the mutations started occurring.

Mel offered to talk to one of the ladies in her club—the woman's husband worked at the visitor center in Kelso and he might have heard something. Torrie would call Morgan and have her find out if Astrid's faculty advisor could shed any light on the research, and Brad would talk to some of the other rangers to see if they had noticed anything suspicious.

Once they had decided on a plan, Torrie leaned back with a sense of relief against the car door and closed her eyes.

Brad patted her arm. "Tired?"

"Tired? Why would I be tired?" She smiled without opening her eyes. Then she sat up and turned to face him. "I guess I'm relieved."

"Relieved about what?" he asked.

"That it said 'Bees' and not 'Brad.'"

"Brad?" he said, puzzled. "Why would it say Brad?"

"I didn't know," she said apologetically. "I just had to consider all possibilities."

It took a moment for the impact of her statement to sink into the recesses of his consciousness. "You mean you suspected *me*?"

She nodded.

He abruptly leaned back and placed an arm on the back seat. "You actually thought I could *murder* someone?"

"I'd just met you. How would I know?"

Mel was concentrating on the winding road leading to the bivouac, and pretending not to be aware of the tension crackling between the two.

Torrie reached over the back of the seat for Brad's hand. "Brad, I . . ." she began.

He impatiently slapped her hand away and turned away from her. He spent the rest of the trip to the mountain top staring wordlessly out the window.

Chapter 20

MACK

Brad still hadn't spoken when they reached the bivouac area. He got out of the car, claimed his own car from the place he had left it, and drove off without even an acknowledgment of the two women, who stood watching him until he was out of sight.

Mel was the first to speak. "He really cares about you."

"Well, he sure has a strange way of showing it," said Torrie.

"That was quite a shock for him."

"Someone thinking him capable of murder?"

Mel nodded. "Especially someone who means a lot to him. I've seen him date others, but it's never meant anything to him the way it has with you."

Torrie was silent as she considered this. She mentally realigned some of her previous conclusions, but still came up muddled and confused. She was in the middle of a string of murders and still didn't know who was on her side. How could she possibly digress in the interest of what was probably a dead-end relationship.

"Well, how does he think *I* feel?" she finally blurted out.

"The police think I might have done it. I could get arrested." Torrie had started to tremble and Mel put a comforting arm around her shoulders. "We'll make sure that doesn't happen," the older woman said.

Torrie allowed herself to be comforted for a minute, then shook herself free from the helpless feeling. "Guess we'd better get going," she said. "We all have a lot to do, and not much time to do it." She glanced at the sun continuing its descent toward the distant coast.

Mel placed a hand on Torrie's arm. "He'll get over it."

"Thanks," said Torrie and retrieved the tool box from Mel's car before she went to the truck.

Mel had already started down the winding road before Torrie arrived at the pickup. To her dismay, the front tire of the pickup was flat. "That's all I need," she exclaimed. She slammed her hand furiously against the fiberglass topper on the back of the truck, and immediately regretted it. She gingerly attempted to soothe her stinging palm and fought back tears as she set to the task of changing the tire.

In her unstable frame of mind, the task took a lot longer than it should have, and more than once she cursed Brad for leaving and herself for voicing her suspicions of him. The job accomplished, she tossed the worthless tire into the back of the pickup, wiped her blackened hands on a rag, and put the tool box on the floor on the passenger's side. After several tries, the engine roared to life, and with a sigh of relief, she eased it into gear. Time to stop feeling sorry for herself, she decided, and get to a phone where she could call Morgan to see if she had found out anything from Astrid's professor—unlikely, if she was anything like Astrid had depicted her.

The pickup jolted and jounced and Torrie checked to

see if she was in the right gear. Second should work fine until I get back on the main road again, she decided, remembering the treacherous descent she still had to maneuver. After a continuing jerky progress toward the exit of the camping area, she realized it wasn't the gears that were causing the problem. Exasperated, she put the truck in neutral, pulled on the emergency brake and got out. She circled the truck, and when she got around to the other side, she found what she had suspected: the other tire was flat.

"This was not an accident," she said aloud and went back and turned off the engine. The tire appeared to be punctured on the side—not something that would happen if you ran over something or picked up a nail. She opened the back of the pickup and inspected the first flat; it was damaged in almost the same way. This was no coincidence. She looked around to see if any felons were lurking in the undergrowth, then mechanically, she began the process again. She had removed the second tire from the axle before she realized she didn't have a second spare. She sat down heavily to the ground beside the truck, sending the lug nuts flying out of the hub cap she had placed them in. Then she started laughing. She laughed hysterically until the inevitable tears came. Then she wiped her eyes and nose on a corner of her new sweatshirt.

"Okay, we've gotten that out of the way. What next?" She studied the situation and her alternatives. She was about to approach one of the support team campers at the other end of the campground when she remembered the toolbox. The toolbox. Of course. Eddie would have been prepared for an emergency like this. He spent enough time off-roading to know that two flat tires would eventually occur at the same time.

Encouraged, she opened the passenger side door and systematically started examining the contents of the toolbox. She soon found what she was looking for—a can of Tire-

Mend with a long flexible tube extending from the mouth of it. "Bless you, Eddie," she said. "You're the only one who did anything right today."

By the time she had finished filling up the second tire with the magic goo, and finished the arduous trek back down the winding back roads, it was getting late, much too late for what she still had to do. It was certainly too late to take the long way around to Randle to check the mail, but she might be able to catch Morgan.

She stopped at Cougar and found a pay phone outside a store that was already closed for the day. She called Morgan, who was understandably dismayed when Torrie brought her up to date on the day's happenings—and that was only what Torrie had chosen to tell her—she hadn't shared any of her suspicions with her. If Morgan had thought she was in danger she would order her to come back to Seattle immediately, or worse yet, come down and take her back as though she were a disobedient child being sent home in disgrace from summer camp. As Torrie had anticipated, Morgan wasn't able to get any information from Astrid's advisor, so she suggested that Morgan try to find the student that Astrid had mentioned. He had been willing to give information to Astrid before, so maybe he would be willing to help out again—if he was still around.

One way or another Torrie was going to get to the bottom of this. With or without the advisor's help. And with or without Brad.

After talking to Morgan, she called Mel. She wanted to let her know what had happened and that she was on her way home. She realized she was actually disappointed when Mel picked up the phone. Mel had some news of her own to share, most of it bad. The only bright spot was that Tasha was adjusting well and was enjoying the run of the fenced-in back yard.

Mel first told her about the message Dr. Li had left on

the answering machine. Torrie waited. The doctor had received the results back from the lab and it was even worse than Torrie had imagined. According to the vet, the mutation present in the Fireweed was the result of a chemical, not a genetic change, so the potential danger was much greater than any of them had realized. A chemical change could be passed on by contact between species, or could even be airborne, whereas a mutated gene was limited to passing on the defect to the next generation. That would explain the dead elk calf and the so-called rabid gopher, and maybe even the disabled bat that had almost betrayed their presence in the lab. And there was no way of knowing how far this terror had spread or how much farther it would go before it could be stopped. Hong was certain they would need more conclusive evidence before the authorities could be convinced to take action—something that posed a threat to the ecosystem, for example, or proof that genetic tampering had taken place within the boundaries of the restricted area in the national park. At least now she could eliminate the vet as a suspect.

Mel saved the worst for last: a deputy had been by the house earlier with a warrant for Torrie's arrest. She advised her that, regrettably, she had probably better not come back to the house until they found some evidence that would clear her. Torrie went numb. She was totally on her own now and time was running out.

Now it was up to her to try to stop this biogenetic nightmare—if it could be stopped. That was the answer she needed from the U-Dub student, and she needed it right away.

Perturbed, Torrie left the phone booth and started around the corner to her truck. She heard voices around back and thought she recognized one. Brad, she wondered? He said he was going to talk to Mack again—no, wait, it was Mack's voice. That's why it sounded familiar. She started around the back of the building, hoping maybe she'd find

Brad with him, but as she turned the corner, the source of the voices was in full view and she stopped cold.

At the far end of the parking lot was an RV, one of the mysterious-looking ones they had seen that were nearly windowless and with no toys attached. Half hidden in the shadows between the vehicle and the vegetation at the edge of the property were two men talking. One of them was Mack, all right. The other was a man in a red suit.

Catching a gasp before it escaped from her lips and betrayed her, Torrie ducked back around to the other side of the building. Her breathing came in quick uncontrollable breaths and she was afraid she was going to hyperventilate. So Mack *was* in on this. Now what were they—or she—going to do? Her first priority was to get out of here before Mack saw her and realized she had discovered his treachery.

She stumbled back to the truck on legs that threatened to buckle, and, with difficulty, inserted the key in the lock and started the truck. She decided she wouldn't turn and look as she drove past the side of the building where the RV was parked. Then if he did see me, she reasoned, he'll think I didn't notice him. Then she realized that if he saw her at all, he'd be obligated to arrest her. She turned the truck sharply and headed back to the forest she now regarded as her refuge. Time to go look for those crumbs . . .

Torrie spent the night in the cab of the pickup huddled in the sleeping bag Morgan had left for her. She had found a little-used gravel road in the approaching darkness and had turned off. When she was certain no one was following her she turned off on an even more remote road, that was little more than a path, and drove until she could no longer see, or be seen, from the main road.

She tried to piece everything together and come up with a strategy. If Mack was involved with the criminal minds that had set up the lab and he knew she had discovered their secret, she was in grave danger. Either he would try to kill her, or accuse her of Astrid's murder and put her in jail. Maybe Brad had reacted the way he had to her suspicions because he really *was* guilty. He and Mack could have been scheming, keeping information from her, and maybe even conspiring to implicate her in Astrid's death. Now that Brad was an unknown, she wasn't sure she had any allies. Except for Mel, and she didn't dare go back to her place. At this point she would even welcome the interference from Morgan that she had found so offensive only days earlier.

At least she would be safe here for the night, locked securely in the truck with no one for miles around. Then by morning she could plan her next move.

She awoke early the next day before the sun was even up. It may have been because of the cheery twittering of the birds just outside her window, but more than likely it was the fact that she urgently needed to find a bathroom. She had ignored the call during the night because she just couldn't bring herself to go out into the cold, thick darkness. Now the need was too pressing and couldn't be postponed for first light.

She dug in her pack but couldn't find the small flashlight she was sure she had brought. Fortunately she did locate the toilet paper and the resealable plastic bag that had become part of her forest imperative. But she had to have a flashlight. No way was she going to be groping around in the dark for a suitable place. No sense adding poison ivy in unspeakable places to her list of woes.

She checked the glove compartment, but no luck. Then she tried to remember if Eddie had one in his toolbox. Of course he did; he had to. He had been obsessively neat and organized. She opened the metal box and there it was, right on top—one of those big bright yellow ones. Now she remembered seeing it before. Almost dancing with urgency, she reached for the flashlight and clicked it. Then clicked it again. Nothing happened. "Oh, Eddie, don't let me down now."

She unscrewed the top to check the bulb and the connections. She had expected to see one of those large square batteries that you can't find anywhere but a hardware store. She knew without looking there wasn't room for any replacements that size in the tool box. However, inside the flashlight she found a plastic casing fitted with four "D" batteries. Yes! She knew she would find that size spares in the toolbox. Sure enough, a brief search turned up the precious commodity and she yanked the casing out so she could remove the dead batteries. In her haste to replace the batteries, she knocked the plastic holder against the tool box and something slid out. At the bottom of the housing was a small drawer she hadn't noticed before. When it opened, out drifted two sheets of crisply folded pieces of paper filled with small, neat handwriting. On the back of one of them was a map.

Chapter 21

WILL

By the time the sun squeezed out its first tentative rays on the barren scene below, Torrie was well on her way to her goal, and wondering every step whether she was doing the right thing.

When she had studied her maps by the flashlight that morning, she had discovered that she was close to the Sheep Canyon trailhead that connected with the same trail she and Brad had traversed two days earlier. Even more importantly, she had found it noted on Eddie's sketchy map and realized that was where they had found his abandoned jeep. It was enough to set her plan in action. She wondered if her plans fell into the category of unacceptable risk. She thought of all the people who would advise her if she asked: Morgan, Brad, Mel. Or back home Myndi, while they were still speaking to each other, Dad, Mom. No, not Mom. She'd never asked Mom's advice for anything. She always knew without asking that they wouldn't be in agreement. But today, her actions would be more in line with her mother's life style—she'd probably tell her to go ahead with this foolhardy scheme. Her dad was the sensible one. He'd advise her to get a lawyer to handle it. Time enough for that when she was arrested.

But in the meantime, like it or not, she was doing exactly what her mom, the journalist, would be doing: taking chances, going into the wilderness and getting the story. Not that Torrie was particularly interested in *getting* a story—she was interested in making the story turn out right.

She had plenty of time to ponder as she trudged along the rim of the spectacular volcano. She was compelled to go back to the feared tunnel and its sinister lab. But this time she would bring back tangible evidence. And this time she knew how much was at stake.

She stopped at the same fallen log to have her makeshift lunch—trail mix and boxed juice. After she passed the deserted bees' nest, she began watching for the steam vent. She hoped she'd be able to find it on her own. She had her notebook handy and kept checking it for landmarks. Then she spotted the vent. It was still sending up puffs of mist into the hot afternoon sunlight. Good, I found it, she thought to herself. At least she hoped it was good. It wasn't too late to abandon her plan. No, that wasn't an option. She dreaded even thinking about what would happen if the pestilence were allowed to leave the confines of this isolated valley. She only hoped the workers wouldn't be in the lab when she arrived. But she could wait until it was deserted—she didn't have anything else to do, and nowhere else to go.

She focused intently on her every step when she reached the cavern that housed the bats. With Eddie's "magic lantern" in hand she carefully illuminated her pathway. She didn't want to slip and alert the subterranean inhabitants to the presence of a human enemy. She passed through the area uneventfully and was grateful when she reached the cleaner, more civilized part of the passageway. When she came to the hidden doorway, she searched for the foot pedal that she had accidentally tripped before.

Swallowing loudly she stepped on the protruding metal bar and waited for the door to swing open. Only one more door until she reached the lab. She hoped that she wouldn't encounter any more of the men in the red suits—and that the lab workers were gone for the day.

She listened quietly just outside the door for a few moments. Satisfied that no one was inside, she pushed the heavy metal door open just a crack. The lab was dark. Good. A definite sign that no one was there. The row of lights from the distant passageway at the other end of the lab provided a dim illumination to the lab itself. Maybe she could find what she needed without turning on the flashlight and alerting anyone who might be around. She wondered if they had a guard on duty. Or a dog. But they hadn't seen one the last time.

After her eyes had adjusted to the dimness, Torrie cautiously felt her way along the counter. The stillness felt as eerie as the darkness. She planned to get a reading from the DNA monitor. According to Eddie's notes, and Hong's suggestion, that should be enough evidence of the genetic tampering that had been going on here. But, just in case, she was going to acquire another sample of the mysterious glowing substance. Come to think of it, she hadn't heard the bubbling of the agitator. Could they have turned it off?

Even if the experiments had been harmless, according to Eddie, they would have been forbidden in this part of the national monument. This was the area that was supposed to be growing back naturally without any interference from man. She reached the counter where she thought she and Brad had studied the strange readings on the machine, but it was not there. She backtracked and checked another one of the counter spaces. Not there, either. In fact, there was nothing on it at all. Not any racks of flasks, or goggles, or any of the things she was sure were there before. Alarmed, Torrie risked turning on the flashlight and shone it around the entire lab. It was empty. Everything was gone.

Nothing remained of the state-of-the-art equipment they had found on their first trip. The controlled environment units that looked like large refrigerators were still there, but there was nothing in them. The agitator where Brad had confiscated his original sample was empty, and silent. That's why the place had seemed so deathly quiet. The Red Suits must have been packing things up to leave when she and Brad had been here before.

Why would they leave? Did someone find out she and Brad had been there and realized their secret hideout had been discovered? No, whatever they were planning, they had already started it before she and Brad discovered the cave. They must be relocating the lab. That would be unthinkable. They couldn't be allowed to move their genetic time bomb to some place where it would be impossible to contain the progress of the mutations. Unless it was too late. They may have already left the mountain.

That phone call that warned her to leave—or die. They *knew* she had been in the lab. But how had they learned where she was staying? And what about Brad? Why hadn't their warning, or threat been directed at him? That pointed more to his involvement. She had to get out of there, fast, and find somebody who would believe her and be willing to take action. First she needed some kind of evidence, some proof. She looked desperately around. Surely they had overlooked some insignificant specimen—something she could take back with her.

She tried to recall the rest of Eddie's microscopic-sized notes. She had read them hurriedly in the early morning light with the help of his flashlight. He had explained the process: living cells were taken from the normal Fireweed plants, that's what the sterile environment with the gloves was for. Then they were placed in a sterile culture and grown for a time in the petri dishes. Or did they put them in that strange machine that looked like a FAX machine next? She couldn't remember for sure. Whichever it was, it accelerated the growth. Then they monitored the culture by taking Polaroid photographs of the developing mutations. She turned, half expecting to see the strange-looking camera still on the counter. It wasn't.

From the passageway behind her she thought she heard a faint rustling. She had left the door ajar so she could retreat quickly if need be. What was that sound? It continued evenly in the distance. It must be the wind . . . or the steam vent. She had neglected to notice normal sounds in the lava tube. How would she recognize the sounds of danger? She would have to train herself to be more observant—or get in the habit of taking pictures. Pictures. Something clicked in her brain.

Then, in her peripheral vision she caught a glimpse of a bright red object shoved back into the corner. The hazardous waste disposal. On an impulse, Torrie picked up a scrap of paper toweling from the counter and gingerly lifted the lid of the container. There were still negatives in it! Heart racing, she extricated two negatives that were not too badly crumpled and wrapped them in the scrap of paper towel. Hoping she wasn't exposing herself to some dangerous chemical or radiation, she slipped them into her shorts pocket. She had been around her mother enough to know that a negative was just as good as the original. If only they weren't too badly mangled to develop.

Convinced she wasn't going to find another shred of evidence, she turned on her flashlight and started back toward the partially-opened door—and safety. Suddenly she realized what that sound had been: bats. She looked at her watch. Late afternoon, but still too early for them to be flying out in search of insects. Something must have disturbed them, or someone. Someone who wasn't acquainted with their habits, or someone who didn't care that their arrival was being announced by the winged creatures. Someone who had been in the cavern at least half an hour earlier.

She turned off the flashlight and ducked behind one of the counters. Her pulse was thumping in her ears, making it difficult for her to discern sounds. She heard faint noises, maybe footsteps in the passageway?

Then, without warning, something sailed over the counter and landed behind her on the floor. Startled, she turned to see if another bat had swooped into her personal space. In the dim light she could barely make out the silhouette of the object lying there. It was the ranger hat she had left when they were here before.

Suddenly the place was flooded with light. She heard bold footsteps approaching. Before she had time to react, a pair of black boots came around the corner and she was confronted by a red-suited man. "Is that what you're looking for?" he asked, indicating the ranger hat.

Torrie remained cowering on the floor, debating whether she could get to the knife which was still secreted in the pocket of her pack.

"Stand up," he ordered before she could take any kind of action.

He didn't seem to be armed, but she stood anyway and faced him warily.

His English was flawless and correct, but she detected a hint of the guttural German entonation she and Brad had heard from the armed workers. She also recognized it as the accent she had heard on the phone when she received the threat.

"Are you pleased with what you have done?" he asked her. He was staring at her with dark inscrutable eyes in a face devoid of expression.

"I remember you," Torrie said tentatively. "You were coming down from Windy Ridge the first day we tried to get a look at the volcano."

"Very astute," he sneered. "Is that why you came sneaking in here with your friend and tried to destroy what we're doing here?"

"What *are* you doing here?" Torrie asked. Keep him talking, she thought. Buy some time to figure out how to get out of this.

"What we *were* doing was highly advanced, sophisticated genetic research."

"Research in what?" She continued her questioning.

"We had discovered a very potent strain of honey. It could only be produced from the special Fireweed that was growing here at Mount St. Helens."

"What do you mean, potent?" Why is he answering my questions, she wondered. He must be planning on killing me.

"Honey naturally has incredible healing powers," he began. "At least in Europe we are aware of that; in America you are not quite so enlightened."

He was moving gradually closer to her as he talked. With each step he took, Torrie inched away from him. She was getting close to the door that led to the other passageway—the one the men had come through last time.

"You're wasting your time," he told her. "You'll never get out of here. You're going to die in this abandoned lava tube and no one will ever know what happened to you."

"Brad will come looking for me," she retorted with a confidence she didn't feel.

"Why would he do that? Now that you've had a little lover's quarrel." He took another step toward her and Torrie moved even closer to the passageway. She noticed a lone hand cart that leaned up against the doorway with a couple of empty crates balanced on it.

"How do you know that?" she demanded.

"I have my sources."

Mack, she thought. One more reason to get out of here

alive. Corruption in the justice system was intolerable. He wasn't going to get away with it. None of them were.

Before she had time to think it through, she bent and picked up the hat and smashed it into his face, right in his eyes. She took advantage of his momentary confusion and turned and ran toward the passageway, knocking the cart and crates onto the floor behind her. The violence of her movement caused something to fall from her pack and thud to the floor, but she didn't have time to stop and retrieve whatever it was. She headed for something else she had observed while edging toward the doorway—the fuse box. In two strides she reached it and wrenched down the lever on the side. The place was plunged into a palpable darkness.

Torrie kept her hand on the wall and slid noiselessly away from the fuse box. She had to get as much space as possible between them before he turned the lights back on; then she might stand a chance of outrunning him in his clumsy boots. Or maybe she could find a hiding place and ambush him with the knife when he came by—if she still had it. That might have been what dropped on the floor during her precipitous flight. Time enough to check later. Right now she had to find a place to hide. With one hand she continued feeling her way along the wall.

As she feared, the lights soon came back on and he roared after her with a spate of German she was glad she couldn't understand. The wall was smooth and damp, much as the one in Ape Cave. No place to hide. Only minutes before he would catch up to where she was.

Then she felt a warm breeze against her legs. Was she close to the other exit? Hope re-ignited, she began to move more quickly along the wall. Suddenly there was no wall. There seemed to be a breach in the cold stone. She shone her light toward the narrow opening. It was worth a try. It might be a branch of the main lava flow that had formed this more recent cave. Their Ape Cave guide had said the hot magma—no not magma, the pyroclastic flow—followed the easiest path, like the course of a river, so this cavern might have a connecting branch, like the tributary of a river.

She ducked into the opening and turned out the flashlight again—just in time; her pursuer rushed by in the dimly lit passageway. Then it was silent. He may have gone outside to look for her. Or maybe he had abandoned his search. Had she actually eluded him that easily? She waited for what seemed like hours in the little niche. There seemed to be currents of air rushing about her, most of them unusually warm. That could mean the space behind her opened into a large cavern. In the silence she heard what seemed to be a gurgling. Could there possibly be a stream locked within the mountainside? If there were, it might be her path to safety.

As she considered her possibilities, the entire place went dark again. He must have turned out the lights. Maybe he thought she'd escaped to the outside and was looking for her in the labyrinth of canyons out there. Or maybe he was just going to leave her to die here while he finished his preparations to leave the area. The terrifying thought came to her that he might have sealed her in.

Then Torrie remembered the other part of her strategy. She had to stop them from leaving with their genetic mutations and their plans to continue their devious plans elsewhere. There wasn't any time to waste; she had to detain him.

With that decided, she turned on her flashlight and stepped back into the corridor. Before she could take even a few steps the lights went back on. "So there you are," came his triumphant voice. She heard his clumping footsteps running down the corridor. "You didn't think you could escape from Will, did you?"

Torrie had no choice but to turn around and take her chances with the beckoning river.

Chapter 22

MUD FLATS

Torrie turned and headed in the direction of the faint gurgling and the puffs of warm air. Much as she hated to, she was forced to use the flashlight to pick her way along the unimproved pathway. If he got too close she could turn it off. Except, of course, he would have his own flashlight—she wouldn't be able to rely on the thick darkness as a cover. She checked for the knife. Good, it was still in the pack. She took it out and continued along the wall with the handle grasped in her perspiring palm.

He yelled at her as he continued his pursuit, and his voice bounced around the walls of the cavern. "You'll never find your way out," he said. "Do you know what it's like to starve to death?" His voice sounded high-pitched and thin. She could see the bobbing light of his flashlight as he made his way along the path she had just come. She heard a scrabble of rocks and a guttural outburst she assumed was cursing in German.

"I can save you from a slow, painful death," he offered. He waved a long narrow object in his free hand. A rifle?

The path was becoming narrower and more congested with loose rocks and she was gaining altitude. The heat was also becoming more oppressive. Then it occurred to Torrie that it should be cooler in the cave, not warmer. Her flashlight revealed what appeared to be a curve in the solid rock river. If she could get around the bend she might find a place to ambush him.

In a burst of determination she lost her concentration and stumbled, knocking loose a shower of rocks. They fell a long ways and she heard them plunk into something far below. It sounded like rocks splashing into a stream, but different somehow. The acoustics in here must be distorting the sounds. But if there were really a stream in here, it had to have an outlet somewhere—maybe even large enough for her to get out.

She rounded the bend and her flashlight shone into nothingness. She found herself on a narrow ledge. Here the gurgling sounds were much louder. She may have found her river. She searched vainly with the flashlight, but the elusive stream was too far below her to discern clearly. But something definitely *was* moving down there.

Her faint glimmer of hope was interrupted by Will's monologue. He was much closer now; she could clearly hear his threatenings. His voice was wavering and cracking; he seemed on the verge of insanity. "How do you want to die, Rangerette?" echoed around the cavern. "You're not even a real ranger. You can't even die honorably in the line of duty."

Torrie turned to examine the dead end she was trapped in. The ledge narrowed to mere inches, then widened again on the other side of a crevasse after making a sharp turn toward the river. On the far side was a small opening, just large enough for a small person to crouch in, maybe deep enough to get out of sight. But the only way she could reach it was to jump. She studied the distance. Only three or four feet—not very far for a track and field event, but stretching over an unknown chasm made it seem like a mile. It had to be heights.

Will's cursing was close behind her. She quickly stuffed the knife in her back pocket. No time to waste. Just jump. She backed a foot or two, then with flashlight clenched in one hand she took a deep breath, made two running strides, and launched herself into the blackness. She landed with a shattering crash and a thud against the sheer cliff face and fell on her side on the narrow ledge. The shattering was the flashlight and the thud was her shoulder. Her left hand groped for the painful shoulder in the dark and came away warm and sticky. It was probably blood—her blood. No time to worry about it now.

She felt around her in the dark for the edge of the narrow space. Much too close. She scooted back against the dank refuge of the cold wall. Where was the opening she had spotted earlier? She was completely disoriented; she didn't know if it was ahead of her or behind. She didn't know which direction she had fallen. She began creeping forward. She had to reach the safety of the little niche before he came around the corner with his flashlight and rifle. Painfully and silently she pulled herself along on her stomach. She was too weak with fear and pain to raise herself up on her hands and knees.

The going was easier if she favored the injured right shoulder and moved her weight along with her strong left arm and her right leg. Just be careful not to move too far to the left and fall into the abyss or too far to the right and scrape this sore shoulder, she coached herself. After several torturous movements her right knee came forward and encountered nothing. The little cave. It was behind her. Of course. She had scraped her right shoulder on the cliff wall, so she was heading away from the cave.

She reversed her course and eased herself into the opening just moments before Will's flashlight beam illuminated the cavern where the stream bubbled below. As she had hoped, the cave was deep enough for her to sequester herself within, but unfortunately not quite deep enough for her to be completely out of sight. She had stopped breathing, but not bleeding, when Will appeared.

He stopped abruptly, as she had, when the ledge narrowed. "So, our little hero has disappeared. Fallen over the cliff, perhaps?" He shined his flashlight into the ravine below. "Without even a whimper? I doubt it." He steadily aimed the beam around the cavernous space—above, below, around, even flitting briefly over her hiding place.

"Uncle Sieg had your friends killed," he said coldly. "Do you think you can get away?"

Uncle Sieg? Eddie's notes had mentioned a Siegfried. He appeared to be the mastermind behind all this. Then she remembered the notes Astrid had copied from the Internet. The DE she had assumed meant Delaware must have stood for Deutschland—Germany. But she had put it all together too late.

"The geologist was so easy to kill," he continued in a flat sinister tone. "We just waited on his favorite beach and saw to it that he suffered an unfortunate drowning. Then we carried him away by boat. No tracks, no evidence. Then we broke into his cabin and took his camping things so no one would suspect anything."

That was your mistake, thought Torrie. You did leave evidence—evidence the investigators apparently chose to ignore. Surely they couldn't have missed the jimmied lock she found at his cabin.

"Your ranger friend will have to die, too. He knows too much."

Brad. Torrie inhaled sharply. He was on her side after all. If only she had trusted him—she wouldn't be in this mess.

"We invested a lot of money in this laboratory," her tormentor continued. "You and your friends spoiled it for us here. But we'll be moving on—a corporate relocation." He laughed. "Yes, that's what it is, a relocation. We've found an even better market for our products."

He stood slowly and swept the beam of the flashlight along the wall near Torrie's refuge. This time he saw the toe of her protruding boot. He continued his threatenings as he described his "business venture."

Risking impelling him to action, Torrie answered his taunts. "Don't you even care about all these animals that are dying?" Torrie asked.

"Animals die," he said. "It's the way of nature."

"Nature," Torrie scoffed. "That's what started this whole mess. You started toying with nature."

"That," he said, "is the nature of man."

Profound philosophy from a murderer.

He sat on the edge of the path directly across from Torrie, set down the object he was carrying, and laid the flashlight beside him. In the beam of his light she got a better look at his weapon—it wasn't a rifle, only a club. Some consolation. He got a small package out of his knapsack and waved it in the air. "Care to join me in lunch?" he asked loudly. He opened the package and waved the contents in the air. "I'd be glad to share my sandwich with you."

Torrie wondered how long she could last without food. She knew that people had survived for days in the wilderness without food.

"Or water," he yelled into the hollow space. "How about some water?" He produced a flask. "I imagine you are *dying* for some water."

He cruelly emphasized "dying," and Torrie felt in her pack. Her water bottle was gone. That must have been what had fallen out when he was pursuing her. He knew she was without water and was sadistically pressing his advantage.

She realized that without her water supply this would have to come to an end—and soon.

He continued his taunts in a lowered voice. "I know you're still here," he began. "There's nowhere to go. As you probably noticed, the path ends here. And there's no place to go but down." He laughed. A mirthless, horrifying laugh. "Do you know what's down there?" he asked into the silence. "Sounds like a river, doesn't it?" He picked up something and tossed it over the ledge. Torrie heard the same thunk she had produced earlier when she had thrown the rock in. This time she noticed that the thunk was followed by a thick swallowing sound.

"Your water bottle," he said. "You may have guessed how you're going to die. I'm going to feed you to the river. The mud river."

Torrie's heart began hammering. It wasn't a river. It was one of those quicksand pits—or mud flats—that Brad had told her about. But those should all be dried up by now. It's been how long? Fifteen years since the eruption? Hadn't Brad said there might still be some in a protected area?

As if hearing her silent question, Will continued. "Just another little surprise the Saint saved for us. Saint Helens. Strange thing for a saint to do, don't you think? Blow her top and kill hundreds of people and animals?"

He finished his sandwich in silence, then tossed the wrapper over the edge. "Here's a peace offering," he shouted into the cavity below. "I'll be sending you something much better." He returned to his conversational tone, addressing Torrie. "Wasn't it your native Americans who made offerings to appease nature? Young maidens, if I remember right."

Torrie was beginning to get angry. She was sure his ravings were supposed to frighten her, intimidate her, force her to make a careless move. Well, he was using the wrong strategy on her. With each comment Torrie was becoming more indignant, more clear-headed, bolder. She felt to see if the knife was still in her pocket.

"She almost got me one time. I bet you didn't know that," he continued. "I was hiking up here and she almost sucked me in. But I was too smart for her." He gave another eerie laugh. "I even stole her honey."

Torrie had had enough. "What are you waiting for?" she shouted in his direction. "Go ahead, throw me to your volcano god."

In one smooth movement, he was on his feet, shining the flashlight in her direction, wildly, up and down the cliff face. At last he found her hiding place.

She glared at the light he was shining full in her face. "Come and get me," she taunted. With determination she secured the weapon she had kept as constant companion for what seemed like a terribly long time. Now she was going to have a chance to find out what she was made of.

"So the little rat is in her burrow," said his voice behind the light. "I think the place for rats is in the sewer."

She could hear him pacing and saw the flashlight beam swerve crazily. She wondered what he would sacrifice to get across the chasm. He'd surely have to keep the flashlight— or the club. Then she saw a second light. The two beams danced around each other for a few moments, the source of one a couple of feet higher than the other. He was wearing a miner's head lamp. Then there was only one.

Torrie raised herself up and positioned herself for action. She heard a scuffling on the facing ledge and then the head lamp was hurtling through the air towards her. She heard the bulk thud to her right—too far away for her to catch him off balance and send him plunging to the mud flats below. He must have anticipated that.

She scrunched deeper into her cubicle and waited. Suddenly he was in front of the entrance, blocking her escape, but perched precariously on the narrow ledge. She was nearly blinded by the light, but she had one advantage—she knew exactly where his throat was.

For an endless moment the adversaries faced each other, muscles tense in the warm moist darkness.

Then he lunged.

Chapter 23

HEROES

The struggle happened too quickly to recall. Torrie remembered the scream coming from her throat, the excruciating pain, and then blackness. In her semi-conscious state she was falling over a waterfall—falling, falling, and never coming to a stop. Brad was at the top throwing her a rope and calling her name. Or was he at the bottom waiting to catch her? Or had he pushed her? In the distance was the barking of a dog. Tasha? Brad's voice in the void became more insistent until she began to regain consciousness and knew it really was his voice. And her body was not floating freely through a watery mist—it was lying firmly, too firmly, on the hard rock beneath her. The crescendoing presence of pain began to prick her brain back into a cognitive state. How far had she fallen? Where was Will? She strained to listen in the darkness, but could not hear breathing, only the now familiar murmuring of the mud flats.

She groaned, trying to rise up on one elbow. A sharp

pain in her shoulder reminded her of the scrape she had received in her escape attempt. Brad's voice was still part of the waking dream. He was closer now, as was the sound of barking. "I'm here," she called weakly, but was sure he hadn't heard. Or maybe he shouldn't hear her. She couldn't remember if he was the good guy or the bad guy, so she lay back down on her stone bed and waited quietly.

She tried to sit up again, this time using her good arm. She took a deep breath that was almost a sob and sat up. She could see flashlights bobbing in the distance, tracing their snaky patterns on the irregular walls and losing themselves in the gaping expanse of the cavern. She didn't know how long she had been here—long enough to be extremely thirsty and to be experiencing rumblings of hunger pangs. She was more aware of the distant voices. Voices, so there were at least two people: Brad and . . . Mack? She *knew* Mack was the enemy. She tried to inventory her belongings in the dark, reaching tentative fingers out in ever widening circles. No backpack. No water. No food. No weapon.

"Torrie." They were closer now. "Are you okay?"

It sounded like concern in his voice. Maybe he was coming to rescue her. But maybe not. She continued her search. She could see them now—at least the pattern their lights were making as they picked their way along the treacherous path. Their flashlights now seemed focused intently on the narrowing path in front of them. They were coming her way. The faint barking she thought she had dreamed accompanied them.

When she had almost exhausted the search of the circumference surrounding her aching body she felt something hard and cold: Will's flashlight. She clasped the long solid piece of metal gratefully—her lone symbol of survival in her dark tomb. If it worked. Maybe it had broken in the fall. But it would still serve as a weapon. She wished she could remember the last minutes before she ended up on this cold slab.

She meandered in the fog of her mind, trying to determine who the enemy was.

Risking discovery, she found the switch and quickly flicked it on and off. Still in working order.

She located the approaching beams again. If they were following the path one illuminated step at a time they might not notice if she turned her light on long enough to survey her immediate situation. She began systematically, rapidly clicking on and off as she scanned the area. To her left was a sheer rock face. Straight ahead a flat narrow space ended abruptly against the wall. No escape that way. The search to her right revealed a vast nothingness. Good thing she hadn't tried to move. Then she remembered. There had been a small depression on the ledge where she and Will had struggled. Was he still there? She listened in the dark for signs of breathing. Cautiously, she adjusted her position so she could check the area behind her.

Her would-be rescuers were close enough that she could hear their footsteps, even the click, click of the dog's paws on stone. They had stopped talking, probably to listen for her.

She turned herself slowly, moving herself one awkward inch at a time with her one good arm, keeping the wall within reach as she moved. She had almost gotten herself into the desired position to turn the light on again, when her hand came across something evenly shaped and manmade. She examined it tentatively with her fingertips. A knife. Possibly her own knife. She felt along it until she could grasp the handle and pick it up. With her other hand she felt the hasp and began a cautious examination of the blade. The sticky substance on it was all too familiar to her now. It was blood. But whose?

In horror she flung it from her and it went clattering noisily to the cave bottom below. The advancing flashlights stopped. "Did you hear that?" she heard Brad ask. "Tasha, where is she, girl?"

Tasha. She was going to be betrayed by the faithful little sheltie she had befriended.

"Sounded like something fell," came the still distant reply. She couldn't be sure of the voice.

But the knife had brought it all flooding back to her. She remembered what had happened.

In the instant that Will had paused, facing her in her den with his light shining in her face, Torrie had repositioned herself. She had held the knife directly in front of her with both hands. When he lunged at her he encountered her slashing blade. In pain and anger he had retreated long enough for her to rethink her position. Her back was against the wall—his was to an open chasm. She rolled onto her back, brought her knees to her chest, and with a fury that shocked her she calculated where his chest would be beneath his miner's light and released her taut body like a spring.

He had had no time to react. The scream she remembered was his as he tumbled to an uncertain fate on the flats below.

Torrie was overcome with a different kind of weakness and all her limbs were trembling. It was over—she remembered her final conversation with Will. With fumbling fingers she turned on the flashlight and waved it. "I'm here, Brad. I'm over here." At almost the instant she spoke, Tasha had leaped over the chasm and was at her side, whining and licking Torrie's face. She buried her face in the silky fur.

Mack had insisted on radioing out for a stretcher, but after suffering the jolts of that contrivance, she almost thought she would have been better off walking out on her own. As it turned out, only her shoulder had suffered any degree of damage and that was just a sprain and a minor festering wound. She had squinted when they finally left the dark tunnels for the brightness of the day. The whole area was bustling with people—good guys.

Little by little they started filling her in on what had happened.

Mack had been working undercover to infiltrate the organization. The department had also been alerted to the presence of an unusual number of RV's in the area—identical RV's, all manned by young men in red suits. No retired couples, no families, just the ubiquitous red suits. Multi-purpose suits for riding motorcycles, working in the cool laboratory, and disposing of miscellaneous bodies. Suits reinforced with Kevlar, that tough miracle fiber, that was, coincidentally, also found in diving suits.

It hadn't been the Cispus divers after all. Torrie and Brad exchanged sheepish looks. He shrugged. "I guess we missed that one."

"Oh, I almost forgot," said Torrie. "In my pocket." She winced as she attempted to reach her pocket with her injured right arm. Brad carefully removed the crushed negative for her while she explained how she found it.

"All right!" exclaimed Brad as he examined the treasure.

"This should seal up a conviction for these creeps," added Mack. "And you'll never guess who was behind the whole thing."

She looked at him and waited.

"It was that quiet, well-mannered Fred, the one who works for Ben."

"Fred?" she said in disbelief. "But he was always so helpful to Astrid. And he's the one who had them . . . killed?"

Mack nodded. "That store has been old Fred's cover for the last fifteen years. His real name is Siegfried Barth. His nephew Wilhelm is the one who originally discovered the mutated honey while he was going to college here in Washington."

"Will," Torrie stated. Astrid said he used to think she should know his relative who was going to U-Dub. Fred must be the 'Uncle Sieg' he was talking about. What happened to him?" She felt herself begin to tremble.

"Uncle Fred?" Mack replied. "We've got him locked up with all his buddies."

"No, I mean Will," stammered Torrie. "I think . . . I think I killed him." Her lip started to quiver, and Brad placed a comforting hand on her arm.

"No. You didn't," Mack said. "The mountain got him."

"The mountain?"

"He fell off that narrow shelf where you were and fell into the quicksand—or quick mud," Mack told her. "He was still alive when we got to him. He told us everything. Seemed a just end, somehow. It was after his original fall in the quicksand that he discovered the healing powers of the honey."

Torrie closed her eyes and placed a forearm over her face. So she hadn't directly killed him, but still . . . still she couldn't bring herself to think about it.

Then Mack told about his undercover scam. He had pretended to take a bribe to help the felons smuggle their equipment out of the area. They had brought in a fleet of specially-equipped RV's and had been ferrying out the laboratory equipment piece by piece by helicopter from its underground hiding place. Will was the pilot. They realized that their biogenetic tampering had gotten out of hand and they were trying to leave the country before their scheme was discovered. "Thanks to you two," he said, "they didn't get away with it. They were planning on moving the entire operation to Australia."

"In RV's?" asked Torrie in amazement.

Mack laughed. "No. They were planning on transporting everything to a remote airstrip where they had a cargo jet waiting."

"These guys have some serious money," added Brad. "They've been marketing their super honey in Europe, actually all over the world, as a miraculous health cure—charging outrageous prices for it."

"Then they got greedy," added Mack. "Decided to alter the genetic makeup of the Fireweed a little to alter the chemical makeup of the pollen. They expected to produce an even better type of honey and charge ten times the amount they were getting."

"Incredible," said Torrie.

"Unfortunately, they hadn't factored in the bees' contribution."

"What do you mean?"

"I don't pretend to understand it," said Mack, "but I guess I'm not the only one. No one knows for sure what process the bees use to convert the pollen into honey, but whatever goes on in those little bee bellies was completely messed up with this new power pollen. Not only did it produce a toxic honey, but the contaminated pollen was being transferred to other species of plants."

"That's what happened to the elk calf," Brad added. "The herd was grazing on some clover that had been infected. The calf's system wasn't developed enough to fight off the toxins, so the poor little fella didn't survive."

"So now we have infected clover?" asked Torrie.

"No," Mack reassured her. "Fortunately this kind of alteration isn't carried on to the next generation. Morgan got in touch with Astrid's former student and he told us what to do. The sheriff's department acquired some flame throwers and wiped out the entire stand of infected plants."

"I thought fire caused the Fireweed to germinate."

"No," Brad explained. "Some larger plants have seeds that have to be burned before they can germinate, but Fireweed just takes advantage of the sterile environment to move in and propagate. We destroyed all the altered parent plants so that should take care of it."

"Oh, you have to see this," said Brad abruptly, and he

darted off toward the waiting helicopter. In a minute he was back with a large, black, alien-looking apparatus. "This is an awesome piece of equipment," he said.

Torrie watched doubtfully as he brought it close to her stretcher. "That's the flame thrower?"

He took her question as permission to launch into a description. "You wear the fuel tank on your back like a backpack, and this hose connects to the trigger. See it? You just pull on it like you would a gun or rifle and it'll blast everything within fifty feet."

Torrie didn't even pretend to be interested—don't encourage him, she thought. But secretly she thought it would have been nice to have something a little more effective than a kitchen knife when she was facing Will all by herself in the dark recesses of the cavern.

She had no more thought Will's name when Mack spoke again.

"We'd better get rolling and get Will carted off to a secure hospital ward."

Like a recurring nightmare. "Will?" she stammered his name with difficulty. "I thought I had . . . I thought he was dead."

"Just some superficial knife wounds and the aftereffects of his mud bath."

She covered her mouth with her hands and slumped back onto the stretcher. "You let me think I had killed him, or the fall had."

"No, you just dumped him into the mud flats," said Mack.

"I wanted to leave him there," said Brad, placing a comforting hand on her arm. "But Mack decided that we'd better rescue him—something about department protocol."

"He had a helicopter waiting to take off after he'd disposed of you," Mack said. "We found Eddie's missing compass and topo maps in there, too. That should implicate him at least in *that* case."

"So it is considered a 'case,'" said Torrie.

"It always has been," Mack explained. "We just couldn't let it get out that we were investigating it as a murder. We didn't want to spook these guys before we had all the evidence we needed. Sorry we had to keep you in the dark."

They were ready to load Torrie's stretcher into the waiting helicopter when she suddenly sat up, wincing with the pain.

"My backpack!" she exclaimed.

"We brought it," Brad said. "It's already in the chopper."

"I have to have it," she said, trying to sit up. The paramedic tried to restrain her.

Mack motioned him off and waited while Brad set down his deadly toy and brought her the pack. "What is it?" Mack asked.

"In the side pocket," she said. "Eddie's notes. I found them and a map. I just realized what his markings meant on the map. At first I thought the Spanish word was "sheep," because it was close to Sheep Canyon, but it was "bees." The two words are almost the same in Spanish: *ovejas* and *abejas*. We've got to get rid of that hidden field of Fireweed."

Mack and Brad looked at her with uncertainty.

"We already destroyed it. We've confiscated all their equipment," Mack said, "along with the shipment of honey they were ready to ship out. Even the bees. We've closed down the operation entirely."

"But that canyon," Torrie said. "The one Eddie had marked on his map. That's where the mutated crop is growing. It's part of the original strain that Astrid was worried about—the ones that mutated when the eruption germinated those prehistoric seeds. The plants in *that* plot can pass on the mutation to the next generations. Remember, Brad? The ones we found glowing in the dark? Those are the ones that have to be destroyed. That's the destructive kind. This nightmare isn't over yet. If we don't find that plot and destroy it, this whole scenario will be repeated."

Chapter 24

AFTERGLOW

Mack was on the helicopter intercom almost before the conversation ended. He was shouting orders to everyone and his crew was scurrying around the mountainside.

In the confusion everybody forgot about Torrie—everybody except Brad. He knelt beside her stretcher with a look of concern on his face. "I was worried about you," he admitted. Tasha sat protectively on the ground beside the stretcher, watching the conversation that took place over her head.

"You should have been. I got myself in a lot of trouble."

"I shouldn't have let you go off by yourself."

"But you came looking for me."

"Thank Tasha for that. She's the one who found you."

The dog rose up on her forelegs at the mention of her name. Torrie patted her head.

"I don't blame you for being upset," Torrie said. "I'm sorry..."

He turned away and made a dismissive gesture with one

hand. He stared at the mountain for awhile without speaking. Finally he turned back. "I've been thinking about . . . what you thought about me."

Torrie started to speak but he continued.

"We were all scared. It's pretty scary to have your friends being killed around you. If the situation had been reversed . . ."

Torrie waited.

"If it had been the other way around . . . I probably would have suspected you, too."

"And I would have forgiven you," said Torrie. "But I can't believe you're going to let them put me on the same helicopter with that . . . monster."

Out of the corner of her eye she saw a flurry of activity on the copter. "It's Will!" she screamed. She turned in time to see the co-pilot as his limp body was flung from the aircraft, and watched incredulously at the struggle going on inside with the pilot. "He's trying to escape."

Brad seemed immobilized and everyone else was scurrying around in response to Mack's earlier directives. For an instant Torrie thought the horror would start again, then with a strength she didn't know she possessed, she snatched up the hose of the flame thrower and without a moment's hesitation aimed and pulled the trigger. The recoil of the blast tumbled her to the ground, but the tongue of flame hit its mark and the cockpit of the aircraft shriveled up like a child's toy tossed into a bonfire. Two figures toppled from the open door and were immediately surrounded by deputies.

Torrie shakily rose to her feet and scarcely dared to breathe until Mack brought a damage report. Will was in custody again—this time in handcuffs. He and the pilot had only suffered first degree burns. Torrie breathed a tremendous sigh of relief. She had escaped becoming a murderer twice in one day.

Brad leaned over and kissed her quickly on the forehead. "Now we need to get you off to the hospital and take care of the rest of this killer Fireweed."

The paramedics had returned to the stretcher and were standing by to put her on the chopper they had confiscated from Will.

"No," she responded firmly. "I'm not going."

Brad looked at her with an expression of surprise mixed with admiration.

"We need to take you back to Kelso," said one of the attendants.

"I'm fine. It's just a superficial wound. Isn't that what you just told me?" she asked the medics. Then to Brad, "You need me to help find that field of Fireweed."

"I can take them there," said Brad.

"Do you remember where it is?"

"Well, yes . . . ," he began.

"Are you sure?" She pinned him with an intense stare.

"Well, sort of."

"We both need to go," she said with finality. "And Tasha. It will take both of us, all three of us, to find the spot again."

Brad attempted to return her stare, but relented. "Okay, guys," he said to the medics. "Take off. The lady says she's going to be all right."

"We'll need to have her sign a release form," said one.

"Well, go get it," he snapped. "We've got to go extinguish some Fireweed."

Torrie sat on the patio with a steaming cup of decaf latte in her hands. Tasha, head resting despondently on her paws, was by her side. Torrie felt she needed to escape the crowd that had converged on Mel's house. Almost everyone who had attended the memorial service for the two young scientists was there: Mack and several other deputies, Kirsten, and a couple of the other rangers, Dave and Dr. Matthews, Ben, and Hong Li. Even Morgan had driven down for the weekend from Seattle. Eddie's parents and his brother had stopped by briefly. They had come for Eddie's jeep, and had wanted to thank Brad and Torrie for their part in discovering what had happened to their son. A subdued Jimmy showed up. He was back from a spontaneous trip to Canada he had taken with a friend. The friend had turned nineteen and they had decided to go drive up to Vancouver and take advantage of the lower drinking age laws. Three days and two serious hangovers later they had returned to Kelso.

Even Marge had slipped into the back row of the service, but she didn't come to the house although she had been invited. Torrie discovered that Marge had mailed a package to Astrid per Eddie's instructions in case anything happened to him. Torrie found Astrid's box number in Tasha's ID that was fastened to her collar and had retrieved Astrid's mail. The package contained the names of people involved in the biogenetic engineering and pictures of their underground lab. There wasn't much chance that any of them would talk their way out of it now.

Torrie was a little embarrassed when greeting some of the people she had considered as suspects, but then, none of them knew they had been on her list. Mel and her husband had wanted to have Astrid and Eddie's friends over to attain a degree of "closure" for the tragic and unexpected deaths of the young people. All had words of praise for Torrie and her bravery. Looking back on it she wondered if it was bravery or merely stupidity. A friend had told her one time she had more luck than sense. After the events of the past week she had to agree she had had plenty of luck. Or maybe it went beyond mere luck . . .

At any rate, she was finding closure in her own way by submitting a story to the local paper on what was being called the "Miracle Honey Scam." After being misquoted by a reporter in an earlier story, she had approached the editor and offered to do an article herself. She would, however, have to leave out the part about the threat to the community posed by the genetically altered plants. "It don't pay to stir up the tourists," she had been admonished. She'd also left out the part about her own role in unraveling the mystery.

She had discussed with Brad and Mel what to include. Torrie couldn't decide how much to say about the divers. Since she and Brad had accused them falsely, she almost felt obligated to mention their research in the article. "They've got some strange theories," Brad had said. "So did Copernicus and Galileo," Mel reminded them. That decided her: she would include the facts and let the readers decide for themselves.

Torrie had thrown herself into the writing and re-writing of the article and was surprised how much she had enjoyed it—and how easily it had come together for her. But the ordeal of the previous week had caught up with her and she was acutely aware of her need to unwind for a few days. She had escaped the medics again when Mel offered to watch over her a few days while she recuperated.

She'd had plenty of time to think through her priorities while Mel was pampering her. One of them was Myndi. She had called her old friend and they promised to get together as soon as Torrie returned to Texas. Dealing with Aaron would have to wait until the time was right, but Torrie was ready to get on with her own life, and that would definitely include one of her closest friends.

She took a break from her writing and bent over to scratch Tasha on the head. "You're the one who's going to miss her the most, aren't you, girl?" The dog responded with an unenthusiastic wag of the tail. Hong had offered to add the animal to the growing menagerie of pets she already had, but at the last minute, Mel had decided to keep her. She needed a jogging partner and Tasha could help run off the critters—it would give her something constructive to do. Torrie was going to miss her companion of the last few days. "You're the hero, here, you know." Tasha looked up with sad eyes as though she understood.

The door of the patio slid open and they both turned to watch Brad cross the stone patio. He sat in a deck chair beside Torrie and smiled comfortably at her. "You sure I can't convince you to stay on as a summer ranger?"

She smiled. "Much as I love myself in uniform, I think I'll have to pass up the opportunity."

They had had their heart-to-heart the night before. Brad had taken her to dinner at a restaurant with a spectacular view of the volcano, then they had gone for a moonlight walk by the river. They were a great team, they decided, but, to resort to a cliché, 'their lives were going in different directions.' She had felt a sense of betrayal when she found out he had dated both Astrid and Hong, but he assured her he had never dated Marge. Torrie was grateful that he had been there to help her get past her feelings for Aaron, but she knew the chemistry—or the geography—wasn't right for a relationship. They made the usual pact to "remain friends" and had ended the evening on a rather melancholy note.

"So, when are you flying back to Texas?" he asked.

"Not for awhile," she said.

He raised an eyebrow and looked quizzically at her.

"Morgan has invited me to spend the rest of the summer with her."

"What about your job?" he asked.

"It'll be there when I get back—if I still want it. That's another advantage of being the boss's daughter." She took a tentative sip of the steaming nut-flavored latte, her new favorite drink. "Besides I'm not sure I want to be in the business world. It looks like I may be cut out for writing after all."

"That's quite a switch, isn't it?"

"I'd say. I spent my life being 'Daddy's little girl' and wanting to do everything he did. Then after all the conflicts

I've had with my mother all my life I end up choosing her career."

"So, what are you going to do in Seattle?"

"Morgan has some contacts. I may just do some temp work until I decide what I want to do with my life."

"Find yourself?" he suggested.

"You might say that."

"Well, you couldn't pick a better place to look—Washington's a great state."

The patio door opened again and Morgan joined them. "What's this you're saying about our state?" she asked Brad.

"I just told Torrie it was a good plan to stay out here."

"I'll drink to that," Morgan said, raising her cup for a toast and taking the seat on the other side of Brad.

"I hear you're from Bellingham," she said, focusing all her attention on him. "I considered going to Western Washington."

"It's a good school. My brother graduated from their business program."

"You know, I've always wanted to get up for the Ski-to-Sea Festival."

"Do you ski?" he turned to Torrie before Morgan could answer. "How about you, Torrie."

"Just once," she replied.

"Where did you go? Vail? Aspen?"

Torrie laughed. "Actually, it wasn't really a mountain. It was kind of a high hill in South Dakota. One winter we spent the holidays at my grandparents' farm and drove up to Sioux Falls for a skiing weekend," she ended lamely.

"You'll have to come out next winter and do some *real* skiing," Morgan said.

Brad didn't give her a chance to answer. "Yes, do. Come on up to Bellingham and my brother and I will take you skiing on Mt. Baker."

"We'd love to," answered Morgan. "What do you say,

Torrie?"

Both looked at her, waiting for her reply.

"I just have one question," she said.

"What is it?" asked Brad.

"I can't possibly give you my answer until I know."

"Well, ask," prompted Morgan impatiently.

She turned to Brad in her best mock-serious manner and asked, "Do they have any Fireweed on Mount Baker?"

Epilogue

MOUNT ST. HELENS: 2000

Twenty years have passed since the devastating blast that altered the futures of so many people in the southwest Washington area. Recovery has been remarkable and the region is reclaiming its share of the tourist business, especially with the addition of numerous visitor centers on the west side of the gaping crater.

Science, too, has been served, as the characters in *Fireweed Glow* suggest. While the plot is fanciful, many of the premises are rooted in scientific fact. The reader is urged to pursue a study of this fascinating region. As this edition goes to press a web page is being prepared to provide links to some of the subjects mentioned. So start your search engines and join Torrie in her attempts to stay out of trouble while she gets to the bottom of things.

Or better yet, start your vehicle engines and head out to Mount St. Helens for your next vacation. It should prove much less eventful than Torrie's trip, and you may even find me hiking around researching for my next novel—the second in the Flowers of the Field series.

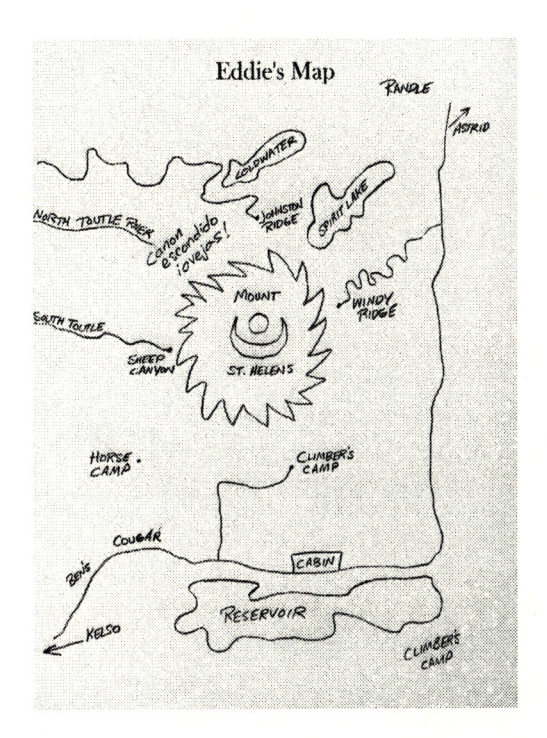

Eddie's Map